AND THERE

JEFFREY ARCHER, whose novels and short stories include *Kane and Abel*, *A Prisoner of Birth* and *Cat O' Nine Tales*, has topped the bestseller lists around the world, with sales of over 270 million copies.

He is the only author ever to have been a number one bestseller in fiction (sixteen times), short stories (four times) and non-fiction (*The Prison Diaries*).

The author is married with two sons, and lives in London and Cambridge.

www.jeffreyarcher.com

ALSO BY JEFFREY ARCHER

NOVELS

Not a Penny More, Not a Penny Less

Shall We Tell the President?   Kane and Abel

The Prodigal Daughter   First Among Equals

A Matter of Honour   As the Crow Flies

Honour Among Thieves

The Fourth Estate   The Eleventh Commandment

Sons of Fortune   False Impression

The Gospel According to Judas
(with the assistance of Professor Francis J. Moloney)

A Prisoner of Birth   Paths of Glory

Only Time Will Tell   The Sins of the Father

SHORT STORIES

A Quiver Full of Arrows   A Twist in the Tale

Twelve Red Herrings   The Collected Short Stories

To Cut a Long Story Short   Cat O' Nine Tales

PLAYS

Beyond Reasonable Doubt   Exclusive   The Accused

PRISON DIARIES

Volume One – Belmarsh: Hell

Volume Two – Wayland: Purgatory

Volume Three – North Sea Camp: Heaven

SCREENPLAYS

Mallory: Walking Off the Map   False Impression

JEFFREY ARCHER

AND THEREBY HANGS A TALE

PAN BOOKS

First published 2010 by Macmillan

This edition first published 2010 by Pan Books
an imprint of Pan Macmillan, a division of Macmillan Publishers Limited
Pan Macmillan, 20 New Wharf Road, London N1 9RR
Basingstoke and Oxford
Associated companies throughout the world
www.panmacmillan.com

ISBN 978-1-4472-2305-4

1 3 5 7 9 8 6 4 2

A CIP catalogue record for this book is available from
the British Library.

Typeset by SetSystems Ltd, Saffron Walden, Essex
Printed and bound by CPI Group (UK) Ltd, Croydon, CR0 4YY

For Simon Bainbridge

Acknowledgements

I would like to thank the following people for their
valuable advice and assistance:

Simon Bainbridge, Rosie de Courcy, Alison Prince,
Billy Little, David Russell, Nisha and Jamwal Singh,
Jerome Kerr-Jarrett, Mari Roberts, Jonathan Ticehurst,
Mark Boyce and Brian Wead.

GRUMIO
First, know my horse is tired, my master and
mistress fallen out.

CURTIS
How?

GRUMIO
Out of their saddles into the dirt, and
thereby hangs a tale.

CURTIS
Let's ha't, good Grumio.

The Taming of the Shrew
IV, i, ll. 47–52.

FOREWORD

During the past six years I have gathered together several of these stories while on my travels around the world. Ten of them are based on known incidents and are marked as in my past collections with an asterisk, while the remaining five are the result of my imagination.

I would like to thank all those people who have inspired me with their tales, and while there may not be a book in every one of us, there is so often a damned good short story.

JEFFREY ARCHER
May 2010

CONTENTS

* Based on true incidents

STUCK ON YOU *

1

JEREMY LOOKED ACROSS the table at Arabella and still couldn't believe she had agreed to be his wife. He was the luckiest man in the world.

She was giving him the shy smile that had so entranced him the first time they met, when a waiter appeared by his side. 'I'll have an espresso,' said Jeremy, 'and my fiancée' – it still sounded strange to him – 'will have a mint tea.'

'Very good, sir.'

Jeremy tried to stop himself looking around the room full of 'at home' people who knew exactly where they were and what was expected of them, whereas he had never visited the Ritz before. It became clear from the waves and blown kisses from customers who flitted in and out of the morning room that Arabella knew everyone, from the maître d' to several of 'the set', as she often referred to them. Jeremy sat back and tried to relax.

They'd first met at Ascot. Arabella was inside the royal enclosure looking out, while Jeremy was on the outside, looking in; that was how he'd assumed it would always be, until she gave him that beguiling smile as she strolled out of the enclosure and whispered as she passed him, 'Put your shirt on Trumpeter.' She then disappeared off in the direction of the private boxes.

Jeremy took her advice, and placed twenty pounds on Trumpeter – double his usual wager – before return-

3

ing to the stands to see the horse romp home at 5–1. He hurried back to the royal enclosure to thank her, at the same time hoping she might give him another tip for the next race, but she was nowhere to be seen. He was disappointed, but still placed fifty pounds of his winnings on a horse the *Daily Express* tipster fancied. It turned out to be a nag that would be described in tomorrow's paper as an 'also-ran'.

Jeremy returned to the royal enclosure for a third time in the hope of seeing her again. He searched the paddock full of elegant men dressed in morning suits with little enclosure badges hanging from their lapels, all looking exactly like each other. They were accompanied by wives and girlfriends adorned in designer dresses and outrageous hats, desperately trying not to look like anyone else. Then he spotted her, standing next to a tall, aristocratic-looking man who was bending down and listening intently to a jockey dressed in red-and-yellow hooped silks. She didn't appear to be interested in their conversation and began to look around. Her eyes settled on Jeremy and he received that same friendly smile once again. She whispered something to the tall man, then walked across the enclosure to join him at the railing.

'I hope you took my advice,' she said.

'Sure did,' said Jeremy. 'But how could you be so confident?'

'It's my father's horse.'

'Should I back your father's horse in the next race?'

'Certainly not. You should never bet on anything unless you're sure it's a certainty. I hope you won enough to take me to dinner tonight?'

If Jeremy didn't reply immediately, it was only because he couldn't believe he'd heard her correctly.

He eventually stammered out, 'Where would you like to go?'

'The Ivy, eight o'clock. By the way, my name's Arabella Warwick.' Without another word she turned on her heel and went back to join her set.

Jeremy was surprised Arabella had given him a second look, let alone suggested they should dine together that evening. He expected that nothing would come of it, but as she'd already paid for dinner, he had nothing to lose.

Arabella arrived a few minutes after the appointed hour, and when she entered the restaurant, several pairs of male eyes followed her progress as she made her way to Jeremy's table. He had been told they were fully booked until he mentioned her name. Jeremy rose from his place long before she joined him. She took the seat opposite him as a waiter appeared by her side.

'The usual, madam?'

She nodded, but didn't take her eyes off Jeremy.

By the time her Bellini had arrived, Jeremy had begun to relax a little. She listened intently to everything he had to say, laughed at his jokes, and even seemed to be interested in his work at the bank. Well, he had slightly exaggerated his position and the size of the deals he was working on.

After dinner, which was a little more expensive than he'd anticipated, he drove her back to her home in Pavilion Road, and was surprised when she invited him in for coffee, and even more surprised when they ended up in bed.

Jeremy had never slept with a woman on a first date before. He could only assume that it was what 'the set' did, and when he left the next morning, he certainly didn't expect ever to hear from her again. But she called that afternoon and invited him over for supper at her place. From that moment, they hardly spent a day apart during the next month.

What pleased Jeremy most was that Arabella didn't seem to mind that he couldn't afford to take her to her usual haunts, and appeared quite happy to share a Chinese or Indian meal when they went out for dinner, often insisting that they split the bill. But he didn't believe it could last, until one night she said, 'You do realize I'm in love with you, don't you, Jeremy?'

Jeremy had never expressed his true feelings for Arabella. He'd assumed their relationship was nothing more than what her set would describe as a fling. Not that she'd ever introduced him to anyone from her set. When he fell on one knee and proposed to her on the dance floor at Annabel's, he couldn't believe it when she said yes.

'I'll buy a ring tomorrow,' he said, trying not to think about the parlous state of his bank account, which had turned a deeper shade of red since he'd met Arabella.

'Why bother to buy one, when you can steal the best there is?' she said.

Jeremy burst out laughing, but it quickly became clear Arabella wasn't joking. That was the moment he should have walked away, but he realized he couldn't if it meant losing her. He knew he wanted to spend the rest of his life with this beautiful and intoxicating woman, and if stealing a ring was what it took, it seemed a small price to pay.

'What type shall I steal?' he asked, still not altogether sure that she was serious.

'The expensive type,' she replied. 'In fact, I've already chosen the one I want.' She passed him a De Beers catalogue. 'Page forty-three,' she said. 'It's called the Kandice Diamond.'

'But have you worked out how I'm going to steal it?' asked Jeremy, studying a photograph of the faultless yellow diamond.

'Oh, that's the easy part, darling,' she said. 'All you'll have to do is follow my instructions.'

Jeremy didn't say a word until she'd finished outlining her plan.

That's how he had ended up in the Ritz that morning, wearing his only tailored suit, a pair of Links cufflinks, a Cartier Tank watch and an old Etonian tie, all of which belonged to Arabella's father.

'I'll have to return everything by tonight,' she said, 'otherwise Pa might miss them and start asking questions.'

'Of course,' said Jeremy, who was enjoying becoming acquainted with the trappings of the rich, even if it was only a fleeting acquaintance.

The waiter returned, carrying a silver tray. Neither of them spoke as he placed a cup of mint tea in front of Arabella and a pot of coffee on Jeremy's side of the table.

'Will there be anything else, sir?'

'No, thank you,' said Jeremy with an assurance he'd acquired during the past month.

'Do you think you're ready?' asked Arabella, her knee brushing against the inside of his leg while she once again gave him the smile that had so captivated him at Ascot.

'I'm ready,' said Jeremy, trying to sound convincing.

'Good. I'll wait here until you return, darling.' That same smile. 'You know how much this means to me.'

Jeremy nodded, rose from his place and, without another word, walked out of the morning room, across the corridor, through the swing doors and out on to Piccadilly. He placed a stick of chewing gum in his mouth, hoping it would help him to relax. Normally Arabella would have disapproved, but on this occasion she had recommended it. He stood nervously on the pavement and waited for a gap to appear in the traffic, then nipped across the road, coming to a halt outside De Beers, the largest diamond merchant in the world. This was his last chance to walk away. He knew he should take it, but just the thought of her made it impossible.

He rang the doorbell, which made him aware that his palms were sweating. Arabella had warned him that you couldn't just stroll into De Beers as if it was a supermarket, and that if they didn't like the look of you, they would not even open the door. That was why he had been measured for his first hand-tailored suit and acquired a new silk shirt, and was wearing Arabella's father's watch, cufflinks and old Etonian tie. 'The tie will ensure that the door is opened immediately,' Arabella had told him, 'and once they spot the watch and the cufflinks, you'll be invited into the private salon, because by then they'll be convinced you're one of the rare people who can afford their wares.'

Arabella turned out to be correct, because when the doorman appeared, he took one look at Jeremy and immediately unlocked the door.

'Good morning, sir. How may I help you?'

'I was hoping to buy an engagement ring.'

'Of course, sir. Please step inside.'

Jeremy followed him down a long corridor, glancing at photographs on the walls that depicted the history of the company since its foundation in 1888. Once they had reached the end of the corridor, the doorman melted away, to be replaced by a tall, middle-aged man wearing a well-cut dark suit, a white silk shirt and a black tie.

'Good morning, sir,' he said, giving a slight bow. 'My name is Crombie,' he added, before ushering Jeremy into his private lair. Jeremy walked into a small, well-lit room. In the centre was an oval table covered in a black velvet cloth, with comfortable-looking leather chairs on either side. The assistant waited until Jeremy had sat down before he took the seat opposite him.

'Would you care for some coffee, sir?' Crombie enquired solicitously.

'No, thank you,' said Jeremy, who had no desire to hold up proceedings any longer than necessary, for fear he might lose his nerve.

'And how may I help you today, sir?' Crombie asked, as if Jeremy were a regular customer.

'I've just become engaged . . .'

'Many congratulations, sir.'

'Thank you,' said Jeremy, beginning to feel a little more relaxed. 'I'm looking for a ring, something a bit special,' he added, still sticking to the script.

'You've certainly come to the right place, sir,' said Crombie, and pressed a button under the table.

The door opened immediately, and a man in an identical dark suit, white shirt and dark tie entered the room.

'The gentleman would like to see some engagement rings, Partridge.'

'Yes, of course, Mr Crombie,' replied the porter, and disappeared as quickly as he had arrived.

'Good weather for this time of year,' said Crombie as he waited for the porter to reappear.

'Not bad,' said Jeremy.

'No doubt you'll be going to Wimbledon, sir.'

'Yes, we've got tickets for the women's semi-finals,' said Jeremy, feeling rather pleased with himself, remembering that he'd strayed off script.

9

A moment later, the door opened and the porter reappeared carrying a large oak box which he placed reverentially in the centre of the table, before leaving without uttering a word. Crombie waited until the door had closed before selecting a small key from a chain that hung from the waistband of his trousers, unlocking the box and opening the lid slowly to reveal three rows of assorted gems that took Jeremy's breath away. Definitely not the sort of thing he was used to seeing in the window of his local H. Samuel.

It was a few moments before he fully recovered, and then he remembered Arabella telling him he would be presented with a wide choice of stones so the salesman could estimate his price range without having to ask him directly.

Jeremy studied the box's contents intently, and after some thought selected a ring from the bottom row with three perfectly cut small emeralds set proud on a gold band.

'Quite beautiful,' said Jeremy as he studied the stones more carefully. 'What is the price of this ring?'

'One hundred and twenty-four thousand, sir,' said Crombie, as if the amount was of little consequence.

Jeremy placed the ring back in the box, and turned his attention to the row above. This time he selected a ring with a circle of sapphires on a white-gold band. He removed it from the box and pretended to study it more closely before asking the price.

'Two hundred and sixty-nine thousand pounds,' replied the same unctuous voice, accompanied by a smile that suggested the customer was heading in the right direction.

Jeremy replaced the ring and turned his attention to a large single diamond that lodged alone in the top row, leaving no doubt of its superiority. He removed it and, as with the others, studied it closely. 'And this magnificent stone,' he said, raising an eyebrow. 'Can you tell me a little about its provenance?'

'I can indeed, sir,' said Crombie. 'It's a flawless, eighteen-point-four carat cushion-cut yellow diamond that was recently extracted from our Rhodes mine. It has been certified by the Gemmological Institute of America as a Fancy Intense Yellow, and was cut from the original stone by one of our master craftsmen in Amsterdam. The stone has been set on a platinum band. I can assure sir that it is quite unique, and therefore worthy of a unique lady.'

Jeremy had a feeling that Mr Crombie might just have delivered that line before. 'No doubt there's a quite unique price to go with it.' He handed the ring to Crombie, who placed it back in the box.

'Eight hundred and fifty-four thousand pounds,' he said in a hushed voice.

'Do you have a loupe?' asked Jeremy. 'I'd like to study the stone more closely.' Arabella had taught him the word diamond merchants use when referring to a small magnifying glass, assuring him that it would make him sound as if he regularly frequented such establishments.

'Yes, of course, sir,' said Crombie, pulling open a drawer on his side of the table and extracting a small tortoiseshell loupe. When he looked back up, there was no sign of the Kandice Diamond, just a gaping space in the top row of the box.

'Do you still have the ring?' he asked, trying not to sound concerned.

'No,' said Jeremy. 'I handed it back to you a moment ago.'

Without another word, the assistant snapped the box closed and pressed the button below his side of the table. This time he didn't indulge in any small talk while he waited. A moment later, two burly, flat-nosed men who looked as if they'd be more at home in a boxing ring than De Beers entered the room. One remained by the door while the other stood a few inches behind Jeremy.

'Perhaps you'd be kind enough to return the ring,' said Crombie in a firm, flat, unemotional voice.

'I've never been so insulted,' said Jeremy, trying to sound insulted.

'I'm going to say this only once, sir. If you return the ring, we will not press charges, but if you do not—'

'And I'm going to say this only once,' said Jeremy, rising from his seat. 'The last time I saw the ring was when I handed it back to you.'

Jeremy turned to leave, but the man behind him placed a hand firmly on his shoulder and pushed him back down into the chair. Arabella had promised him there would be no rough stuff as long as he cooperated and did exactly what they told him. Jeremy remained seated, not moving a muscle. Crombie rose from his place and said, 'Please follow me.'

One of the heavyweights opened the door and led Jeremy out of the room, while the other remained a pace behind him. At the end of the corridor they stopped outside a door marked 'Private'. The first guard opened the door and they entered another room which once again contained only one table, but this time it wasn't covered in a velvet cloth. Behind it sat a man who looked as if he'd been waiting for them. He didn't invite Jeremy to sit, as there wasn't another chair in the room.

'My name is Granger,' the man said without expression. 'I've been the head of security at De Beers for the past fourteen years, having previously served as a detective inspector with the Metropolitan Police. I can tell you there's nothing I haven't seen, and no story I haven't heard before. So do not imagine even for one moment that you're going to get away with this, young man.'

How quickly the fawning *sir* had been replaced by the demeaning *young man*, thought Jeremy.

Granger paused to allow the full weight of his words to sink in. 'First, I am obliged to ask if you are willing to assist me with my inquiries, or whether you would prefer us to call in the police, in which case you will be entitled to have a solicitor present.'

'I have nothing to hide,' said Jeremy haughtily, 'so naturally I'm happy to cooperate.' Back on script.

'In that case,' said Granger, 'perhaps you'd be kind enough to take off your shoes, jacket and trousers.'

Jeremy kicked off his loafers, which Granger picked up and placed on the table. He then removed his jacket and handed it to Granger as if he was his valet. After taking off his trousers he stood there, trying to look appalled at the treatment he was being subjected to.

Granger spent some considerable time pulling out every pocket of Jeremy's suit, then checking the lining and the seams. Having failed to come up with anything other than a handkerchief – there was no wallet, no credit card, nothing that could identify the suspect, which made him even more suspicious – Granger placed the suit back on the table. 'Your tie?' he said, still sounding calm.

Jeremy undid the knot, pulled off the old Etonian tie and put it on the table. Granger ran the palm of his right hand across the blue stripes, but again, nothing. 'Your shirt.' Jeremy undid the buttons slowly, then handed his shirt over. He stood there shivering in just his pants and socks.

As Granger checked the shirt, for the first time the hint of a smile appeared on his lined face when he touched the collar. He pulled out two silver Tiffany collar stiffeners. Nice touch, Arabella, thought Jeremy as Granger placed them on the table, unable to mask his disappointment. He handed the shirt back to Jeremy, who replaced the collar stiffeners before putting his shirt and tie back on.

'Your underpants, please.'

Jeremy pulled down his pants and passed them across. Another inspection which he knew would reveal nothing. Granger handed them back and waited for him to pull them up before saying, 'And finally your socks.'

Jeremy pulled off his socks and laid them out on the table. Granger was now looking a little less sure of himself, but he still checked them carefully before turning his attention to Jeremy's loafers. He spent some time tapping, pushing and even trying to pull them apart, but there was nothing to be found. To Jeremy's surprise, he once again asked him to remove his shirt and tie. When he'd done so, Granger came around from behind the table and stood directly in front of him. He raised both his hands, and for a moment Jeremy thought the man was going to hit him. Instead, he pressed his fingers into Jeremy's scalp and ruffled his hair the way his father used to do when he was a child, but all he ended up with was greasy nails and a few stray hairs for his trouble.

'Raise your arms,' he barked. Jeremy held his arms high in the air, but Granger found nothing under his armpits. He then stood behind Jeremy. 'Raise one leg,' he ordered. Jeremy raised his right leg. There was nothing taped underneath the heel, and nothing between the toes. 'The other leg,' said Granger, but he ended up with the same result. He walked round to face him once again. 'Open your mouth.' Jeremy opened wide as if he was in the dentist's chair. Granger shone a pen-torch around his cavities, but didn't find so much as a gold tooth. He could not hide his discomfort as he asked Jeremy to accompany him to the room next door.

'May I put my clothes back on?'

'No, you may not,' came back the immediate reply.

Jeremy followed him into the next room, feeling apprehensive about what torture they had in store for him. A man in a long white coat stood waiting next to what looked like a sun bed. 'Would you be kind enough to lie down so that I can take an X-ray?' he asked.

'Happily,' said Jeremy, and climbed on to the machine. Moments later there was a click and the two men studied the results on a screen. Jeremy knew it would reveal nothing. Swallowing the Kandice Diamond had never been part of their plan.

'Thank you,' said the man in the white coat courteously, and Granger added reluctantly, 'You can get dressed now.'

Once Jeremy had his new school tie on, he followed Granger back into the interrogation room, where Crombie and the two guards were waiting for them.

'I'd like to leave now,' Jeremy said firmly.

Granger nodded, clearly unwilling to let him go, but he no longer had any excuse to hold him. Jeremy turned to face Crombie, looked him straight in the eye and said, 'You'll be hearing from my solicitor.' He thought he saw him grimace. Arabella's script had been flawless.

The two flat-nosed guards escorted him off the premises, looking disappointed that he hadn't tried to escape. As Jeremy stepped back out on to the crowded Piccadilly pavement, he took a deep breath and waited for his heartbeat to return to something like normal before crossing the road. He then strolled confidently back into the Ritz and took his seat opposite Arabella.

'Your coffee's gone cold, darling,' she said, as if he'd just been to the loo. 'Perhaps you should order another.'

'Same again,' said Jeremy when the waiter appeared by his side.

'Any problems?' whispered Arabella once the waiter was out of earshot.

'No,' said Jeremy, suddenly feeling guilty, but at the same time exhilarated. 'It all went to plan.'

'Good,' said Arabella. 'So now it's my turn.' She rose from her seat and said, 'Better give me the watch and the cufflinks. I'll need to put them back in Daddy's room before we meet up this evening.'

Jeremy reluctantly unstrapped the watch, took out the cufflinks and handed them to Arabella. 'What about the tie?' he whispered.

'Better not take it off in the Ritz,' she said. She leaned over and kissed him gently on the lips. 'I'll come to your place around eight, and you can give it back to me then.' She gave him that smile one last time before walking out of the morning room.

A few moments later, Arabella was standing outside De Beers. The door was opened immediately: the Van Cleef & Arpels necklace, the Balenciaga bag and the Chanel watch all suggested that this lady was not in the habit of being kept waiting.

'I want to look at some engagement rings,' she said shyly before stepping inside.

'Of course, madam,' said the doorman, and led her down the corridor.

During the next hour, Arabella carried out almost the same routine as Jeremy, and after much prevarication she told Mr Crombie, 'It's hopeless, quite hopeless.

16

I'll have to bring Archie in. After all, he's the one who's going to foot the bill.'

'Of course, madam.'

'I'm joining him for lunch at Le Caprice,' she added, 'so we'll pop back this afternoon.'

'We'll look forward to seeing you both then,' said the sales associate as he closed the jewel box.

'Thank you, Mr Crombie,' said Arabella as she rose to leave.

Arabella was escorted to the front door by the sales associate without any suggestion that she should take her clothes off. Once she was back on Piccadilly, she hailed a taxi and gave the driver an address in Lowndes Square. She checked her watch, confident that she would be back at the flat long before her father, who would never find out that his watch and cufflinks had been borrowed for a few hours, and who certainly wouldn't miss one of his old school ties.

As she sat in the back of the taxi, Arabella admired the flawless yellow diamond. Jeremy had carried out her instructions to the letter. She would of course have to explain to her friends why she'd broken off the engagement. Frankly, he just wasn't one of our set, never really fitted in. But she had to admit she would quite miss him. She'd grown rather fond of Jeremy, and he was very enthusiastic between the sheets. And to think that all he'd get out of it was a pair of silver collar stiffeners and an old Etonian tie. Arabella hoped he still had enough money to cover the bill at the Ritz.

She dismissed Jeremy from her thoughts and turned her attention to the man she'd chosen to join her at Wimbledon, whom she had already lined up to assist her in obtaining a matching pair of earrings.

◄◦►

When Mr Crombie left De Beers that night, he was still trying to work out how the man had managed it. After all, he'd had no more than a few seconds while his head was bowed.

'Goodnight, Doris,' he said as he passed a cleaner who was vacuuming in the corridor.

'Goodnight, sir,' said Doris, opening the door to the viewing room so she could continue to vacuum. This was where the customers selected the finest gems on earth, Mr Crombie had once told her, so it had to be spotless. She turned off the machine, removed the black velvet cloth from the table and began to polish the surface; first the top, then the rim. That's when she felt it.

Doris bent down to take a closer look. She stared in disbelief at the large piece of chewing gum stuck under the rim of the table. She began to scrape it off, not stopping until there wasn't the slightest trace of it left, then dropped it into the rubbish bag attached to her cleaning cart before placing the velvet cloth back on the table.

'Such a disgusting habit,' she muttered as she closed the viewing-room door and continued to vacuum the carpet in the corridor.

THE QUEEN'S
BIRTHDAY TELEGRAM *

2

Her Majesty the Queen sends her congratulations to
Albert Webber on the occasion of his 100th birthday,
and wishes him many more years of good health
and happiness.

ALBERT WAS STILL SMILING after he'd read the
message for the twentieth time.

'You'll be next, ducks,' he said as he passed the royal
missive across to his wife. Betty only had to read the
telegram once for a broad smile to appear on her face
too.

The festivities had begun a week earlier, culminating
in a celebration party at the town hall. Albert's photograph had appeared on the front page of the *Somerset
Gazette* that morning, and he had been interviewed on
BBC Points West, his wife seated proudly by his side.

His Worship the Mayor of Street, Councillor Ted
Harding, and the leader of the local council, Councillor
Brocklebank, were waiting on the town hall steps to
greet the centenarian. Albert was escorted to the
mayor's parlour where he was introduced to Mr David
Heathcote-Amory, the local Member of Parliament, as
well as the local MEP, although when asked later he
couldn't remember her name.

After several more photographs had been taken,

Albert was ushered through to a large reception room where over a hundred invited guests were waiting to greet him. As he entered the room he was welcomed by a spontaneous burst of applause, and people he'd never met before began shaking hands with him.

At 3.27 p.m., the precise minute Albert had been born in 1907, the old man, surrounded by his five children, eleven grandchildren and nineteen great-grandchildren, thrust a silver-handled knife into a three-tier cake. This simple act was greeted by another burst of applause, followed by cries of *speech, speech, speech!*

Albert had prepared a few words, but as quiet fell in the room, they went straight out of his head.

'Say something,' said Betty, giving her husband a gentle nudge in the ribs.

He blinked, looked around at the expectant crowd, paused and said, 'Thank you very much.'

Once the assembled gathering realized that was all he was going to say, someone began to sing 'Happy Birthday', and within moments everyone was joining in. Albert managed to blow out seven of the hundred candles before the younger members of the family came to his rescue, which was greeted by even more laughter and clapping.

Once the applause had died down, the mayor rose to his feet, tugged at the lapels of his black and gold braided gown and cleared his throat, before delivering a far longer speech.

'My fellow citizens,' he began, 'we are gathered together today to celebrate the birthday, the one hundredth birthday, of Albert Webber, a much-loved member of our community. Albert was born in Street on the fifteenth of April 1907. He married his wife Betty at Holy Trinity Church in 1931, and spent his working life at C. and J. Clark's, our local shoe factory. In fact,' he continued, 'Albert has spent his entire life in Street, with the notable exception of four years when he served as a private soldier in the Somerset Light Infantry. When the war ended in 1945, Albert was discharged from the army and returned to Street to take up his old job as a leather cutter at Clark's. At the age of sixty, he retired as Deputy Floor Manager. But you can't get rid of Albert that easily, because he then took on part-time work as a night watchman, a responsibility he carried out until his seventieth birthday.'

The mayor waited for the laughter to fade before he continued. 'From his early days, Albert has always been a loyal supporter of Street Football Club, rarely missing a Cobblers' home game, and indeed the club has recently made him an honorary life member. Albert also played darts for the Crown and Anchor, and was a member of that team when they were runners-up in the town's pub championship.

'I'm sure you will all agree,' concluded the mayor, 'that Albert has led a colourful and interesting life, which we all hope will continue for many years to come, not least because in three years' time we will be celebrating the same landmark for his dear wife Betty. It's hard to believe, looking at her,' said the mayor, turning towards Mrs Webber, 'that in 2010 she will also be one hundred.'

'Hear, hear,' said several voices, and Betty shyly bowed her head as Albert leaned across and took her hand.

After several other dignitaries had said a few words, and many more had had their photograph taken with Albert, the mayor accompanied his two guests out of the town hall to a waiting Rolls-Royce, and instructed the chauffeur to drive Mr and Mrs Webber home.

Albert and Betty sat in the back of the car holding hands. Neither of them had ever been in a Rolls-Royce before, and certainly not in one driven by a chauffeur.

By the time the car drew up outside their council house in Marne Terrace, they were both so exhausted and so full of salmon sandwiches and birthday cake that it wasn't long before they retired to bed.

The last thing Albert murmured before turning out his bedside light was, 'Well, it will be your turn next, ducks, and I'm determined to live another three years so we can celebrate your hundredth together.'

'I don't want all that fuss made over me when my time comes,' she said. But Albert had already fallen asleep.

◄◦►

Not a lot happened in Albert and Betty Webber's life during the next three years: a few minor ailments, but nothing life-threatening, and the birth of their first great-great-grandchild, Jude.

When the historic day approached for the second Webber to celebrate a hundredth birthday, Albert had become so frail that Betty insisted the party be held at their home and only include the family. Albert reluctantly agreed, and didn't tell his wife how much he'd been looking forward to returning to the town hall and once again being driven home in the mayor's Rolls-Royce.

The new mayor was equally disappointed, as he'd anticipated that the occasion would guarantee his photograph appearing on the front page of the local paper.

When the great day dawned, Betty received over a hundred cards, letters and messages from well-wishers, but to Albert's profound dismay, there was no telegram from the Queen. He assumed the Post Office was to blame and that it would surely be delivered the following day. It wasn't.

'Don't fuss, Albert,' Betty insisted. 'Her Majesty is a very busy lady and she must have far more important things on her mind.'

But Albert did fuss, and when no telegram arrived the next day, or the following week, he felt a pang of disappointment for his wife who seemed to be taking the whole affair in such good spirit. However, after another week, and still no sign of a telegram, Albert decided the time had come to take the matter into his own hands.

Every Thursday morning, Eileen, their youngest daughter, aged seventy-three, would come to pick up Betty and drive her into town to go shopping. In reality this usually turned out to be just window shopping, as Betty couldn't believe the prices the shops had the nerve to charge. She could remember when a loaf of bread cost a penny, and a pound a week was a working wage.

That Thursday Albert waited for them to leave the house, then he stood by the window until the car had disappeared around the corner. Once they were out of sight, he shuffled off to his little den, where he sat by the phone, going over the exact words he would say if he was put through.

After a little while, and once he felt he was word perfect, he looked up at the framed telegram on the wall above him. It gave him enough confidence to pick up the phone and dial a six-digit number.

'Directory Enquiries. What number do you require?'

'Buckingham Palace,' said Albert, hoping his voice sounded authoritative.

There was a slight hesitation, but the operator finally said, 'One moment please.'

Albert waited patiently, although he quite expected to be told that the number was either unlisted or ex-directory. A moment later the operator was back on the line and read out the number.

'Can you please repeat that?' asked a surprised Albert as he took the top off his biro. 'Zero two zero, seven seven six six, seven three zero zero. 'Thank you,' he said, before putting the phone down. Several minutes passed before he gathered enough courage to pick it up again. Albert dialled the number with a shaky hand. He listened to the familiar ringing tone and was just about to put the phone back down when a woman's voice said, 'Buckingham Palace, how may I help you?'

'I'd like to speak to someone about a one hundredth birthday,' said Albert, repeating the exact words he had memorized.

'Who shall I say is calling?'

'Mr Albert Webber.'

'Hold the line please, Mr Webber.'

This was Albert's last chance of escape, but before he could put the phone down, another voice came on the line.

'Humphrey Cranshaw speaking.'

The last time Albert had heard a voice like that was when he was serving in the army. 'Good morning, sir,' he said nervously. 'I was hoping you might be able to help me.'

'I certainly will if I can, Mr Webber,' replied the courtier.

'Three years ago I celebrated my hundredth birth-day,' said Albert, returning to his well-rehearsed script.

'Many congratulations,' said Cranshaw.

'Thank you, sir,' said Albert, 'but that isn't the reason why I'm calling. You see, on that occasion Her Majesty the Queen was kind enough to send me a telegram, which is now framed on the wall in front of me, and which I will treasure for the rest of my life.'

'How kind of you to say so, Mr Webber.'

'But I wondered,' said Albert, gaining in confidence, 'if Her Majesty still sends telegrams when people reach their hundredth birthday?'

'She most certainly does,' replied Cranshaw. 'I know that it gives Her Majesty great pleasure to continue the tradition, despite the fact that so many more people now attain that magnificent milestone.'

'Oh, that is most gratifying to hear, Mr Cranshaw,' said Albert, 'because my dear wife celebrated her hundredth birthday some two weeks ago, but sadly has not yet received a telegram from the Queen.'

'I am sorry to hear that, Mr Webber,' said the courtier. 'It must be an administrative oversight on our part. Please allow me to check. What is your wife's full name?'

'Elizabeth Violet Webber, née Braithwaite,' said Albert with pride.

'Just give me a moment, Mr Webber,' said Cranshaw, 'while I check our records.'

This time Albert had to wait a little longer before Mr Cranshaw came back on the line. 'I am sorry to have kept you waiting, Mr Webber, but you'll be pleased to learn that we have traced your wife's telegram.'

'Oh, I'm so glad,' said Albert. 'May I ask when she can expect to receive it?'

There was a moment's hesitation before the courtier said, 'Her Majesty sent a telegram to your wife to congratulate her on reaching her hundredth birthday some five years ago.'

Albert heard a car door slam, and moments later a key turned in the lock. He quickly put the phone down, and smiled.

HIGH HEELS*

3

I WAS AT LORD'S for the first day of the Second Test against Australia when Alan Penfold sat down beside me and introduced himself.

'How many people tell you they've got a story in them?' he asked.

I gave him a closer look before I replied. He must have been around fifty years old, slim and tanned. He looked fit, the kind of man who goes on playing his chosen sport long after he's past his peak, and as I write this story, I recall that his handshake was remarkably firm.

'Two, sometimes three a week,' I told him.

'And how many of those stories make it into one of your books?'

'If I'm lucky, one in twenty, but more likely one in thirty.'

'Well, let's see if I can beat the odds,' said Penfold as the players left the field for tea. 'In my profession,' he began, 'you never forget your first case.'

◄○►

Alan Penfold put the phone gently back on the hook, hoping he hadn't woken his wife. She stirred when he slipped stealthily out of bed and began to dress in yesterday's clothes, as he didn't want to put the light on.

'And where do you think you're going at this time in the morning?' she demanded.

'Romford,' he replied.

Anne tried to focus on the digital clock on her side of the bed.

'At ten past eight on a Sunday morning?' she said with a groan.

Alan leaned over and kissed her on the forehead. 'Go back to sleep, I'll tell you all about it over lunch.' He quickly left the room before she could question him any further.

Even though it was a Sunday morning, he calculated that it would take him about an hour to get to Romford. At least he could use the time to think about the phone conversation he'd just had with the duty reports officer.

Alan had joined Redfern & Ticehurst as a trainee actuary soon after he'd qualified as a loss adjuster. Although he'd been with the firm for over two years, the partners were such a conservative bunch that this was the first time they'd allowed him to cover a case without his supervisor, Colin Crofts.

Colin had taught him a lot during the past two years, and it was one of his comments, oft repeated, that sprang to Alan's mind as he headed along the A12 towards Romford: 'You never forget your first case.'

All the reports officer had told him over the phone were the basic facts. A warehouse in Romford had caught fire during the night and by the time the local brigade had arrived, there wasn't a lot that could be done other than to dampen down the embers. Old buildings like that often go up like a tinderbox, the reports officer said matter-of-factly.

The policy holders, Lomax Shoes (Import and Export) Ltd, had two insurance policies, one for the building, and the other for its contents, each of them for approximately two million pounds. The reports officer didn't consider it to be a complicated assignment, which was probably why he allowed Alan to cover the case without his supervisor.

Even before he reached Romford, Alan could see where the site must be. A plume of black smoke was hovering above what was left of the hundred-year-old company. He parked in a side street, exchanged his shoes for a pair of Wellington boots and headed towards the smouldering remains of Lomax Shoes (Import and Export) Ltd. The smoke was beginning to disperse, the wind blowing it in the direction of the east coast. Alan walked slowly, because Colin had taught him that it was important to take in first impressions.

When he reached the site, there was no sign of any activity other than a fire crew who were packing up and preparing to return to brigade headquarters. Alan tried to avoid the puddles of sooty water as he made his way across to the engine. He introduced himself to the duty officer.

'So where's Colin?' the man asked.

'He's on holiday,' Alan replied.

'That figures. I can't remember when I last saw him on a Sunday morning. And he usually waits for my report before he visits the site.'

'I know,' said Alan. 'But this is my first case, and I was hoping to have it wrapped up before Colin comes back from his holiday.'

'You never forget your first case,' said the fire officer as he climbed up into the cab. 'Mind you, this one's unlikely to make any headlines, other than in the *Romford Recorder*. I certainly won't be recommending a police inquiry.'

'So there's no suggestion of arson?' said Alan.

'No, none of the usual tell-tale signs to indicate that,' said the officer. 'I'm betting the cause of the fire will turn out to be faulty wiring. Frankly, the whole electrical system should have been replaced years ago.' He paused and looked back at what remained of the site. 'It was just fortunate for us that it was an isolated building and the fire broke out in the middle of the night.'

'Was there anyone on the premises at the time?'

'No, Lomax sacked the night watchman about a year ago. Just another victim of the recession. It will all be in my report.'

'Thanks,' said Alan. 'I don't suppose you've seen any sign of the rep from the insurance company?' he asked as the fire chief slammed his door closed.

'If I know Bill Hadman, he'll be setting up his office in the nearest pub. Try the King's Arms on Napier Road.'

Alan spent the next hour walking around the water-logged site searching for any clue that might prove the fire chief wrong. He wasn't able to find anything, but he couldn't help feeling that something wasn't right. To start with, where was Mr Lomax, the owner, whose business had just gone up in smoke? And why wasn't the insurance agent anywhere to be seen, when he was going to have to pay out four million pounds of his company's money? Whenever things didn't add up, Colin always used to say, 'It's often not what you *do* see that matters, but what you *don't* see.'

After another half-hour of not being able to work out what it was he couldn't see, Alan decided to take the fire chief's advice and headed for the nearest pub.

When he walked into the King's Arms just before eleven, there were only two customers seated at the bar, and one of them was clearly holding court.

'Good morning, young man,' said Bill Hadman. 'Come and join us. By the way, this is Des Lomax. I'm trying to help him drown his sorrows.'

'It's a bit early for me,' said Alan after shaking hands with both men, 'but as I didn't have any breakfast this morning, I'll settle for an orange juice.'

'It's unusual to see someone from your office on site this early.'

'Colin's on holiday and it's my first case.'

'You never forget your first case,' sighed Hadman, 'but I fear this one won't be something to excite your grandchildren with. My company has insured the Lomax family from the day they first opened shop in 1892, and the few claims they've made over the years have never raised an eyebrow at head office, which is more than I can say for some of my other clients.'

'Mr Lomax,' said Alan, 'can I say how sorry I am that we have to meet in such distressing circumstances?' That was always Colin's opening line, and Alan added, 'It must be heartbreaking to lose your family business after so many years.' He watched Lomax carefully to see how he would react.

'I'll just have to learn to live with it, won't I?' said Lomax, who didn't look at all heartbroken. In fact, he appeared remarkably relaxed for someone who'd just lost his livelihood but had still found the time to shave that morning.

'No need for you to hang around, old fellow,' said Hadman. 'I'll have my report on your desk by Wednesday, Thursday at the latest, and then the bargaining can begin.'

'Can't see why there should be any need for bargaining,' snapped Lomax. 'My policy is fully paid up, and as the world can see, I've lost everything.'

'Except for the tiny matter of insurance policies totalling around four million pounds,' said Alan after he'd drained his orange juice. Neither Lomax nor Hadman commented as he placed his empty glass on the bar. He shook hands with them both again and left without another word.

'Something isn't right,' Alan said out loud as he walked slowly back to the site. What made it worse was that he had a feeling Colin would have spotted it by now. He briefly considered paying a visit to the local police station, but if the fire officer and the insurance representative weren't showing any concern, there wasn't much chance of the police opening an inquiry. Alan could hear the chief inspector saying, 'I've got enough real crimes to solve without having to follow up one of your "something doesn't feel right" hunches.'

As Alan climbed behind the wheel of his car, he repeated, 'Something isn't right.'

━◦━

Alan arrived back in Fulham just in time for lunch. Anne didn't seem particularly interested in how he'd spent his Sunday morning, until he mentioned the word shoes. She then began to ask him lots of questions, one of which gave him an idea.

At nine o'clock the following morning, Alan was standing outside the claim manager's office. 'No, I haven't read your report,' Roy Kerslake said, even before Alan had sat down.

'That might be because I haven't written it yet,' said Alan with a grin. 'But then, I'm not expecting to get a copy of the fire report or the insurance evaluation before the end of the week.'

'Then why are you wasting my time?' asked Kerslake, not looking up from behind a foot-high pile of files.

'I'm not convinced the Lomax case is quite as straightforward as everyone on the ground seems to think it is.'

'Have you got anything more substantial to go on other than a gut feeling?'

'Don't let's forget my vast experience,' said Alan.

'So what do you expect me to do about it?' asked Kerslake, ignoring the sarcasm.

'There isn't a great deal I can do before the written reports land on my desk, but I was thinking of carrying out a little research of my own.'

'I smell a request for expenses,' said Kerslake, looking up for the first time. 'You'll need to justify them before I'll consider parting with a penny.'

Alan told him in great detail what he had in mind, which resulted in the claims manager putting his pen down.

'I will not advance you a penny until you come up with something more than a gut feeling by the next time I see you. Now go away and let me get on with my job ... By the way,' he said as Alan opened the door, 'if I remember correctly, this is your first time flying solo?'

'That's right,' said Alan, but he'd closed the door before he could hear Kerslake's response.

'Well, that explains everything.'

<o>

Alan drove back to Romford later that morning, hoping that a second visit to the site might lift the scales from his eyes, but still all he could see were the charred remains of a once-proud company. He walked slowly across the deserted site, searching for the slightest clue, and was pleased to find nothing.

At one o'clock he returned to the King's Arms, hoping that Des Lomax and Bill Hadman wouldn't be propping up the bar as he wanted to chat to one or two locals in the hope of picking up any gossip that was doing the rounds.

He plonked himself down on a stool in the middle of the bar and ordered a pint and a ploughman's lunch. It didn't take him long to work out who were the regulars and who, like him, were passing trade. He noticed that one of the regulars was reading about the fire in the local paper.

'That must have been quite a sight,' said Alan, pointing to the photograph of a warehouse in flames which took up most of the front page of the *Romford Recorder*.

'I wouldn't know,' said the man after draining his glass. 'I was tucked up in bed at the time, minding my own business.'

'Sad, though,' said Alan, 'an old family company like that going up in flames.'

'Not so sad for Des Lomax,' said the man, glancing at his empty glass. 'He pockets a cool four million and then swans off on holiday with his latest girlfriend. Bet we never see him around these parts again.'

'I'm sure you're right,' said Alan and, tapping his glass, he said to the barman, 'Another pint, please.' He turned to the regular and asked, 'Would you care to join me?'

'That's very civil of you,' said the man, smiling for the first time.

An hour later, Alan left the King's Arms with not a great deal more to go on, despite a second pint for his new-found friend and one for the barman.

Lomax, it seemed, had flown off to Corfu with his new Ukrainian girlfriend, leaving his wife behind in Romford. Alan had no doubt that Mrs Lomax would be able to tell him much more than the stranger at the bar, but he knew he'd never get away with it. If the company were to find out that he'd been to visit the policyholder's wife, it would be his last job as well as his first. He dismissed the idea, although it worried him that Lomax could be found in a pub on the morning after the fire and then fly off to Corfu with his girlfriend while the embers were still smouldering.

When Alan arrived back at the office he decided to give Bill Hadman a call and see if he had anything that might be worth following up.

'Tribunal Insurance,' announced a switchboard voice.

'It's Alan Penfold from Redfern and Ticehurst. Could you put me through to Mr Hadman, please?'

'Mr Hadman's on holiday. We're expecting him back next Monday.'

'Somewhere nice, I hope,' said Alan, flying a kite.

'I think he said he was going to Corfu.'

–◄o►–

Alan leaned across and stroked his wife's back, wondering if she was awake.

'If you're hoping for sex, you can forget it,' Anne said without turning over.

'No, I was hoping to talk to you about shoes.'

Anne turned over. 'Shoes?' she mumbled.

'Yes, I want you to tell me everything you know about Manolo Blahnik, Prada and Roger Vivier.'

Anne sat up, suddenly wide awake.

'Why do you want to know?' she asked hopefully.

'What size are you, for a start?'

'Thirty-eight.'

'Is that inches, centimetres or—'

'Don't be silly, Alan. It's the recognized European measurement, universally accepted by all the major shoe companies.'

39

'But is there anything distinctive about . . .' Alan went on to ask his wife a series of questions, all of which she seemed to know the answers to.

◄○►

Alan spent the following morning strolling around the first floor of Harrods, a store he usually only visited during the sales. He tried to remember everything Anne had told him, and spent a considerable amount of time studying the vast department devoted to shoes, or to be more accurate, to women.

He checked through all the brand names that had been on Lomax's manifest, and by the end of the morning he had narrowed down his search to Manolo Blahnik and Roger Vivier. Alan left the store a couple of hours later with nothing more than some brochures, aware that he couldn't progress his theory without asking Kerslake for money.

When Alan returned to the office that afternoon, he took his time double-checking Lomax's stock list. Among the shoes lost in the fire were two thousand three hundred pairs of Manolo Blahnik and over four thousand pairs of Roger Vivier.

'How much do you want?' asked Roy Kerslake, two stacks of files now piled up in front of him.

'A thousand,' said Alan, placing yet another file on the desk.

'I'll let you know my decision once I've read your report,' Kerslake said.

'How do I get my report to the top of the pile?' asked Alan.

'You have to prove to me that the company will benefit from any further expenditure.'

'Would saving a client two million pounds be considered a benefit?' asked Alan innocently.

Kerslake pulled the file back out from the bottom of the pile, opened it and began to read. 'I'll let you know my decision within the hour.'

<o>

Alan returned to Harrods the next day, after he'd had another nocturnal chat with his wife. He took the escalator to the first floor and didn't stop walking until he reached the Roger Vivier display. He selected a pair of shoes, took them to the counter and asked the sales assistant how much they were. She studied the coded label.

'They're part of a limited edition, sir, and this is the last pair.'

'And the price?' said Alan.

'Two hundred and twenty pounds.'

Alan tried not to look horrified. At that price, he realized he wouldn't be able to buy enough pairs to carry out his experiment.

'Do you have any seconds?' he asked hopefully.

'Roger Vivier doesn't deal in seconds, sir,' the assistant replied with a sweet smile.

'Well, if that's the case, what's the cheapest pair of shoes you have?'

'We have some pairs of ballerinas at one hundred and twenty pounds, and a few penny loafers at ninety.'

'I'll take them,' said Alan.

'What size?'

'It doesn't matter,' said Alan.

It was the assistant's turn to look surprised. She leaned across the counter and whispered, 'We have five pairs of size thirty-eight in store, which I could let you have at a reduced price, but I'm afraid they're last season's.'

'I'm not interested in the season,' said Alan, and

happily paid for five pairs of Roger Vivier shoes, size thirty-eight, before moving across the aisle to Manolo Blahnik.

The first question he asked the sales assistant was, 'Do you have any of last season's, size thirty-eight?'

'I'll just check, sir,' said the girl, and headed off in the direction of the stockroom. 'No, sir, we've sold out of all the thirty-eights,' she said when she returned. 'The only two pairs left over from last year are a thirty-seven and a thirty-five.'

'How much would you charge me if I take both pairs?'

'Without even looking at them?'

'All I care about is that they're Manolo Blahnik,' said Alan, to another surprised assistant.

Alan left Harrods carrying two bulky green carrier bags containing seven pairs of shoes. Once he was back in the office, he handed the receipts to Roy Kerslake, who looked up from behind his pile of files when he saw how much Alan had spent.

'I hope your wife's not a size thirty-eight,' he said with a grin. The thought hadn't even crossed Alan's mind.

◄○►

While Anne was out shopping on Saturday morning, Alan built a small bonfire at the bottom of the garden. He then disappeared into the garage and removed the two carrier bags of shoes and the spare petrol can from the boot of his car.

He had completed his little experiment long before Anne returned from her shopping trip. He decided not to tell her that Manolo Blahnik had been eliminated from his findings, because, although he had a spare pair left over, sadly they were not her size. He locked the boot of his car, just in case she discovered the four remaining pairs of Roger Vivier, size thirty-eight.

◄◦►

On Monday morning, Alan rang Des Lomax's secretary to arrange an appointment with him once he'd returned from his holiday. 'I just want to wrap things up,' he explained.

'Of course, Mr Penfold,' said the secretary. 'We're expecting him back in the office on Wednesday. What time would suit you?'

'Would eleven o'clock be convenient?'

'I'm sure that will be just fine,' she replied. 'Shall we say the King's Arms?'

'No, I'd prefer to see him on site.'

◄◦►

Alan woke early on Wednesday morning and dressed without waking his wife. She'd already supplied him with all the information he required. He set off for Romford soon after breakfast, allowing far more time for the journey than was necessary. He made one stop on the way, dropping into his local garage to refill the spare petrol can.

When Alan drove into Romford he went straight to the site and parked on the only available meter. He decided that an hour would be more than enough. He opened the boot, took out the Harrods bag and the can of petrol, and walked on to the middle of site where he waited patiently for the chairman of Lomax Shoes (Import and Export) Ltd to appear.

Des Lomax drove up twenty minutes later and parked his brand-new red Mercedes E-Class Saloon on

43

a double yellow line. When he stepped out of the car, Alan's first impression was that he looked remarkably pale for someone who'd just spent ten days in Corfu.

Lomax walked slowly across to join him, and didn't apologize for being late. Alan refused his outstretched hand and simply said, 'Good morning, Mr Lomax. I think the time has come for us to discuss your claim.'

'There's nothing to discuss,' said Lomax. 'My policy was for four million, and as I've never missed a payment, I'm looking forward to my claim being paid in full, and sharpish.'

'Subject to my recommendation.'

'I don't give a damn about your recommendation, sunshine,' said Lomax, lighting a cigarette. 'Four million is what I'm entitled to, and four million is what I'm going to get. And if you don't pay up pretty damn quick, you can look forward to our next meeting being in court, which might not be a good career move, remembering that this is your first case.'

'You may well prove to be right, Mr Lomax,' said Alan. 'But I shall be recommending to your insurance broker that they settle for two million.'

'Two million?' said Lomax. 'And when did you come up with that Mickey Mouse figure?'

'When I discovered that you hadn't spent the last ten days in Corfu.'

'You'd better be able to prove that, sunshine,' snapped Lomax, 'because I've got hotel receipts, plane tickets, even the hire car agreement. So I wouldn't go down that road if I were you, unless you want to add a writ for libel to the one you'll be getting for non-payment of a legally binding contract.'

'Actually, I admit that I don't have any proof you weren't in Corfu,' said Alan. 'But I'd still advise you to settle for two million.'

44

'If you don't have any proof,' said Lomax, his voice rising, 'what's your game?'

'What we're discussing, Mr Lomax, is your game, not mine,' said Alan calmly. 'I may not be able to prove you've spent the last ten days disposing of over six thousand pairs of shoes, but what I *can* prove is that those shoes weren't in your warehouse when you set fire to it.'

'Don't threaten me, sunshine. You have absolutely no idea who you're dealing with.'

'I know only too well who I'm dealing with,' said Alan as he bent down and removed four boxes of Roger Vivier shoes from the Harrods bag and lined them up at Lomax's feet.

Lomax stared down at the neat little row of boxes. 'Been out buying presents, have we?'

'No. Gathering proof of your nocturnal habits.'

Lomax clenched his fist. 'Are you trying to get yourself thumped?'

'I wouldn't go down that road, if I were you,' said Alan, 'unless you want to add a charge of assault to the one you'll be getting for arson.'

Lomax unclenched his fist, and Alan unscrewed the cap on the petrol can and poured the contents over the boxes. 'You've already had the fire officer's report, which confirms there was no suggestion of arson,' said Lomax, 'so what do you think this little fireworks display is going to prove?'

'You're about to find out,' said Alan, suddenly cursing himself for having forgotten to bring a box of matches.

'Might I add,' said Lomax, defiantly tossing his cigarette stub on to the boxes, 'that the insurance company has already accepted the fire chief's opinion.'

'Yes, I'm well aware of that,' said Alan. 'I've read both reports.'

45

'Just as I thought,' said Lomax, 'you're bluffing.'

Alan said nothing as flames began to leap into the air, causing both men to take a pace back. Within minutes, the tissue paper, the cardboard boxes and finally the shoes had been burnt to a cinder, leaving a small cloud of black smoke spiralling into the air. When it had cleared, the two men stared down at all that was left of the funeral pyre – eight large metal buckles.

'It's often not what you do see, but what you don't see,' said Alan without explanation. He looked up at Lomax. 'It was my wife,' continued Alan, 'who told me that Catherine Deneuve made Roger Vivier buckles famous when she played a courtesan in the film *Belle de Jour*. That was when I first realized you'd set fire to your own warehouse, Mr Lomax, because if you hadn't, according to your manifest, there should have been several thousand buckles scattered all over the site.'

Lomax remained silent for some time before he said, 'I reckon you've still only got a fifty-fifty chance of proving it.'

'You may well be right, Mr Lomax,' said Alan. 'But then, I reckon you've still only got a fifty-fifty chance of not being paid a penny in compensation and, even worse, ending up behind bars for a very long time. So as I said, I will be recommending that my client settles for two million, but then it will be up to you to make the final decision, sunshine.'

◄◊►

'So what do you think?' asked Penfold as a bell sounded and the players began to stroll back out on to the field.

'You've undoubtedly beaten the odds,' I replied, 'even if I was expecting a slightly different ending.'

'So how would you have ended the story?' he asked.

'I would have held on to one pair of Roger Vivier shoes,' I told him.

'What for?'

'To give to my wife. After all, it was her first case as well.'

BLIND DATE

4

THE SCENT OF JASMINE was the first clue: a woman.

I was sitting alone at my usual table when she came and sat down at the next table. I knew she was alone, because the chair on the other side of her table hadn't scraped across the floor, and no one had spoken to her after she'd sat down.

I sipped my coffee. On a good day, I can pick up the cup, take a sip and return it to the saucer, and if you were sitting at the next table, you'd never know I was blind. The challenge is to see how long I can carry out the deception before the person sitting next to me realizes the truth. And believe me, the moment they do, they give themselves away. Some begin to whisper, and, I suspect, nod or point; some become attentive; while a few are so embarrassed they don't speak again. Yes, I can even sense that.

I hoped someone would be joining her, so I could hear her speak. I can tell a great deal from a voice. When you can't see someone, the accent and the tone are enhanced, and these can give so much away. Pause for a moment, imagine listening to someone on the other end of a phone line, and you'll get the idea.

Charlie was heading towards us. 'Are you ready to order, madam?' asked the waiter, his slight Cornish burr leaving no doubt that he was a local. Charlie is tall, strong and gentle. How do I know? Because when he guides me back to the pavement after my morning coffee, his voice comes from several inches above me, and I'm five foot ten. And if I should accidentally bump against him, there's no surplus weight, just firm muscle. But then, on Saturday afternoons he plays rugby for the Cornish Pirates. He's been in the first team for the past seven years, so he must be in his late twenties, possibly early thirties. Charlie has recently split up with his girlfriend and he still misses her. Some things you pick up from asking questions, others are volunteered.

The next challenge is to see how much I can work out about the person sitting at the next table before they realize I cannot see them. Once they've gone on their way, Charlie tells me how much I got right. I usually manage about seven out of ten.

'I'd like a lemon tea,' she replied, softly.

'Certainly, madam,' said Charlie. 'And will there be anything else?'

'No, thank you.'

Thirty to thirty-five would be my guess. Polite, and not from these parts. Now I'm desperate to know more, but I'll need to hear her speak again if I'm to pick up any further clues.

I turned to face her as if I could see her clearly. 'Can you tell me the time?' I asked, just as the clock on the church tower opposite began to chime.

She laughed, but didn't reply until the chimes had stopped. 'If that clock is to be believed,' she said, 'it's exactly ten o'clock.' The same gentle laugh followed.

'It's usually a couple of minutes fast,' I said, staring blankly up at the clock face. 'Although the church's perpendicular architecture is considered as fine an example of its kind as any in the West Country, it's not the building itself that people flock to see, but the

Madonna and Child by Barbara Hepworth in the Lady Chapel,' I added, casually leaning back in my chair.

'How interesting,' she volunteered, as Charlie returned and placed a teapot and a small jug of milk on her table, followed by a cup and saucer. 'I was thinking of attending the morning service,' she said as she poured herself a cup of tea.

'Then you're in for a treat. Old Sam, our vicar, gives an excellent sermon, especially if you've never heard it before.'

She laughed again before saying, 'I read somewhere that the *Madonna and Child* is not at all like Hepworth's usual work.'

'That's correct,' I replied. 'Barbara would take a break from her studio most mornings and join me for a coffee,' I said proudly, 'and the great lady once told me that she created the piece in memory of her eldest son, who was killed in a plane crash at the age of twenty-four while serving in the RAF.'

'How sad,' said the woman, but added no further comment.

'Some critics say,' I continued, 'that it's her finest work, and that you can see Barbara's devotion for her son in the tears in the Virgin's eyes.'

The woman picked up her cup and sipped her tea before she spoke again. 'How wonderful to have actually known her,' she said. 'I once attended a talk on the St Ives School at the Tate, and the lecturer made no mention of the *Madonna and Child*.'

'Well, you'll find it tucked away in the Lady Chapel. I'm sure you won't be disappointed.'

As she took another sip of tea, I wondered how many out of ten I'd got so far. Clearly interested in art, probably lives in London, and certainly hasn't come to St Ives to sit on the beach and sunbathe.

'So, are you a visitor to these parts?' I ventured, searching for further clues.

'Yes. But my aunt is from St Mawes, and she's hoping to join me for the morning service.'

I felt a right chump. She must have already seen the *Madonna and Child*, and probably knew more about Barbara Hepworth than I did, but was too polite to embarrass me. Did she also realize I was blind? If so, those same good manners didn't even hint at it.

I heard her drain her cup. I can even tell that. When Charlie returned, she asked him for the bill. He tore off a slip from his pad and handed it to her. She passed him a banknote, and he gave her back some coins.

'Thank you, madam,' said Charlie effusively. It must have been a generous tip.

'Goodbye,' she said, her voice directed towards me. 'It was nice to talk to you.'

I rose from my place, gave her a slight bow and said, 'I do hope you enjoy the service.'

'Thank you,' she replied. As she walked away I heard her say to Charlie, 'What a charming man.' But then, she had no way of knowing how acute my hearing is.

And then she was gone.

I sat waiting impatiently for Charlie to return. I had so many questions for him. How many of my guesses would turn out to be correct this time? From the buzz of cheerful chatter in the café, I guessed there were a lot of customers in that morning, so it was some time before Charlie was once again standing by my side.

'Will there be anything else, Mr Trevathan?' he teased.

'There most certainly will be, Charlie,' I replied. 'For a start, I want to know all about the woman who was sitting next to me. Was she tall or short? Fair or dark? Was she slim? Good-looking? Was she—'

Charlie burst out laughing.

'What's so funny?' I demanded.

'She asked me exactly the same questions about you.'

WHERE THERE'S A WILL*

5

NOW, YOU'VE ALL HEARD the story about the beautiful young nurse who takes care of a bedridden old man, convinces him to change his will in her favour, and ends up with a fortune, having deprived his children of their rightful inheritance. I confess that I thought I'd heard every variation on this theme; at least that was until I came across Miss Evelyn Beattie Moore, and even that wasn't her real name.

Miss Evelyn Mertzberger hailed from Milwaukee. She was born on the day Marilyn Monroe died, and that wasn't the only thing they had in common: Evelyn was blonde, she had the kind of figure that makes men turn and take a second look, and she had legs you rarely come across other than in an ad campaign for stockings.

So many of her friends from Milwaukee commented on how like Marilyn Monroe she looked that it wasn't surprising when as soon as Evelyn left school she bought a one-way ticket to Hollywood. On arrival in the City of Angels, she changed her name to Evelyn Beattie Moore (half Mary Tyler Moore and half Warren Beatty), but quickly discovered that, unlike Marilyn, she didn't have any talent as an actress, and no number of directors' couches was going to remedy that.

Once Evelyn had accepted this – not an easy thing for any aspiring young actress to come to terms with –

she began to look for alternative employment – which was difficult in the city of a thousand blondes.

She had spent almost all of her savings renting a small apartment in Glendale and buying a suitable wardrobe for auditions, agency photographs and the endless parties young hopefuls had to be seen at.

It was after she'd checked her latest bank statement that Evelyn realized a decision had to be made if she was to avoid returning to Milwaukee and admitting she wasn't quite as like Marilyn as her friends had thought. But what else could she do?

The idea never would have occurred to Evelyn if she hadn't come across the entry while she was flicking through the Yellow Pages looking for an electrician. It was some time before she was willing to make the necessary phone call, and then only after a final demand for the last three months' rent dropped through her mailbox.

The Happy Hunting agency assured Evelyn that their escorts were under no obligation to do anything other than have dinner with the client. They were a professional agency that supplied charming young ladies as companions for discreet gentlemen. However, it was none of their business if those young ladies chose to come to a private arrangement with the client. As the agency took 50 per cent of the booking fee, Evelyn got the message.

She decided at first that she would only sleep with a client if she felt there was a chance of their developing a long-term relationship. However, she quickly discovered that most men's idea of a long-term relationship was about an hour, and in some cases half an hour. But at least her new job made it possible for her to pay off the landlord, and even to open a savings account.

When Evelyn celebrated – or, to be more accurate, remained silent about – her thirtieth birthday, she decided the time had come to take revenge on the male species.

While not quite as many men were turning to give her a second look, Evelyn had accumulated enough money to enjoy a comfortable lifestyle. But not enough to ensure that that lifestyle would continue once she reached her fortieth birthday, and could no longer be sure of a first look.

Evelyn disappeared, and once again she changed her name. Three months later, Lynn Beattie turned up in Florida, where she registered for a diploma course at the Miami College of Nursing.

You may well ask why Lynn selected the Sunshine State for her new enterprise. I think it can be explained by some statistics she came across while carrying out her research. An article she read in *Playboy* magazine revealed that Florida was the state with the greatest number of millionaires per capita, and that the majority of them had retired and had a life expectancy of less than ten years. However, she quickly realized that she would need to carry out much more research if she hoped to graduate top of that particular class, as she was likely to come up against some pretty formidable rivals who had the same thing in mind as she did.

In the course of a long weekend spent with a middle-aged married doctor, Lynn discovered, without once having to refer to a textbook, not only that Jackson Memorial Hospital was the most expensive rest home in the state, but also that it didn't offer special rates for deserving cases.

Once Lynn had graduated with a nursing diploma, and a grade which came as a surprise to her fellow students but not to her professor, she applied for a job at Jackson Memorial.

She was interviewed by a panel of three, two of whom, including the Medical Director, were not convinced that Ms Beattie came from the right sort of background to be a Jackson nurse. The third bumped into her in the car park on his way home, and the following morning he was able to convince his colleagues to change their minds.

Lynn Beattie began work as a probationary nurse on the first day of the following month. She did not rush the next part of her plan, aware that if the Medical Director found out what she was up to, he would dismiss her without a second thought.

From the first day, Lynn went quietly and conscientiously about her work, melting into the background while keeping her eyes wide open. She quickly discovered that a hospital, just like any other workplace, has its gossip-mongers, who enjoy nothing more than to pass on the latest snippet of information to anyone willing to listen. Lynn was willing to listen. After a few weeks Lynn had discovered the one thing she needed to know about the doctors, and, later, a great deal more about their patients.

There were twenty-three doctors who ministered to the needs of seventy-one residents. Lynn had no interest in how many nurses there were, because she had no plans for them, provided she didn't come across a rival.

The gossip-monger told her that three of the doctors assumed that every nurse wanted to sleep with them, which made it far easier for Lynn to continue her research. After another few weeks, which included several 'stopovers', she found out, without ever being able to make a note, that sixty-eight of the residents were married, senile or, worse, received regular visits from their devoted relatives. Lynn had to accept the fact that 90 per cent of women either outlive their husbands or end up divorcing them. It's all part of the American dream. However, Lynn still managed to come up with a shortlist of three candidates who suffered from none of these deficiencies: Frank Cunningham Jr, Larry Schumacher III and Arthur J. Sommerfield.

Frank Cunningham was eliminated when Lynn discovered that he had two mistresses, one of whom was pregnant and had recently served a paternity suit on him, demanding that a DNA test be carried out.

Larry Schumacher III also had to be crossed off the list when Lynn found out he was visited every day by his close friend Gregory, who didn't look a day over fifty. Come to think of it, not many people in Florida do.

However, the third candidate ticked all her boxes.

Arthur J. Sommerfield was a retired banker whose worth according to *Forbes* magazine – a publication which had replaced *Playboy* as Lynn's postgraduate reading – was estimated at around a hundred million dollars: a fortune that had grown steadily through the assiduous husbandry of three generations of Sommerfields. Arthur was a widower who had only been married once (another rarity in Florida), to Arlene, who had died of breast cancer some seven years earlier. He had two children, Chester and Joni, both of whom lived abroad. Chester worked for an engineering company in Brazil, and was married with three children, while his sister Joni had recently become engaged to a landscape gardener in Montreal. Although they both wrote to their father regularly, and phoned most Sundays, visits were less frequent.

Six weeks later, after a slower than usual courtship, Lynn was transferred to the private wing of Dr William

Grove, who was the personal physician of her would-be victim.

Dr Grove was under the illusion that the only reason Lynn had sought the transfer was so she could be near him. He was impressed by how seriously the young nurse took her responsibilities. She was always willing to work unsociable hours, and never once complained about having to do overtime, especially after he'd informed her that poor Mr Sommerfield didn't have much longer to live.

Lynn quickly settled into a daily routine that ensured her patient's every need was attended to. Mr Sommerfield's preferred morning paper, the *International Herald Tribune*, and his favourite beverage, a mug of hot chocolate, were to be found on his bedside table moments after he woke. At ten, she would help Arthur – he insisted she call him Arthur – to get dressed. At eleven, they would venture out for their morning constitutional around the grounds, during which he would always cling on to her. She never once complained about which part of her anatomy he clung on to.

After lunch she would read to the old man until he fell asleep, occasionally Steinbeck, but more often Chandler. At five, Lynn would wake him so that he could watch repeats of his favourite television sitcom, *The Phil Silvers Show*, before enjoying a light supper.

At eight, she allowed him a single glass of malt whisky – it didn't take her long to discover that only Glenmorangie was acceptable – accompanied by a Cuban cigar. Both were frowned upon by Dr Grove, but encouraged by Lynn.

'We just won't tell him,' Lynn would say before turning out the light. She would then slip a hand under the sheet, where it would remain until Arthur had fallen into a deep, contented sleep. Something else she didn't tell the doctor about.

◄○►

One of the tenets of the Jackson Memorial Hospital was to make sure that patients were sent home when it became obvious they had only a few weeks to live.

'Much more pleasant to spend your final days in familiar surroundings,' Dr Grove explained to Lynn. 'And besides,' he added in a quieter voice, 'it doesn't look good if everyone who comes to Jackson Memorial dies here.'

On hearing the news of his imminent discharge – which, loosely translated, meant demise – Arthur refused to budge unless Lynn was allowed to accompany him. He had no intention of employing an agency nurse who didn't understand his daily routine.

'So, how would you feel about leaving us for a few weeks?' Dr Grove asked her in the privacy of his office.

'I don't want to leave you, William,' she said, taking his hand, 'but if it's what you want me to do . . .'

'We wouldn't be apart for too long, honey,' Dr Grove said, taking her in his arms. 'And in any case, as his physician, I'd have to visit the old man at least twice a week.'

'But he could live for months, possibly years,' said Lynn, clinging to him.

'No, darling, that's not possible. I can assure you it will be a few weeks at the most.' Dr Grove was not able to see the smile on Lynn's face.

◄○►

Ten days later, Arthur J. Sommerfield was discharged from Jackson Memorial and driven to his home in Bel Air.

65

He sat silently in the back seat, holding Lynn's hand. He didn't speak until the chauffeur had driven through a pair of crested wrought-iron gates and up a long driveway, and brought the car to a halt outside a vast redbrick mansion.

'This is the family home,' said Arthur proudly.

And it's where I'll be spending the rest of my life, thought Lynn as she gazed in admiration at the magnificent house situated in several acres of manicured lawns, bordered by flower beds and surrounded by hundreds of trees, the likes of which Lynn had only ever seen in a public park.

She soon settled into the room next door to Arthur's master suite and continued to carry out her routine, always completing the day with a happy-ending massage, as they used to call it at the agency.

It was on a Thursday evening, after his second whisky (only allowed when Lynn was certain Dr Grove wouldn't be visiting his patient that day), that Arthur said, 'I know I don't have much longer to live, my dear.' Lynn began to protest, but the old man waved a dismissive hand before adding, 'And I'd like to leave you a little something in my will.'

A little something wasn't exactly what Lynn had in mind. 'How considerate of you,' she replied. 'But I don't want anything, Arthur . . .' She hesitated. 'Except perhaps . . .'

'Yes, my dear?'

'Perhaps you could make a donation to some worthy cause? Or a bequest to your favourite charity in my name?'

'How typically thoughtful of you, my dear. But wouldn't you also like some personal memento?'

Lynn pretended to consider the offer for some time before she said, 'Well, I've grown rather attached to

66

your cane with the silver handle, the one you used to take on our afternoon walks at Jackson Memorial. And if your children wouldn't object, I'd also like the photo of you that's on your desk in the study – the one taken when you were a freshman at Princeton. You were so handsome, Arthur.'

The old man smiled. 'You shall have both of them, my dear. I'll speak to my lawyer tomorrow.'

◄◦►

Mr Haskins, the senior partner of Haskins, Haskins & Purbright, was not the kind of man who would easily have succumbed to Miss Beattie's charms. However, he wholeheartedly approved when his client expressed the desire to add several large donations to selected charities and other institutions to his will – after all, he was a Princeton man himself. And he certainly didn't object when Arthur told him that he wanted to leave his cane with the silver handle, and a photo of himself when he was at Princeton, to his devoted nurse, Miss Lynn Beattie.

'Just a keepsake, you understand,' Lynn murmured as the lawyer wrote down Arthur's words.

'I'll send the documents to you within a week,' Mr Haskins said as he rose to leave, 'in case there are any further revisions you might wish to consider.'

'Thank you, Haskins,' Arthur replied, but he had fallen asleep even before they'd had a chance to shake hands.

◄◦►

Mr Haskins was as good as his word, and a large legal envelope, marked Private & Confidential, arrived by courier five days later. Lynn took it straight to her room, and once Arthur had fallen asleep she studied every

67

syllable of the forty-seven-page document carefully. After she had turned the last page, she felt that only one paragraph needed to be amended before the old man put his signature to it.

When Lynn brought in Arthur's breakfast tray the following morning, she handed him his newspaper and said, 'I don't think Mr Haskins likes me.'

'What makes you say that, my dear?' asked Arthur as he unfolded the *Herald Tribune*.

She placed a copy of the will on his bedside table and said, 'There's no mention of your cane with the silver handle, or of my favourite photo of you. I'm afraid I won't have anything to remember you by.'

'Damn the man,' said Arthur, spilling his hot chocolate. 'Get him on the phone immediately.'

'That won't be necessary,' said Lynn. 'I'll be passing by his office later this afternoon. I'll drop the will off and remind him of your generous offer. Perhaps he simply forgot.'

'Yes, why don't you do that, my dear. But be sure you're back in time for Phil Silvers.'

Lynn did indeed pass by the Haskins, Haskins & Purbright building that afternoon, on her way to the office of a Mr Kullick, whom she had rung earlier to arrange an appointment. She had chosen Mr Kullick for two reasons. The first was that he had left Haskins, Haskins & Purbright some years before, having been passed over as a partner. There were several other lawyers in the town who had suffered the same fate, but what tipped the balance in Mr Kullick's favour was the fact that he was the vice-president of the local branch of the National Rifle Association.

Lynn took the lift to the fourth floor. As she entered the lawyer's office, Mr Kullick rose to greet her, ushering his potential client into a chair. 'How can I help you, Miss Beattie?' he asked even before he'd sat down.

'You can't help me,' said Lynn, 'but my employer is in need of your services. He's unable to attend in person because, sadly, he's bedridden.'

'I'm sorry to hear that,' said Mr Kullick. 'However, I'll need to know who it is that I'd be representing.' When he heard the name, he sat bolt upright in his chair and straightened his tie.

'Mr Sommerfield has recently executed a new will,' said Lynn, 'and he wishes one paragraph on page thirty-two to be amended.' She passed over the will that had been prepared by Mr Haskins, and the reworded paragraph she had neatly typed on Arthur's headed notepaper above a signature he had scrawled after a third whisky.

Once Mr Kullick had read the emendation, he remained silent for some time. 'I will happily draw up a new will for Mr Sommerfield, but of course I'll need to be present when he signs the document.' He paused. 'It will also have to be countersigned by an independent witness.'

'Of course,' said Lynn, who had not anticipated this problem and realized she would need a little time to find a way round it. 'Shall we say next Thursday afternoon at five o'clock, Mr Kullick?'

The lawyer checked his diary, crossed something out and entered the name Sommerfield in its place. Lynn rose from her chair.

'I see that this will was originally drawn up by Haskins, Haskins & Purbright,' said Kullick.

'That is correct, Mr Kullick,' Lynn said just before she reached the door. She turned back and smiled sweetly. 'Mr Sommerfield felt that Mr Haskins's charges had become . . . exorbitant, I think was the word he used.' She opened the door. 'I do hope you don't make the same mistake, Mr Kullick, as we may be in need of your services at some time in the future.' She closed the door quietly behind her.

◄◦►

By four o'clock the following Thursday, Lynn felt confident that she had addressed all the problems posed by Mr Kullick's demands and that everything was in place. She knew if she made the slightest mistake she would have wasted almost a year of her life, and all she would have to show for it would be a cane with a silver handle and a photograph of a young man at Princeton whom she didn't particularly like.

As she and Arthur sat and watched yet another episode in the life of Sergeant Bilko, Lynn went over the timing in her mind, trying to think of anything that might crop up at the last moment and derail her. Mr Kullick would need to be on time if her plan was to work. She checked her watch every few minutes.

When the show finally came to an end, with Bilko somehow managing to outsmart Colonel John T. Hall once again, Lynn turned off the television, poured Arthur a generous measure of whisky and handed him a Havana cigar.

'What have I done to deserve this?' he asked, patting her on the bottom.

'Someone's coming to see you, Arthur, so you mustn't fall asleep.'

'Who?' demanded Arthur, but not before he'd taken a sip of his whisky.

'A Mr Kullick. He's one of Mr Haskins's associates.'

'What does he want?' he asked as Lynn lit a match and held it up to the cigar.

70

'He's bringing over the latest version of your will, so you can sign it. Then you won't have to bother about it again.'

'Has he included my bequests to you this time?'

'He assured me that your wishes would be carried out to the letter, but he needed them confirmed in person,' said Lynn as the doorbell rang.

'Good,' said Arthur, taking another swig of whisky before Lynn plumped up his pillows and helped him to sit up.

Moments later there was a gentle knock on the bedroom door and a maid entered, accompanied by Mr Kullick. Arthur peered intently at the intruder through a cloud of smoke.

'Good afternoon, Mr Sommerfield,' said the lawyer as he walked towards the bed. He had intended to shake hands with the old man, but when he saw the look of disdain on his face, he decided against it. 'My name is Kullick, sir,' he said, remaining at the foot of the bed.

'I know,' said Arthur. 'And you've come about my will.'

'Yes, sir, I have, and—'

'And have you remembered to include the bequests for my nurse this time?'

'Yes, he has, Arthur,' interrupted Lynn. 'I told you all about it after I'd returned from visiting Mr Kullick last week.'

'Ah, yes, I remember,' said Arthur, draining his glass.

'You've given me everything – ' she paused ' – that I asked for.'

'Everything?' said Arthur.

'Yes,' she said, 'which is so much more than I deserve. But if you want to change your mind . . .' she added as she refilled his glass.

'No, no, you've more than earned it.'

71

'Thank you, Arthur,' she said, taking him by the hand.

'Let's get on with it,' said the old man wearily, turning his attention back to Kullick.

'Would you like me to take you through the will clause by clause, sir?'

'Certainly not. Haskins took long enough doing that last time.'

'As you wish, sir. Then all that remains to be done is for you to sign the document. But, as I explained to Ms Beattie, that will require a witness.'

'I'm sure Mr Sommerfield's personal maid will be happy to act as witness,' said Lynn as the front doorbell rang again.

'I'm afraid that won't be possible,' said Kullick.

'But why not?' demanded Lynn, who had already given Paula twenty dollars to carry out the task.

'Because she's a beneficiary of the will,' said Kullick, 'and therefore ineligible to be a witness.'

'She is indeed,' said Arthur. Turning to Lynn he explained, 'I've left her the silver-plated dinner service.' He leaned across and whispered, 'But I can assure you, my dear, that the silver cane is, like you, sterling.'

Lynn smiled as she desperately tried to think who could take Paula's place. Her first thought was the chauffeur, but then she remembered that he was also a beneficiary – Arthur's ancient car. She didn't want to risk going through the whole process again, but she couldn't think of anyone suitable to take the maid's place at such short notice.

'Could you come back this time tomorrow?' she asked, trying to remain calm. 'By then I'm sure—' She was interrupted by a knock on the door and Dr Grove strode into the room.

'How are you, Arthur?' he asked.

'Not too bad,' said Arthur. 'I'd be even better if you felt able to witness my signature. Or is Grove also a beneficiary of my will?' he asked Kullick.

'Certainly not,' said Dr Grove before the lawyer could speak. 'It's against company policy for any employee of Jackson Memorial to benefit from a bequest left by a patient.'

'Good, then you can earn your fee for a change, Grove. That is, assuming Kullick agrees you're acceptable.'

'Eminently so, Mr Sommerfield,' said Kullick as he opened his briefcase and extracted three thick documents. He slowly turned the pages, pointing to the small pencil crosses at the bottom of each page indicating where both signatures should be placed.

Although Lynn had taken a step back so as not to appear too involved in the process, her heartbeat didn't return to normal until the last page of all three copies had been signed and witnessed.

Once the ceremony had been completed, Kullick gathered up the documents, placed one copy in his briefcase and handed the other two to Mr Sommerfield, who waved them away, so Lynn placed them in the drawer by his bed.

'I'll take my leave, sir,' said Kullick, still not confident enough to shake hands with his latest client.

'Give Haskins my best wishes,' said Arthur as he screwed the top back on his fountain pen.

'But I no longer work for—'

'Just be sure to tell Mr Haskins when you next see him,' Lynn said quickly, 'that he obviously didn't fully appreciate Mr Sommerfield's wishes when it came to the very generous bequest he had in mind for me. But at the same time, do assure him I am not someone who bears grudges.'

Dr Grove frowned, but said nothing.

'Very magnanimous of you in the circumstances, my dear,' said Arthur.

'When I next see him,' Kullick repeated. Then he added, 'I feel it's my duty to point out to you, Mr Sommerfield, that your children may feel they are entitled to—'

'Not you as well, Kullick. When will you all accept that I've made my decision, and nothing you can say will change my mind? Now please leave us.'

'As you wish, sir,' said Kullick, stepping back as Dr Grove stuck a thermometer into his patient's mouth.

Lynn accompanied the lawyer to the door. 'Thank you, Mr Kullick, the maid will show you out.'

Kullick left without another word and after Lynn had closed the door behind him she returned to Arthur's bedside where Dr Grove was studying the thermometer.

'Your temperature is up a little, Arthur, but that's hardly surprising, considering all the excitement you've just been put through.' Turning to Lynn, he added, 'Perhaps we should leave him to have a little rest before supper.' Lynn nodded. 'Goodbye, Arthur,' he said in a louder voice. 'See you in a few days' time.'

'Good day, Grove,' said Arthur, switching the television back on.

'He's looking very frail,' said Dr Grove as Lynn accompanied him down the stairs. 'I'm going to advise his children to fly home in the next few days. I can't believe it will be much longer.'

'I'll make sure their rooms are ready,' said Lynn, 'and that Mr Sommerfield's driver picks them up at the airport.'

'That's very thoughtful of you,' said Dr Grove as they walked across the hall. 'I want you to know, Lynn, how much I appreciate all you're doing for Arthur.

When you come back to Jackson Memorial, I'm going to recommend to the medical director that you're given a promotion and a rise in salary to go with it.'

'Only if you think I'm worth it,' said Lynn coyly.

'You're more than worth it,' Grove said. 'But you do realize,' he added, lowering his voice when he spotted the maid coming out of the kitchen, 'that if Arthur left you anything in his will, however small, you would lose your job?'

'I would lose so much more than that,' said Lynn, squeezing his hand.

Grove smiled as the maid opened the door for him. 'Goodbye, honey,' he whispered.

'Goodbye, Dr Grove,' Lynn said, for the last time.

She ran back up the stairs and into the bedroom to find Arthur, cigar in one hand and an empty glass in the other, watching *The Johnny Carson Show*. Once she'd poured him a second whisky, Lynn sat down by his side. Arthur had almost fallen asleep when Carson bade goodnight to his thirty million viewers with the familiar words, 'See you all at the same time tomorrow.' Lynn turned off the TV, deftly removed the half-smoked cigar from Arthur's fingers and placed it in an ashtray on the side table, then switched off the light by his bed.

'I'm still awake,' said Arthur.

'I know you are,' said Lynn. She bent down and kissed him on the forehead before slipping an arm under the sheet. She didn't comment when a stray hand moved slowly up the inside of her leg. She stopped when she heard the familiar sigh, that moments later was followed by steady breathing. She removed her hand from under the sheet and strolled into the bathroom, wondering how many more times she would have to . . .

75

Sadly, the children arrived home just a few hours after Arthur passed away peacefully in his sleep.

◄◦►

Mr Haskins removed the half-moon spectacles from the end of his nose, put down the will and looked across his desk at his two clients.

'So all I get,' said Chester Sommerfield, not attempting to hide his anger, 'is a silver-handled cane, while Joni ends up with just a picture of Dad taken when he was a freshman at Princeton?'

'While all his other worldly goods,' confirmed Mr Haskins, 'are bequeathed to a Miss Lynn Beattie.'

'And what the hell has she done to deserve that?' demanded Joni.

'To quote the will,' said Haskins, looking back down at it, 'she has acted as "my devoted nurse and close companion".'

'Are there no loopholes for us to exploit?' asked Chester.

'That's most unlikely,' said Haskins, 'because, with the exception of one paragraph, I drew up the will myself.'

'But that one paragraph changes the whole outcome of the will,' said Joni. 'Surely we should take this woman to court. Any jury will see that she is nothing more than a fraudster who tricked my father into signing a new will only days after you had amended the old one for him.'

'You may well be right,' said Haskins, 'but, given the circumstances, I couldn't advise you to contest the validity of the will.'

'But your firm's investigators have come up with irrefutable evidence that Ms Beattie was nothing more than a common prostitute,' said Chester, 'and her nursing qualifications were almost certainly exaggerated. Once the court learns the truth, surely our claim will be upheld.'

'In normal circumstances I would agree with you, Chester, but these are not normal circumstances. As I have said, I could not advise you to take her on.'

'But why not?' came back Joni. 'At the very least we could show that my father wasn't in his right mind when he signed the will.'

'I'm afraid we'd be laughed out of court,' said Haskins, 'when the other side points out that the will was witnessed by a highly respected doctor who was at your father's bedside right up until the day he died.'

'I'd still be willing to risk it,' said Chester. 'Just look at it from her perspective. She's a penniless whore who has recently been dismissed from her job without a reference, and she sure won't want her past activities aired in court and then reported on the early evening news followed by the front page of every morning paper.'

'You may well be right,' said Haskins. 'But it's still my duty as a lawyer to inform my clients when I believe their case cannot be won.'

'But you can't be worried about taking on Kullick in court,' said Chester. 'After all, you didn't even think he was good enough to be a partner in your firm.'

Haskins raised an eyebrow. 'That may well be the case, but it wouldn't be Mr Kullick I would be up against.' He replaced his half-moon spectacles on the end of his nose and once again picked up the will, then turned over several pages before identifying the relevant clause. He looked solemnly at his clients before he began to read.

'"I also bequeath ten million dollars to my alma mater, Princeton University; five million dollars to the

Veterans Association of America; five million dollars to the Conference of Presidents, to assist their work in Israel; five million dollars to the Republican Party, which I have supported all my life; and finally five million dollars to the National Rifle Association, the aims of which I approve, and which I have always supported."'

The old lawyer looked up. 'I should point out to you both that none of these bequests was in your father's original will,' he said, before adding, 'and although I am in no doubt that we could beat Mr Kullick if he was our only opponent, I can assure you that we would have little chance of defeating five of the largest and most prestigious law firms in the land. Between them they would have bled you dry long before the case came to court. I fear I can only recommend that you settle for a cane with a silver handle and a photograph of your father at Princeton.'

'While she walks away with a cool seventy million dollars,' said Joni.

'Having sacrificed thirty million to ensure she would never have to appear in court,' said Haskins as he placed the will back on his desk. 'Clever woman, Ms Lynn Beattie, and that wasn't even her real name.'

DOUBLE-CROSS *

6

THE JUDGE LOOKED DOWN at the defendant and frowned.

'Kevin Bryant, you have been found guilty of armed robbery. A crime you clearly planned with considerable skill and ingenuity. During your trial it has become clear that you knew exactly when to carry out the attack upon your chosen victim, Mr Neville Abbott, a respected diamond merchant from Hatton Garden. You held up the security guard at his workshop with a shotgun, and forced him to open the strongroom where Mr Abbott was showing a dealer from Holland a consignment of uncut diamonds he had recently purchased from South Africa for just over ten million pounds.

'Thanks to outstanding police work, you were arrested within days, although the diamonds have never been found. During the seven months you have spent in custody you have been given every opportunity to reveal the whereabouts of the diamonds, but you have chosen not to do so.

'Taking that fact, as well as your past record, into consideration, I am left with no choice but to sentence you to twelve years in prison. However, Mr Bryant, I would consider a reduction to your sentence if at any time you should change your mind and decide to inform the police where the diamonds are. Take the prisoner down.'

Detective Inspector Matthews frowned as he watched

Bryant being led down to the cells before being shipped off to Belmarsh prison. As a policeman, you're meant to feel a certain professional pride, almost pleasure, when you've been responsible for banging up a career criminal, but this time Matthews felt no such pride, and wouldn't until he got his hands on those diamonds. He was convinced Bryant hadn't had enough time to sell them on and must have hidden them somewhere.

Detective Inspector Matthews had attempted to make a deal with Bryant on more than one occasion. He even offered to downgrade his charge to aggravated burglary, which carries a far shorter sentence, but only if he pleaded guilty and told him where the diamonds were. But Bryant always gave the same reply: 'I'll do my bird, guv.'

If Bryant wasn't willing to make a deal with him, Matthews knew someone doing time in the same prison who was.

◄○►

Benny Friedman, known to his fellow inmates as Benny the Fence, was serving a six-year sentence for handling stolen goods. A burglar would bring him the gear and Benny would pay him 20 per cent of its value in cash, then sell it on to a middle man for about 50 per cent, walking away with a handsome profit.

From time to time Benny got caught and had to spend some time in the nick. But as he didn't pay a penny in tax, was rarely out of work and had no fears of being made redundant, he considered the occasional spell in prison no more than part of the job description. But if the police ever offered him an alternative to going back inside, Benny was always willing to listen. After all, why would you want to spend more time behind bars than was necessary?

'Drugs check,' bellowed the wing officer as he pulled open the heavy door of Benny's cell.

'I don't do drugs, Mr Chapman,' said Benny, not stirring from his bunk.

'Get your arse upstairs, Friedman, and sharpish. Once they've checked your piss you can come back down and enjoy a well-earned rest. Now move it.'

Benny folded his copy of the *Sun*, lowered himself slowly off the bottom bunk, strolled out of his cell into the corridor and made his way up to the medical wing. No officer ever bothered to accompany him while he was out of his cell, as he never caused any trouble. You can have a reputation, even in prison.

When Benny arrived at the medical wing, he was surprised to find that none of the usual reprobates was waiting in line to be checked for drugs. In fact, he seemed to be the only inmate in sight.

'This way, Friedman,' said an officer he didn't recognize. Moments after he had entered the hospital, he heard a key being turned in the lock behind him. He looked around and saw his old friend Detective Inspector Matthews, who had arrested him many times in the past, sitting on the end of one of the beds.

'To what do I owe this honour, Mr Matthews?' Benny asked without missing a beat.

'I need your help, Benny,' said the detective inspector, not suggesting that the old lag should sit down.

'That's a relief, Mr Matthews. For a minute I thought you were being tested for drugs.'

'Don't get lippy with me, Benny,' said Matthews sharply. 'Not when I've come to offer you a deal.'

'And what are you proposing this time, Mr Matthews? A packet of fags in exchange for a serial killer?'

Matthews ignored the question. 'You're coming up for appeal in a few months' time,' he said, lighting a cigarette but not offering Benny one. 'I might be able to arrange for a couple of years to be knocked off your sentence.' He took a deep drag and blew out a cloud of smoke before adding, 'Which would mean you could be out of this hell hole in six months' time.'

'How very thoughtful of you, Mr Matthews,' said Benny. 'What are you expecting me to do in return for such munificence?'

'There's a con on his way to Belmarsh from the Old Bailey. He should be checking in any moment now. His name's Bryant, Kevin Bryant, and I've arranged for him to be your new cellmate.'

—◆—

When the cell door was pulled open, Benny looked up from his copy of the *Sun* and watched as Bryant swaggered into the cell. The man didn't say a word, just flung his kit bag on the top bunk. New prisoners always start off on the top bunk.

Benny went back to his paper while Bryant placed a thin bar of white soap, a green flannel, a rough green towel and a Bic razor on the ledge above the washbasin. Benny put his paper down and studied the new arrival more closely. Bryant was every inch the armed robber. He was about five foot five, stockily built, with a shaved head. He unbuttoned his blue-and-white striped prison shirt to reveal a massive tattoo of a red devil. Not much doubt which football team Bryant supported. On the fingers of one hand were tattooed the letters HATE, and on the other, LOVE.

Bryant finally glanced across at Benny. 'My name's Kev.'

'Mine's Benny. Welcome to Belmarsh.'

'It's not my first time in the slammer,' said Bryant. 'I've been here before.' He chuckled. 'Several times, actually. And you?' he asked once he'd climbed up on to the top bunk and settled down.

'Fourth time,' said Benny. 'But then, I don't like to hang around for too long.'

Bryant laughed for the first time. 'So what are you in for?' he asked.

Benny was surprised that Bryant had broken one of prison's golden rules: never ask a fellow con what he's in for. Wait for him to volunteer the information. 'I'm a fence,' he replied.

'What do you fence?'

'Almost anything. But I draw the line at drugs, and that includes marijuana, and I won't handle porn, hard or soft. You've got to have some standards.'

Bryant was silent for some time. Benny wondered if he'd fallen asleep, which would be unusual on your first day inside, even for a regular. 'You haven't asked me what I'm in for,' said Bryant eventually.

'No need to, is there?' said Benny. 'Your mugshot's been on the front page of the tabloids every day for the past week. Everyone at Belmarsh knows what you're in for.'

Bryant didn't speak again that night, but Benny was in no hurry. The one thing you've got plenty of in prison is time. As long as you're patient, everything will eventually come out, however secretive an inmate imagines he is.

◄○►

Benny didn't much like being in jail, but most of all he dreaded the weekends, when you could be banged up for eighteen hours at a stretch, with only a short break to collect an oily meal of spam fritters and chips from the hotplate.

The screws allowed the prisoners out for a forty-five-minute break in the afternoon. Benny could choose between watching football on television or taking a stroll around the yard, whatever the weather. He had no interest in football, but as Bryant always went straight to the yard, he settled for watching television. He was grateful for any break he could get in this hastily arranged marriage, and if Bryant was ever going to say anything about where the diamonds were, it was more likely to be in the privacy of their cell than in the bustling, noisy, overcrowded yard where other prisoners could eavesdrop.

Benny was reading an article about how the Italian Prime Minister spent his weekends when Bryant broke into his thoughts. 'Why don't you ever ask me about the diamonds?'

'None of my business,' said Benny, not looking up from his paper.

'But you must be curious about what I've done with them?'

'According to the *Sun*'s crime correspondent,' said Benny, 'you sold them to a middle man for half a million.'

'Half a million?' said Bryant. 'Do I look that fuckin' stupid?'

'So how much did you sell 'em for?'

'Nothin'.'

'Nothin'?' repeated Benny.

'Because I've still got 'em, haven't I?'

'Have you?'

'Yeah. And I can tell you one thing. The fuzz ain't never gonna find out where I stashed 'em, however hard they look.'

Benny pretended to go on reading his paper. He'd reached the sports pages by the time Bryant spoke again.

'It's all part of my retirement plan, innit? Most of the muppets in this place will walk out with nothin', while I've got myself a guaranteed income for life, haven't I?'

Benny waited patiently, but Bryant didn't utter another word before lights out, four hours later. Benny would have liked to ask Bryant just one more question, but he knew he couldn't risk it.

'What do you think about this guy Berlusconi?' he asked finally.

'What's he in for?' asked Bryant.

◄○►

Benny always attended the Sunday morning service held in the prison chapel, not because he believed in God, but because it got him out of his cell for a whole hour. The long walk to the chapel on the other side of the prison, the body search for drugs – by a female officer if you got lucky – the chance for a gossip with some old lags, a sing-song, followed by a saunter back to your cell in time for lunch, were a welcome break from the endless hours of being banged up.

Benny settled down in his usual place in the third row, opened his hymn sheet and, when the organ struck up, joined in lustily with 'Fight the good fight'.

Once the prison chaplain had delivered his regular sermon on repentance and forgiveness, followed by the final blessing, the cons began to make their way slowly out of the chapel and back to their cells.

'Can you spare me a moment, Friedman?' asked the chaplain after Benny had handed in his hymn sheet.

'Of course, Father,' said Benny, feeling a moment of apprehension that the chaplain might ask him to sign up for his confirmation class. If he did, Benny would have to come clean and admit he was Jewish. The only reason he'd ticked the little box marked C of E was so he could escape from his cell for an hour every Sunday morning. If he'd admitted he was a Jew, a Rabbi would have visited him in his cell once a month, because not enough Jews end up in prison to hold a service for them.

The chaplain asked Benny to join him in the vestry. 'A friend has asked to see you, Benny. I'll leave you alone for a few minutes.' He closed the vestry door and returned to those repenting souls who did want to sign up for his confirmation class.

'Good morning, Mr Matthews,' said Benny, taking an unoffered seat opposite the detective inspector. 'I had no idea you'd taken up holy orders.'

'Cut the crap, Friedman, or I may have to let your wing officer know that you're really a Jew.'

'If you did, Inspector, I'd have to explain to him how I'd seen the light on the way to Belmarsh.'

'And you'll see my boot up your backside if you waste any more of my time.'

'So, to what do I owe this pleasure?' asked Benny innocently.

'Has he sold the diamonds?' asked Matthews, not wasting another word.

'No, Inspector, he hasn't. In fact, he claims they're still in his possession. The story about selling them for half a million was just a smokescreen.'

'I knew it,' said Matthews. 'He would never have sold them for so little. Not after all the trouble he went to.' Benny didn't comment. 'Have you managed to find out where he's stashed them?'

'Not yet,' said Benny. 'I've got a feeling that might take a little longer, unless you want me to—'

'Don't press him,' interrupted Matthews. 'It'll only

make him suspicious. Bide your time and wait for him to tell you himself.'

'And when I've elicited this vital piece of evidence, Inspector, I'll get two years knocked off my sentence, as you promised?' Benny reminded him.

'Don't push your luck, Friedman. I accept that you've earned a year off, but you won't get the other year until you find out where those diamonds are. So get back to your cell, and keep your ears open and your mouth shut.'

◄◦►

It was on a Saturday morning that Bryant asked Benny, 'Have you ever fenced any diamonds?'

Benny had waited weeks for Bryant to ask that question. 'From time to time,' he said. 'I've got a reliable dealer in Amsterdam, but I'd need to know a lot more before I'd be willing to contact him. What sort of numbers are we talkin' about?'

'Is ten mill out of your league?' asked Bryant.

'No, I wouldn't say that,' said Benny, trying not to rise, 'but it might take a little longer than usual.'

'All I've got is time,' said Bryant, slipping back into one of his long, contemplative silences. Benny prayed that it wasn't going to be another six weeks before he asked the next question.

'What percentage would you pay me if I let you fence the diamonds?' asked Bryant.

'My usual terms are twenty per cent of the face value, strictly cash.'

'And how much do you sell them on for?'

'Usually around fifty per cent of face value.'

'And how much will your contact make?'

'I've got no idea,' said Benny. 'He doesn't ask me

where it comes from, and I don't ask him how much he makes out of it. As long as we all make a profit, the less anyone knows the better.'

'Does it matter what kind of stones they are?'

'The smaller the better,' said Benny. 'Always avoid the big stuff. If you brought me the Crown Jewels, I'd tell you to fuck off, because I'd never find a buyer. Small stones aren't easy to trace, you can lose them on the open market.'

'So you'd cough up a couple of mill, if I deliver?'

'If they're worth ten million, yes, but I'd need to see them first.'

'Why wouldn't they be?' asked Bryant, looking Benny straight in the eye.

'Because figures reported in the press aren't always reliable. Crime reporters like numbers with lots of noughts, and they only ever round them up.'

'But they were insured for ten million,' said Bryant, 'and don't forget the insurance company paid up in full.'

'I won't make an offer until I've seen the goods,' said Benny.

Bryant fell silent again.

'So where are they?' asked Benny, trying to make the words sound unrehearsed.

'It doesn't matter where they are,' said Bryant.

'It matters if you expect me to give you a valuation,' snapped Benny.

'What if I could show you half a dozen of them right now?'

'Stop pissing me about, Kev. If you're serious about doin' a deal, tell me where they are. If not, fuck off.' Not tactics Inspector Matthews would have approved of, but with his appeal coming up in a few days' time, Benny couldn't afford to wait another six weeks before Bryant spoke again.

'I'm serious,' said Bryant quietly. 'So shut up and listen for a minute, unless you're doing a bigger deal this week?' Benny thought about another year being knocked off his sentence and remained silent. 'While I was banged up on remand, one of the cons was arrested for possession. Heroin, class A.'

'So what?' said Benny. 'People get arrested for possession every day.'

'Not while they're in prison, they don't.'

'But how did he get the gear in?' asked Benny, suddenly taking an interest.

'This con picks up the stuff from a mate while he's on trial at the Old Bailey. Durin' one of the breaks he asks to go to the toilet, knowing that the guard has to stay outside while he's in the cubicle. While he's on the john, he stuffs the gear into a condom, ties a knot in it and swallows it.'

'But if the condom split open in his stomach,' said Benny, 'he'd be history.'

'Yeah, but if he gets it into prison, he can make a grand. Five times what he'd pick up on the out.'

'Tell me something I don't know,' said Benny.

'Once he's banged up in here, he waits till the middle of the night, sits on the toilet, where the screws can't see him through the spy hole, and—'

'Spare me the details.'

After another long pause, Bryant said, 'On the day I was sentenced I did the same thing.'

'You swallowed two ounces of heroin?' asked Benny in disbelief.

'No, you stupid bugger, you've not been payin' attention.' Benny remained silent while Bryant rolled a cigarette then kept him waiting until he'd lit it and inhaled several times. 'I swallowed six of the diamonds, didn't I?'

'Why in Gawd's name would you do that?'

'Prison currency, in case I ever found myself dealin' with a bent screw, or in need of a favour from an old lag.'

'So where are they now?' asked Benny, pushing his luck.

'They've been in this cell for the past three months, and you haven't even set eyes on them.'

Benny said nothing as Bryant climbed down from the top bunk and took a plastic fork from the table. He slowly began to unstitch the centre strip that ran down the side of his Adidas tracksuit bottoms. It was some time before he was able to extract one small diamond. Benny's eyes lit up when he saw it sparkle under the naked light bulb.

'Six stripes means six diamonds,' Bryant said in triumph. 'If any screw checked my tracksuit, he would have found more stashed in there than he earns in a year.'

Bryant handed the diamond over to Benny, who took it across to the tiny barred window and studied it closely while he tried to think.

'So, what do you think?' asked Bryant.

'Can't be sure yet, but there's one way to find out. Let me see your watch.'

'Why?' asked Bryant, holding out his arm.

Benny didn't reply, but ran the edge of the stone across the glass, leaving a thin scratch on the surface.

'Hey, what's your game?' said Bryant, pulling his arm away. 'I paid good money for that watch.'

'And I won't be wasting good money on this piece of shit,' said Benny, handing the stone back to Bryant before returning to the bottom bunk and pretending to read his newspaper.

'Why the fuck not?' asked Bryant.

'Because it's not a diamond,' said Benny. 'If it was, it would have shattered the glass on your watch, not just left a scratch on the surface. You've been robbed, my friend,' said Benny, 'and by a very clever man who's palmed you off with paste.'

Bryant stared at his watch. It was some time before he stammered out, 'But I saw Abbott fill the bag with diamonds from his safe.'

'I've no doubt you saw him fill the bag with something, Kevin, but whatever it was, it wasn't diamonds.'

Bryant collapsed on to the only chair in the cell. Eventually he managed to ask, 'So how much are they worth?'

'Depends how many you've got.'

'A sugar bag full. It weighed about two pounds.'

Benny wrote down some numbers on the back of his newspaper before offering his considered opinion. 'Two grand perhaps, three at the most. I'm sorry to say, Kev, that Mr Abbott saw you coming.'

Bryant began picking at the remaining stripes on his tracksuit bottoms with the plastic fork. Each time a new stone fell out, he rubbed it across his watch. The result was always the same: a faint scratch, but the glass remained firmly intact.

'Twelve years for a few fuckin' grand,' Bryant shouted as he paced up and down the tiny cell like a caged animal. 'If I ever get my hands on that bastard Abbott, I'll tear him apart limb from limb.'

'Not for another twelve years you won't,' said Benny helpfully.

Bryant began thumping the cell door with his bare fists, but he knew that no one could hear him except Benny.

Benny didn't say another word until lights out at ten o'clock, by which time Bryant had calmed down a little, and had even stopped banging his head against the wall.

Benny had spent the time working out exactly what he was going to say next. But not before he was convinced that Bryant was at his most vulnerable, which was usually about an hour after lights out. 'I think I know how you could get revenge on your friend Mr Abbott,' whispered Benny, not sure if Bryant was still awake.

Bryant leapt off the top bunk and, towering over Benny, their noses almost touching, shouted, 'Tell me. Tell me. I'll do anything to get even with that bastard!'

'Well, if you don't want to wait twelve years before you next bump into him, you've got it in your power to make him come to you.'

'Stop talking in fuckin' riddles,' said Bryant. 'How can I get Abbott to come to Belmarsh? He's hardly likely to apply for a visiting order.'

'I was thinking of something more permanent than a visit,' said Benny. It was Bryant's turn to wait impatiently for his cellmate to continue. 'You told me the judge offered to reduce your sentence if you told where you stashed the diamonds.'

'That's right. But have you forgotten they ain't diamonds no more?' shouted Bryant, inching even closer towards him.

'Exactly my point,' said Benny, not flinching, 'so it shouldn't take the police long to work out that they've been taken for a ride, while Abbott has ended up with ten million of insurance money in exchange for two pounds of paste.'

'You're fuckin' right,' said Bryant, clenching his fist.

'As soon as the police realize the diamonds aren't kosher, they're gonna throw the book at Abbott: fraud, theft, criminal deception, not to mention perverting the course of justice. I wouldn't be surprised if he was sent down for at least ten years.' Benny lit a cigarette and slowly inhaled before he added, 'And there's only one place he's heading once he leaves the Old Bailey.'

'Belmarsh!' said Bryant, punching his fist in the air as if Manchester United had just won the Cup.

◄○►

The physical instruction officer at Belmarsh had never seen this particular con in the gym before, despite the fact that he clearly needed some exercise, nor, for that matter, the police officer he was deep in conversation with, who clearly didn't. The governor had told him to lock the gym door and make sure that no one, screw or con, entered while the two men were together.

'Bryant has made a full confession,' said Detective Inspector Matthews, 'including where we'd find the diamonds. Half a dozen of them were missing, of course. I presume there's no chance of retrieving them.'

'None,' said Benny with a sigh. 'It broke my heart to watch him flushing them down the toilet. But, Inspector Matthews, I was thinking of the bigger picture.'

'The one where you leave this place in a few weeks' time?' suggested the detective inspector.

'I admit it had crossed my mind,' said Benny. 'But I'm still curious to know what happened to the rest of the diamonds?'

'The insurance company sold them back to Mr Abbott at a slightly reduced price, on the understanding that neither side would refer to the matter again.'

'That's a relief,' said Benny, 'because I've got a favour to ask you, Inspector Matthews.'

'Isn't two years off your sentence enough to be going on with?'

'It certainly is, Inspector Matthews, and don't think I'm not grateful, but it won't be long before Bryant works out the reason you haven't arrested Abbott is because the diamonds *are* kosher, and I double-crossed him.'

'Go on,' said the detective inspector.

'I just wondered if you could find it in your heart, Mr Matthews, if I was ever foolish enough to be found wanting again, to make sure that I'm never sent back to Belmarsh.'

Matthews rose from the bench at the far end of the gym and looked down at the old con. 'Not a hope, Benny,' he said with a grin. 'I can't think of a better way of ensuring that you finally get yourself a proper job and stay on the straight and narrow. And by the way, there may even come a time when you want to come back to Belmarsh.'

'You must be joking, Mr Matthews. Why would I ever want to come back to this shit hole?'

'Because the judge was as good as his word,' said Matthews. 'He's cut Bryant's sentence in half. So, with good behaviour, he should be out in a couple of years' time. And when he is, Benny, I have a feeling it won't be Mr Abbott he comes looking for.'

'I WILL SURVIVE'*

7

WHEN THE DOORBELL RANG, Julian Farnsdale looked up.

The first decision he always had to make was whether to engage a potential customer in conversation, or simply leave them to browse. There were several golden rules that you adopted after so many years in the trade. If the customer looked as if he needed some assistance, Julian would rise from behind his desk and say either, 'Can I help you?' or, 'Would you prefer just to browse?' If they only wanted to browse, he would sit back down, and although he would keep an eye on them, he wouldn't speak again until they began a conversation.

Julian wasn't in any doubt that this customer was a browser, so he remained seated and said nothing. Browsers fall into three categories: those simply passing the time of day who stroll around for a few minutes before leaving without saying anything; dealers who know exactly what they are looking for but don't want you to know they're in the trade; and, finally, genuine enthusiasts hoping to come across something a little special to add to their collections.

This particular customer unquestionably fell into the third category.

Julian studied him out of the corner of one eye, an art he had perfected over the years. He decided he was probably an American – the tailored blazer, neatly pressed chinos and striped preppy tie. The man may have been a browser but he was a browser with real knowledge and taste because he only stopped to consider the finest pieces: the Adam fireplace, the Chippendale rocking chair and the Delft plate. Julian wondered if he would spot the one real treasure in his shop.

A few moments later, the customer came to a halt in front of the egg. He studied the piece for some time before looking across at Julian. 'Has it been signed by the master?'

Julian rose slowly from his chair. Another golden rule: don't appear to be in a hurry when you're hoping to sell something very expensive.

'Yes, sir,' said Julian as he walked towards him. 'You'll find Carl Fabergé's signature on the base. And of course the piece is listed in the catalogue raisonné.'

'Date and description?' enquired the customer, continuing to study the egg.

'1910,' said Julian. 'It was made to celebrate the Tsarina's thirty-eighth birthday, and is one of a series of Easter eggs commissioned by Tsar Nicholas the Second.'

'It's magnificent,' said the customer. 'Quite magnificent. But probably out of my price range.'

Julian immediately recognized the bargaining ploy, so he mentally added 20 per cent to the asking price to allow a little room for manoeuvre.

'Six hundred and eighty thousand,' he said calmly.

'Pounds?' asked the man, raising an eyebrow.

'Yes,' said Julian without further comment.

'So, about a million dollars,' said the customer, confirming that he was American.

Julian didn't reply. He was distracted by a screeching sound outside, as if a car was trying to avoid a collision. Both men glanced out of the window to see a black stretch limousine that had come to a halt on the double yellow line outside the shop. A woman dressed in a stylish red coat and wearing a diamond necklace, matching earrings and dark glasses stepped out of the back of the car.

'Is that who I think it is?' asked Julian.

'Looks like it is,' said the customer, as the woman stopped to sign an autograph.

'Gloria Gaynor.' Julian sighed as she disappeared into the jewellery shop next door. 'Lucky Millie,' he added without explanation.

'I think she's doing a gig in town this week,' said the customer.

'She's performing at the Albert Hall on Saturday,' said Julian. 'I tried to get a ticket but it's completely sold out.'

The customer was clearly more interested in the jewel-encrusted egg than the jewel-covered pop star so Julian snapped back into antique-dealer mode.

'What's the lowest price you'd consider?' asked the American.

'I suppose I could come down to six hundred and fifty thousand.'

'My bet is that you'd come down to five hundred thousand,' said the American.

'Six hundred and twenty-five thousand,' said Julian. 'I couldn't consider a penny less.'

The American nodded. 'That's a fair price. But my partner will need to see it before I can make a final decision.' Julian tried not to look disappointed. 'Would it be possible to reserve the piece at six twenty-five?'

'Yes, of course, sir.' Julian pulled open a drawer in his desk, removed a small green sticker and placed it on the little description card fixed to the wall. 'And when might we expect to see you again, sir?'

'My partner flies in from the States on Friday, so possibly Friday afternoon. But as he suffers badly from jetlag it's more likely to be Saturday afternoon. What time do you close on Saturdays?'

'Around five, sir,' said Julian.

'I'll make sure we're with you before then,' said the American.

Julian opened the door to allow his customer to leave just as Miss Gaynor walked out of the jewellery shop. Once again she stopped to sign autographs for a little group that had gathered on the pavement outside. The chauffeur ran to open the door of the limousine and she disappeared inside. As the car slipped out into the traffic, Julian found himself waving, which was silly because he couldn't see a thing through the smoked-glass windows.

Julian was about to return to his shop when he noticed that his next-door neighbour was also waving. 'What was she like, Millie?' he asked, trying not to sound too much like an adoring fan.

'Charming. And so natural,' Millie replied, 'considering all that she's been through. A real star.'

'Did you learn anything interesting?' asked Julian.

'She's staying at the Park Lane Hotel, and she's off to Paris on Sunday for the next leg of her tour.'

'I already knew that,' said Julian. 'Read it in Londoner's Diary last night. Tell me something I don't know.'

'On the day of a concert she never leaves her room and won't speak to anyone, even her manager. She likes to rest her voice before going on stage.'

'Fascinating,' said Julian. 'Anything else?'

'The air conditioning in her room has to be turned off, because she's paranoid about catching a cold and not being able to perform. She once missed a concert in Dallas when she came off the street at a hundred degrees straight into an air-conditioned room, and ended up coughing and sneezing for a week.'

'Why's she staying at the Park Lane,' asked Julian, 'and not Claridges or the Ritz where all the big stars stay?'

'It's only a five-minute drive from the Albert Hall and she has a dread of being held up in a traffic jam and being late for a concert.'

'You're beginning to sound like an old friend,' said Julian.

'Well, she was very chatty,' said Millie.

'But did she buy anything?' asked Julian, ignoring a man carrying a large package who strolled past him and through the open door of his antique shop.

'No, but she did put a deposit down on a pair of earrings and a watch. She said she'd be back tomorrow.' Millie gave her next-door neighbour a warm smile. 'And if you buy me a coffee, I'll tell her about your Fabergé egg.'

'I think I may already have a buyer for that,' said Julian. 'But I'll still get you a coffee, just as soon as I've got rid of Lenny.' He smiled and stepped back into his shop, not bothering to close the door.

'I thought you might be interested in this, Mr Farnsdale,' said a scruffily dressed man, handing him a heavy helmet. 'It's Civil War, circa 1645. I could let you have it for a reasonable price.'

Julian studied the helmet for a few moments.

'Circa 1645 be damned,' he pronounced. 'More like circa 1995. And if you picked it up in the Old Kent Road, I can even tell you who made it. I've been around far too long to be taken in by something like that.'

Lenny left the shop, head bowed, still clutching the helmet. Julian closed the door behind him.

◄○►

Julian was bargaining with a lady over a small ceramic figure of the Duke of Wellington in the shape of a boot (circa 1817). He wanted £350 for the piece but she was refusing to pay more than £320, when the black stretch limousine drew up outside. Julian left his customer and hurried over to the window just in time to see Miss Gaynor step out on to the pavement and walk into the jewellery shop without glancing in his direction. He sighed and turned to find that his customer had gone, and so had the Duke of Wellington.

Julian spent the next hour standing by the door so he wouldn't miss his idol when she left the jewellery shop. He was well aware that he was breaking one of his golden rules: you should never stand by the door. It frightens off the customers and, worse, it makes you look desperate. Julian was desperate.

Miss Gaynor finally strolled out of the jewellery shop clutching a small red bag which she handed to her chauffeur. She stopped to sign an autograph, then walked straight past the antique shop and into Art Pimlico, on the other side of Julian's shop. She was in there for such a long time that Julian began to wonder if he'd missed her. But she couldn't have left the gallery because the limousine was still parked on the double yellow lines, the chauffeur seated behind the wheel.

When Miss Gaynor finally emerged she was followed by the gallery owner, who was carrying a large Warhol silk-screen print of Chairman Mao. Lucky Susan, thought Julian, to have had a whole hour with Gloria. The chauffeur leapt out, took the print from Susan and placed it in the boot of the limousine. Miss Gaynor paused to sign a few more autographs before taking the opportunity to escape. Julian stared out of the window and didn't move until she'd climbed into the back of the car and had been whisked away.

Once the car was out of sight, Julian joined Millie and Susan on the pavement. 'I see you sold the great lady a Warhol,' he said to Susan, trying not to sound envious.

'No, she only took it on appro,' said Susan. 'She wants to live with it for a couple of days before she makes up her mind.'

'Isn't that a bit of a risk?' asked Julian.

'Hardly,' said Susan. 'I can just see the headline in the *Sun*: Gloria Gaynor steals Warhol from London gallery. I don't think that's the kind of publicity she'll be hoping for on the first leg of her European tour.'

'Did you manage to sell her anything, Millie?' asked Julian, trying to deflect the barb.

'The earrings and the watch,' said Millie, 'but far more important, she gave me a couple of tickets for her concert on Saturday night.'

'Me too,' said Susan, waving her tickets in triumph.

'I'll give you two hundred pounds for them,' said Julian.

'Not a chance,' said Millie. 'Even if you offered double, I wouldn't part with them.'

'How about you, Susan?' Julian asked desperately.

'You must be joking.'

'You may change your mind when she doesn't return your Chairman Mao,' said Julian, before flouncing back into his shop.

--◦--

The following morning, Julian hovered by the door of his shop, but there was no sign of the stretch limousine.

He didn't join Millie and Susan in Starbucks for coffee at eleven, claiming he had a lot of paperwork to do.

He didn't have a single customer all day, just three browsers and a visit from the VAT inspector. When he locked up for the night, he had to admit to himself that it hadn't been a good week so far. But all that could change if the American returned on Saturday with his partner.

On Thursday morning the stretch limousine drove up and parked outside Susan's gallery. The chauffeur stepped out, removed Chairman Mao from the boot and carried the Chinese leader inside. A few minutes later he ran back on to the street, slammed the boot shut, jumped behind the steering wheel and drove off, but not before a parking ticket had been placed on his windscreen. Julian laughed.

—◦—

The next morning, while Julian was discussing the Adam fireplace with an old customer who was showing some interest in the piece, the doorbell rang and a woman entered the shop.

'Don't worry about me,' she said in a gravelly voice. 'I just want to look around. I'm not in any hurry.'

'Where did you say you found it, Julian?'

'Buckley Manor in Hertfordshire, Sir Peter,' said Julian without adding the usual details of its provenance.

'And you're asking eighty thousand?'

'Yes,' said Julian, not looking at him.

'Well, I'll think about it over the weekend,' said the customer, 'and let you know on Monday.'

'Whatever suits you, Sir Peter,' said Julian, and without another word he strode off towards the front of the shop, opened the door and remained standing by it until the customer had stepped back out on to the pavement, a puzzled look on his face. If Sir Peter had looked round, he would have seen Julian close the door and switch the OPEN sign to CLOSED.

'Stay cool, Julian, stay cool,' he murmured to himself as he walked slowly towards the lady he'd been hoping to serve all week.

'I was in the area a couple of days ago,' she said, her voice husky and unmistakable.

I know you were, Gloria, Julian wanted to say. 'Indeed, madam,' was all he managed.

'Millie told me all about your wonderful shop, but I just didn't have enough time.'

'I understand, madam.'

'Actually, I haven't come across anything I really like this week. I was hoping I might be luckier today.'

'Let's hope so, madam.'

'You see, I try to take home some little memento from every city I perform in. It always brings back so many happy memories.'

'What a charming idea,' said Julian, beginning to relax.

'Of course, I could hardly fail to admire the Adam fireplace,' she said, running a hand over the marble nymphs, 'but I can't see it fitting in to my New York condo.'

'I'm sure you're right, madam,' said Julian.

'The Chippendale rocking chair is unquestionably a masterpiece, but sadly it would look somewhat out of place in a Beverly Hills mansion. And Delft isn't to my taste.' She continued to look around the room, until her eyes came to rest on the egg. 'But I do love your Fabergé egg.' Julian smiled ingratiatingly. 'What does the green dot mean?' she asked innocently.

'That it's reserved for another customer, madam; an American gentleman I'm expecting tomorrow.'

'What a pity,' she said, staring lovingly at the egg. 'I'm working tomorrow, and flying to Paris the following day.' She smiled sweetly at Julian and said, 'It clearly wasn't meant to be. Thank you.' She began walking slowly towards the door.

Julian hurried after her. 'It's possible, of course, that the customer won't come back. They often don't, you know.'

She paused by the door. 'And how much did he agree to pay for the egg?' she asked.

'Six hundred and twenty-five thousand,' said Julian.

'Pounds?'

'Yes, madam.'

She walked back and took an even longer look at the egg. 'Would six hundred and fifty thousand convince you that he won't be returning?' she asked, giving him that same sweet smile.

Julian beamed as she sat down at his desk and took a chequebook out of her bag. 'Whom shall I make it out to?' she asked.

'Julian Farnsdale Fine Arts Ltd,' he said, placing one of his cards in front of her.

She wrote out the name and the amount slowly, and double-checked them before signing 'Gloria Gaynor' with a flourish. She handed the cheque to Julian who tried to stop his hand from shaking.

'If you're not doing anything special tomorrow night,' she said as she rose from her chair, 'perhaps you'd like to come to my concert?'

'How kind of you,' said Julian.

She took two tickets out of her bag and passed them across to him. 'And perhaps you'd care to join me backstage for a drink after the show?'

Julian was speechless.

'Good,' she said. 'I'll leave your name at the stage door. Please don't tell Millie or Susan. There just isn't enough room for everyone. I'm sure you understand.'

'Of course, Miss Gaynor. You can rely on me. I won't say a word.'

'And if I could ask you for one small favour?' she said as she closed her bag.

'Anything,' said Julian. 'Anything.'

'I wonder if you'd be kind enough to deliver the egg to the Park Lane Hotel, and ask a porter to send it up to my room.'

'You could take it with you now if you wish, Miss Gaynor.'

'How kind of you,' she said, 'but I'm lunching with Mick . . .' She hesitated. 'I'd prefer if it could be delivered to the hotel.'

'Of course,' said Julian. He accompanied her out of the shop to the waiting car, where the chauffeur was holding open the back door.

'How silly of me to forget,' she said just before stepping into the car. She turned back to Julian and whispered into his ear, 'For security reasons, my room is booked in the name of Miss Hampton.' She smiled flirtatiously. 'Otherwise I'd never get a moment's peace.'

'I quite understand,' said Julian. He couldn't believe it when she bent down and kissed him on the cheek.

'Thank you, Julian,' she said. 'I look forward to seeing you after the show,' she added as she climbed into the back seat.

Julian stood there shaking as Millie and Susan joined him on the pavement.

'Did she give you any tickets for her show?' asked Millie as the car drove away.

'I'm not at liberty to say,' said Julian, then walked back into his shop and closed the door.

-<o>-

The smartly dressed young man writing down some figures in a little black book reminded her of the rent collector from her youth. 'How much did it cost us this time?' she asked quietly.

'Five days at the Park Lane came to three thousand three hundred, including tips, the stretch limo was two hundred pounds an hour, sixteen hundred in all.' His forefinger continued down the handwritten inventory. 'The two items you purchased from the jewellery shop came to fifteen hundred.' She touched a pearl earring and smiled. 'Meals along with other expenses, including five extras from the casting agency, five autograph books and a parking fine, came to another nine hundred and twenty-two pounds. Six tickets for tonight's concert purchased from a tout, a further nine hundred pounds, making eight thousand, two hundred and twenty-two pounds in all, which, at today's exchange rate, comes to about thirteen thousand three hundred and sixty-nine dollars. Not a bad return,' he concluded as he smiled across at her.

She glanced at her watch. 'Dear sweet Julian should be arriving at the Albert Hall about now,' she said. 'Let's at least hope he enjoys the show.'

'I would have liked to go with him.'

'Behave yourself, Gregory,' she teased.

'When do you think he'll find out?'

'When he turns up at the stage door after the show and finds his name isn't on the guest list, would be my guess.'

Neither of them spoke while Gregory went over the figures a second time, then finally closed his little book and placed it in an inside pocket.

'I must congratulate you on your research this time,' she said. 'I must admit I'd never heard of Robert Adam, Delft or Chippendale before you briefed me.'

Gregory smiled. 'Napoleon once said that time spent on reconnaissance is rarely wasted.'

'So where does Napoleon stay when he's in Paris?'

'The Ritz Carlton,' Gregory replied matter-of-factly.

'That sounds expensive.'

'We don't have much choice,' he replied. 'Miss Gaynor has booked a suite at the Ritz because it's convenient for the Pleyel concert hall. In any case, it gives the right image for someone who's planning to steal a Modigliani.'

'This is your captain speaking,' said a voice over the intercom. 'We've been cleared for landing at Charles de Gaulle airport, and should be on the ground in around twenty minutes. All of us at British Airways hope you've had a pleasant flight and that you enjoy your stay in Paris, whether it be for business or pleasure.'

A flight attendant leaned over and said, 'Would you be kind enough to fasten your seat belt, madam? We'll be beginning our descent very shortly.'

'Yes, of course,' she said smiling up at the flight attendant.

The attendant took a second look at the passenger and said, 'Has anyone ever told you that you look just like Gloria Gaynor?'

A GOOD EYE

8

THERE HAVE BEEN Grebenars living in the small town of Hertzendorf, nestled in the Bavarian hills, for more than three hundred years.

The first Grebenar of any note was Hans Julius, born in 1641, the youngest son of a miller. Hans worked diligently as a pupil at the town's only school, and became the first member of the family to attend university. After four years of conscientious study, the young man left Heidelberg with a law degree. Despite this achievement, Hans did not hanker after the cosmopolitan life of Munich or even the more gentle charm of Friedrichsville. Rather, he returned to the place of his birth, where he rented a set of rooms in the centre of the town and opened his own law practice.

As the years went by, Hans Julius was elected to the local council, later becoming a freeman of the town as well as an elder of the parish church. Towards the end of his days he was responsible for establishing the town's first municipal museum. If that had been all Herr Grebenar achieved, commendable though it was, he would have gone to his grave unworthy of even a short story. However, there is more to be said about this man because God had given him a rare gift: a good eye.

Young Grebenar began to take an interest in paintings and sculptures while he was at university, and once he'd seen everything Heidelberg had to offer (several times), he took every opportunity to travel to other cities in order to view their treasures.

During his bachelor years he put together a small but worthy collection, his limited means not allowing him to acquire anything of real significance. That changed the day he prosecuted Friedrich Bloch, who appeared before the court on a charge of being drunk and disorderly.

Herr Grebenar wouldn't have given the uncouth ruffian a second thought had Bloch not described himself on the court sheet as a painter. Curiosity got the better of the prosecutor, and after Bloch had been fined ten marks, an amount he was ordered to pay within seven days or face a three-month jail sentence, Grebenar decided to follow him back to his home in the hope of finding out if he painted walls or canvases.

Over the years, Grebenar had come to admire the works of Caravaggio, Rubens and Bruegel, and on one occasion he had even travelled to Amsterdam to view the works of Rembrandt at his studio, but the moment he set eyes on his first Bloch, *Child Pushing a Wheelbarrow*, he realized that he was in the presence of a remarkable talent.

An hour later, the lawyer left Bloch's studio with an empty purse but in possession of two self-portraits in oil, as well as *Child Pushing a Wheelbarrow*. He then went straight to the guild house, where he withdrew a large enough sum of money to cause the clerk to raise an eyebrow.

After a light lunch he returned to court, where he discharged the artist's fine, which caused several more raised eyebrows, because he had successfully prosecuted the miscreant only that morning.

When the court rose later that afternoon, Grebenar, still wearing his long black gown and wing collar, took a carriage back to the artist's home. Bloch was surprised to see the prosecutor for a third time that day, and was even more surprised when he handed over the largest number of coins the artist had ever seen, in return for every painting, drawing and notebook that bore Bloch's signature.

—◄○►—

Herr Grebenar did not come across Friedrich Bloch again until the artist was arrested a year later, on the far more serious charge of attempted murder.

Grebenar visited the artist in prison where he languished while awaiting trial. He informed an incredulous Bloch that he was willing to defend him against the charge of attempted murder, but should he get him off, he would require a rather unusual recompense. Bloch, having gone through all his money, agreed to the lawyer's terms without question.

On the morning of the trial Herr Grebenar was inspired; he had rarely experienced a better day in court. He argued that as at least twelve men had been involved in the drunken brawl, how could the constable, who had arrived some time after the victim had been stabbed, possibly know which one of them had been responsible for the crime?

The jury agreed, and Bloch was acquitted on the charge of attempted murder, although he was found guilty of the lesser offence of drunken affray and sentenced to six months in prison.

When Bloch was released, Herr Grebenar was waiting for him in his carriage outside the prison gates. Grebenar outlined his terms during the journey to the artist's home and Bloch listened intently, nodding from time to time. He made only one request of his patron. Grebenar readily agreed to supply him with a large canvas, several new brushes and any pigments and powders he required. He also paid Bloch a weekly stipend to ensure that he could live comfortably, but not excessively, while carrying out his commission.

It took Bloch almost a year to complete the work and Grebenar accepted it was the weekly stipend that had caused him to take his time. However, when the lawyer saw the oil painting *Christ's Sermon on the Mount* he did not begrudge the artist one mark, as even an untutored eye would have been left in no doubt of its genius.

Grebenar was so moved by the work that he immediately offered the young maestro a further commission, even though he realized it might take him several years to execute. 'I want you to paint twelve full-length portraits of Our Lord's disciples,' he told the artist with a collector's enthusiasm.

Bloch happily agreed, as the commission would ensure a regular supply of money for years to come.

He began his commission with a portrait of St Peter standing at the gates of Jerusalem holding crossed keys. The sadness in the eyes of the saint revealed how ashamed he was for betraying Our Lord.

Grebenar visited the artist's home from time to time, not to study any unfinished canvases, but to check that Bloch was in his studio, working. If he discovered the artist was not at his easel, the weekly stipend was suspended until the lawyer was convinced Bloch had returned to work.

The portrait of St Peter was presented to Herr Grebenar a year later, and the prosecutor made no complaint about its cost, or the amount of time it had taken. He simply rejoiced in his good fortune.

St Peter was followed by Matthew sitting at the seat of Custom, extracting Roman coins from the Jews;

another year. John followed, a painting that some critics consider Bloch's finest work: indeed, three centuries later Sir Kenneth Clark has compared the brushwork to Luini's. However, no scholar at the time was able to offer an opinion, as Bloch's works were only seen by one man, so the artist grew neither in fame nor reputation – a problem Matisse was to face two hundred years later.

This lack of recognition didn't seem to worry Bloch so long as he continued to receive a weekly income, which allowed him to spend his evenings in the ale house surrounded by his friends. In turn, Grebenar never complained about Bloch's nocturnal activities, as long as the artist was sober enough to work the next day.

Ten months later, James followed his brother John, and Grebenar thanked God that he had been chosen to be the artist's patron. Doubting Thomas staring in disbelief as he placed a finger in Christ's wound took the maestro only seven months. Grebenar was puzzled by the artist's sudden industry, until he discovered that Bloch had fallen for a steatopygous barmaid from a local tavern and had asked her to marry him.

James the son of Alphaeus appeared just weeks before their first child was born, and Andrew, the fisher of men, followed soon after their second.

After Bloch, his wife and their two children moved into a small house on the outskirts of Hertzendorf, Philip of Galilee and Simon the Zealot followed within months, as the rent collector needed to be paid. What pleased Grebenar most was that the quality of each new canvas remained consistent, whatever travails or joys its creator was going through at the time.

There was then an interval of nearly two years when no work was forthcoming. Then, without warning,

Thaddaeus and Bartholomew followed in quick succession. Some critics have suggested that each new canvas coincided with the appearance of the latest mistress in Bloch's life, although there is little or no historical evidence to back up their claims.

Herr Grebenar was well aware that Bloch had deserted his wife, returned to his old lodgings and was once again frequenting the ale houses at night. He feared that the next time he came across his protégé it would be in court.

Grebenar only needed one more disciple to complete the twelve, but when no new canvas had appeared for over a year and Bloch was never to be found in his studio during the day, the lawyer decided the time had come to withhold his weekly allowance. But it was not until every ale house in Hertzendorf had refused to serve him before his slate had been cleared that Bloch reluctantly returned to work.

Five months later he produced a dark, forbidding image of Judas Iscariot, thirty pieces of silver scattered on the floor around his feet. Historians have suggested the portrait mirrored the artist's own mood at the time, as the face is thought to be in the image of his patron. Grebenar was amused by Bloch's final effort, and bequeathed the twelve portraits of Christ's disciples to the town's recently built museum, so that they could be enjoyed by the local citizens long after both the artist and his patron had departed this world.

◄○►

It was over a game of chess with his friend Dr Müller that Grebenar learned his protégé had contracted syphilis and had only months to live – a year at the most.

'Such a waste of a truly remarkable talent,' said Dr Müller.

'Not if I have anything to do with it,' retorted Grebenar, as he removed the doctor's queen from the board.

The following morning Herr Grebenar visited Bloch in his rooms and was horrified to discover the state the artist was in. He was lying flat on his back, fully clothed, stinking of ale, his arms and legs covered in raw, pustulous scabs.

The lawyer perched on the end of the bed. 'It's Herr Grebenar,' he said softly. 'I'm distressed to find you in this sorry state, old friend,' he added to a man who was only thirty-four. 'Is there anything I can do to help?'

Bloch turned to face the wall, like an animal who knows death approaches.

'Dr Müller tells me you're unable to pay his bills, and it's no secret you've been running up debts all over town and no one will grant you any more credit.'

Not even the usual cursory grunt followed this observation. Grebenar began to wonder if Bloch could hear him. The lawyer leaned over and whispered in his ear, 'If you paint one last picture for me, I'll clear all your debts and make sure the doctor supplies you with any drugs you need.'

Bloch still didn't move.

Grebenar saved his trump card until last, and when he'd played it, the artist turned over and smiled for the first time in weeks.

◄○►

It took Bloch nearly a month to recover enough strength to pick up a paintbrush, but when he finally managed it, he was like a man possessed. No drink, no women, no debts. Just hour after hour spent working on the canvas that he knew would be his final work.

He completed the painting on 17 March, 1679, a few days before he died, drunk, in a whore's bed.

When Grebenar first set eyes on *The Last Supper* he recalled the final words he had spoken to the artist: 'If you achieve what you are capable of, Friedrich, unlike me you will be guaranteed immortality.'

Grebenar couldn't take his eyes off the haunting image. The twelve disciples were seated around a table, with Christ at the centre breaking the communion bread. Although each one of the Apostles sat in different poses and leaned at different angles, they were unmistakably the same twelve men whose portraits Bloch had painted during the past decade. Grebenar marvelled at how Bloch had achieved such a feat since once they had left his studio, the artist had never set eyes on them again. Grebenar decided there was only one place worthy of such a masterpiece.

Herr Grebenar fulfilled the Maker's contract of three score years and ten. As he approached death, he had only one interest left in life: to ensure that his protégé's works would remain on permanent display in the town museum, so that in time everyone would acknowledge Friedrich Bloch's genius, and he himself would at least be guaranteed a footnote in history.

◄○►

Two hundred and ninety-eight years later . . .

It all began when a drop of rain fell on the chief sidesman's forehead during Monsignor Grebenar's Sunday morning sermon. Several members of the congregation looked up at the roof and one of the choirboys pointed to a small crack.

Once Monsignor Grebenar had delivered his final blessing and the congregation began to depart, he approached an elder of the church to seek his advice.

The master builder promised the priest he would climb up on to the roof and inspect the timbers the following morning.

A preliminary opinion and a rough estimate as to the costs of repair were delivered to the Grebenars' family home on the Wednesday afternoon, along with a warning that if the church council did not act quickly, the roof might well collapse. Monsignor Grebenar received confirmation of the master builder's opinion from above when, during Vespers on the following Sunday, a steady trickle of rain began to fall on the front row of the choir as they chanted the 'Nunc Dimittis'.

Monsignor Grebenar fell on his knees in front of the altar, looked up at Friedrich Bloch's *Last Supper* and prayed for guidance.

The collection that followed raised the princely sum of 412 euros, which wasn't going to make much of an impression on the master builder's estimate of the 700,000 euros needed to repair the roof.

If Monsignor Grebenar had been a more worldly man, he might not have considered what happened next to be divine intervention. When he had finished praying, he crossed himself, rose from his knees, bowed to the altar and turned to find someone he had never seen before seated in the front pew.

'I understand you have a problem, Father,' the man said, looking up at the roof. 'And I think I may be able to help you solve it.'

Monsignor Grebenar looked more closely at the stranger. 'What did you have in mind, my son?' he asked.

'I would be willing to pay you seven hundred thousand euros for that painting,' he said, glancing up at *The Last Supper*.

'But it's been in my family for over three hundred years,' replied Monsignor Grebenar, turning to look at the painting.

'I'll leave you to think it over,' said the stranger. When the priest turned round, he was gone.

Monsignor Grebenar once again fell to his knees and sought God's guidance, but his prayer had not been answered by the time he rose to his feet an hour later. In fact, if anything, he was in even more of a dilemma. Had the stranger really existed, or had he imagined the whole thing?

During the following week Monsignor Grebenar canvassed opinion among his parishioners, some of whom attended the following Sunday's service with umbrellas. Once the service was over, he sought advice from a lawyer, another elder of the church.

'Your father left the painting to you in his will, as did his father before him,' said the lawyer. 'Therefore it is yours to dispose of as you wish. But if I may offer you one piece of advice,' he added.

'Yes, of course, my son,' said the priest hopefully.

'Whatever you decide, Father, you should place the painting in the town's museum before it's damaged by water leaking from the roof.'

'Do you consider seven hundred thousand a fair price?' asked the priest.

'I have no idea, Father. I'm a lawyer, not an art dealer. You should seek advice from an expert.'

As Monsignor Grebenar did not have an art dealer among his flock, he phoned the leading auction house in Frankfurt the following day. The head of the Renaissance department did not assist matters when he told him there was no way of accurately estimating the true value of Bloch's masterpiece, since none of his works had ever come on the market. Every known example was hanging in one museum, with the notable exception of *The Last Supper*. The priest was about to thank him and put down the phone when the man added, 'There is, of course, one way you could find out its true value.'

'And what might that be?'

'Allow the painting to come under the hammer in our next Renaissance sale.'

'When is that?'

'Next October, in New York. We're preparing the catalogue at the moment, and I can assure you your painting would attract considerable interest.'

'But that's not for another six months,' said the priest. 'By then I may not have a roof, just a swimming pool.'

When the service the following Sunday had to be moved to a church on the other side of town, Grebenar felt that Our Lord was giving him a sign, and most of his parishioners agreed with him. However, like the lawyer, when it came to selling the painting they felt it had to be his decision.

Once again, the Monsignor prostrated himself before the masterpiece, wondering what his great-great-great-great-great-great-great-great-great-great-grandfather would have done if faced with the same dilemma. His eyes settled on the thirty pieces of silver scattered around Judas's feet. When he finally rose and crossed himself, he was still undecided. He was about to leave the church, when he found the stranger once again sitting in the front pew. The stranger smiled, but did not speak. He extracted a cheque for seven hundred thousand euros from an inside pocket, handed it over to the priest, then left without a word.

When they were told about the chance meeting, several of Monsignor Grebenar's parishioners described it as a miracle. How else could the man have known the exact sum that was needed to repair the roof? Others looked upon the stranger as their Good Samaritan. When a part of the roof caved in the following day, the priest handed the cheque to the master builder.

The stranger returned within the hour and took away the painting.

◄o►

This tale might well have ended here, but for a further twist that Monsignor Grebenar surely would have described as divine intervention, but would have caused Herr Grebenar to become suspicious.

On the day the new roof was finally completed, Monsignor Grebenar held a service of thanksgiving. The church was packed to hear his sermon. The words 'miracle', 'Good Samaritan' and 'divine intervention' could be heard on the lips of several members of the congregation.

When Monsignor Grebenar had given the final blessing and his flock had departed, he once again thanked God for guiding him in his hour of need. He looked briefly at the blank, newly painted white wall behind the altar and sighed. He then turned his eyes to the brand new roof and smiled, thanking the Almighty a second time.

After returning home for a simple lunch prepared by his housekeeper, the priest settled down by the fire to enjoy the *Hertzendorfer Gazette*, an indulgence he allowed himself once a week. He read the headline several times before he fell to his knees and thanked God once again.

Grebenar Museum burnt to the ground
Police suspect arson

The London *Times* described the loss of Friedrich Bloch's work as devastating, and far more significant than the destruction of the museum itself. After all, the arts correspondent pointed out, Hertzendorf could always build another museum, while the portraits of Christ and his twelve disciples were works of true genius, and quite irreplaceable.

During his closing prayers the following Sunday, Monsignor Grebenar thanked God that he had not taken the lawyer's advice and transferred *The Last Supper* to the museum for safe-keeping; another miracle, he suggested.

'Another miracle,' murmured the congregation in unison.

◄◦►

Six months later, *The Last Supper* by Friedrich Bloch (1643–1679) came under the hammer at one of the leading auction houses in New York. In the catalogue were Bloch's *Christ's Sermon on the Mount* (1662), while the portraits of the twelve disciples were displayed on separate pages. The cover of the catalogue carried an image of *The Last Supper*, and its unique provenance reminded potential buyers of the tragic loss of the rest of Bloch's work in a fire earlier that year. The foreword to the catalogue suggested this tragedy had greatly increased the historic significance, and value, of Bloch's only surviving work.

The following day a headline in the arts pages of the *New York Times* read:

Bloch's masterpiece, *The Last Supper*, sells for $42,000,000.

MEMBERS ONLY*

9

'PINK FORTY-THREE.'

'You've won first prize,' said Sybil excitedly as she looked down at the little strip of pink raffle tickets on the table in front of her husband.

Sidney frowned. He'd wanted to win the second prize – a set of gardening implements which included a wheelbarrow, a rake, a spade, a trowel, a fork and a pair of shears. Far more useful than the first prize, he thought, especially when you've spent a pound on the tickets.

'Go and collect your prize, Sidney,' said Sybil sharply. 'You mustn't keep the chairman waiting.'

Sidney rose reluctantly from his place. A smattering of applause accompanied him as he made his way through the crowded tables and up to the front of the hall.

Shouts of 'Well done, Sidney', 'I never win anything' and 'You're a lucky bastard' greeted him as he climbed up on to the stage.

'Good show, Sidney,' said the chairman of Southend Rotary Club, handing over a brand new set of golf clubs to the winner.

'Blue one hundred and seven,' the chairman announced as Sidney left the stage and headed back to his table, the golf clubs slung over his right shoulder. He slumped down in his chair and managed a smile when his friends, including the member who had won the gardening implements, came over to congratulate him on drawing first prize in the annual raffle.

Once midnight struck and the band had played the last waltz, everyone stood and joined in a lusty rendering of 'God Save the King'.

As Mr and Mrs Chapman made their way home, Sidney received some strange looks from passers-by who had rarely seen a man carrying a set of golf clubs along the seafront, and certainly not at twenty to one on a Sunday morning.

'Well, Sidney,' said Sybil as she took the front door key out of her handbag, 'who would have thought you'd win first prize?'

'What use is a set of golf clubs when you don't play golf?' Sidney moaned as he followed his wife into the house.

'Perhaps you should take up the game,' suggested Sybil. 'After all, it's not long before you retire.'

Sidney didn't bother to respond as he climbed the stairs. When he reached the landing he pushed open the hatch in the ceiling, pulled down the folding ladder, climbed the steps and dumped the golf clubs in the loft. He didn't give them another thought until the family sat down for Christmas dinner six months later.

◄o►

Christmas dinner at the Chapman household wouldn't have differed greatly from that in a thousand other homes in Southend in 1921.

Once grace had been said, Sidney rose from his place at the top of the table to carve the turkey. Sybil sat proudly at the other end of the table while their two sons, Robin and Malcolm, waited impatiently for their plates to be laden with turkey, Brussels sprouts, roast potatoes and sage and onion stuffing. Once Sidney had finished carving the bird, he drowned his plate with thick Bisto gravy until the meat was almost floating.

'Superb, quite superb,' declared Sidney, digging into a leg. After a second mouthful he added, 'But then, Sybil, everyone knows you're the finest cook in Southend.'

Sybil beamed with satisfaction, even though her husband had paid her the same compliment every Christmas Day for the past eighteen years.

Only snippets of conversation passed between the Chapman family as they dug contentedly into their well-filled plates. It wasn't until second helpings had been served that Sidney addressed them again.

'It's been another capital year for Chapman's Cleaning Services,' he declared as he emptied the gravy boat over the second leg, 'even if I do say so myself.' The rest of the family didn't comment, as they were well aware that the chairman had only just begun his annual speech to the shareholders.

'The company enjoyed a record turnover, and declared slightly higher profits than last year,' said Sidney, placing his knife and fork on his plate, 'despite the Chancellor of the Exchequer, in his wisdom, raising taxes to fifteen per cent,' he added solemnly. Sidney didn't like Mr Lloyd George's coalition government. He wanted the Conservatives to return to power and bring stability back to the country. 'And what's more,' Sidney continued, nodding in the direction of his older son, 'Robin is to be congratulated on passing his Higher Certificate. Southend Grammar School has done him proud,' he added, raising a glass of sherry that the boy wouldn't be allowed to sample for another year. 'We can only hope that young Malcolm' – he turned his attention to the other side of the table – 'will, in time, follow in his brother's footsteps. And talking of following in another's footsteps, when the school year is over I look forward to welcoming Robin into the firm where he will begin work as an apprentice, just as I did thirty-six years ago.' Sidney raised his glass a second time. 'Let us never forget the company's motto: "Cleanliness is next to Godliness."'

This was the signal that the annual speech had come to an end, which was always followed by Sidney rolling a cigar lovingly between his fingers. He was just about to light up when Sybil said firmly, 'Not until after you've had your Christmas pudding, dear.'

Sidney reluctantly placed the cigar back on the table as Sybil disappeared into the kitchen.

She reappeared a few moments later, carrying a large Christmas pudding which she placed in the centre of the table. Once again, Sidney rose to conduct the annual ceremony. He slowly uncorked a bottle of brandy that had not been touched since the previous year, poured a liberal amount over the burnt offering, then lit a match and set light to the pudding as if he were a high priest performing a pagan sacrifice. Little blue flames spluttered into the air and were greeted by a round of applause.

Once second helpings had been devoured and Sidney had lit his cigar, the boys became impatient to pull their crackers and discover what treasures awaited them.

The four of them stood up, crossed hands and held firmly on to the ends of the crackers. An almighty tug was followed by four tiny explosions, which, as always, caused a ripple of laughter before each member of the family sat back down to discover what awaited them.

Sybil was rewarded with a sewing kit. 'Always useful,' she remarked.

For Sidney, a bottle opener. 'Very satisfactory,' he declared.

Malcolm didn't look at all pleased with his India rubber, the same offering two years in a row.

The rest of the family turned their attention to Robin, who was shaking his cracker furiously, but nothing was forthcoming, until a golf ball fell out and rolled across the table.

None of them could have known that this simple gift would change the young man's whole life. But then, as you are about to discover, this tale is about Robin Chapman, not his father, mother or younger brother.

◄○►

Although Robin Chapman was not a natural games player, his sports master often described him as a good team man.

Robin regularly turned out as the goalkeeper for the school's Second XI hockey team during the winter, while in the summer he managed to secure a place in the cricket First XI as a bit of an all-rounder. However, none of those seated around that Christmas dinner table in 1921 could have predicted what was about to take place.

Robin waited until Tuesday morning before he made his first move, and then only after his father had left for work.

'Always a lot of dry-cleaning to be done following the Christmas holiday,' Mr Chapman declared before kissing his wife on the cheek and disappearing off down the driveway.

Once his father was safely out of sight, Robin climbed the stairs, pushed open the ceiling hatch and dragged the dust-covered golf bag out of the loft. He carried the clubs back to his room and set about removing the dust and grime that had accumulated over the past six months with a zeal he'd never displayed in the kitchen; first the leather bag followed by the nine clubs, each one of which bore the signature of someone called Harry Vardon. Once he had completed the task, he slung the bag over his shoulder, crept down the stairs, slipped out of the house and headed towards the seafront.

When he reached the beach, Robin dropped the bag on the ground and placed the little white ball on the sand by his feet. He then studied the array of shining clubs, not sure which one to select. He finally chose one with the word 'mashie' stamped on its head. He focused on the ball and took a swing at it, causing a shower of sand to fly into the air, while the ball remained resolutely in place. After several more attempts he finally made contact with the ball, but it only advanced a few feet to his left.

Robin chased after it and repeated the exercise again and again, until the ball finally launched into the air and landed with a plop a hundred yards in front of him. By the time he'd returned home for lunch, late, he considered himself to be the next Harry Vardon. Not that he had any idea who Harry Vardon was.

Robin didn't go back to the beach that afternoon, but instead paid a visit to the local library, where he went straight to the sports section. As he could only take out two books on his library card, he needed to be selective. After much deliberation, he removed from the shelf, *Golf for Beginners* and *The Genius of Harry Vardon*.

Back at home, he locked himself in his bedroom and didn't reappear until he heard his mother calling up the stairs, 'Supper, boys', by which time he knew the difference between a putter, a cleek, a niblick and a brassie. After supper he leafed through the pages of the other book, and discovered that Harry Vardon hailed from Jersey in the Channel Islands, which Robin hadn't even realized was part of the British Empire. He also found out that Mr Vardon had won the Open Championship on six separate occasions, a record that had never been equalled and, in the author's opinion, never would be.

The following morning, Robin returned to the beach. He placed the book on the ground, open at a photograph of Harry Vardon in mid-swing. He dropped the ball at his feet and managed to hit it over a hundred yards on several occasions, if not always in a straight line. Once again he steadied himself, checked the photograph, raised his club and addressed the ball, an expression regularly repeated in *Golf for Beginners*.

He was about to take another swing when he heard a voice behind him say, 'Keep your eye on the ball, my boy, and don't raise your head until you've completed the shot. That way you'll find the ball goes a lot further.'

Robin obeyed the instruction without question, and was indeed rewarded with the promised result, although the ball disappeared into the sea, never to be seen again.

He turned to see his instructor smiling.

'Young man,' he said, 'even Harry Vardon occasionally needed more than one ball. You have potential. If you present yourself at the Southend Golf Club at nine o'clock on Saturday morning, the club's professional will try to turn that potential into something a little more worthwhile.' Without another word the gentleman strode off down the beach.

Robin had no idea where the Southend Golf Club was, but he did know that the local library had always managed to answer all his questions in the past.

On Saturday morning he took the number eleven bus to the outskirts of town and was waiting outside the clubhouse a few minutes before the appointed hour.

Thus began a hobby which turned into a passion, and finally became an obsession.

◄◦►

Robin joined his father as an apprentice at Chapman's Cleaning Services a few days after he left school and, despite working long hours, he could still be found on the beach at six o'clock every morning practising his swing, or putting at a target on his bedroom carpet late into the night.

His progress at Chapman's Cleaning Services and at the town's golf club went hand in hand. On his twenty-first birthday Robin was appointed as a trainee manager with the firm, and a few weeks later he was invited to play for Southend in the annual fixture against Brighton. When he stood on the first tee the following Saturday, he was so nervous he hit his opening shot into the nearest flower bed, and he didn't fare much better for the next nine holes. By the turn, he'd left it far too late to recover and was well beaten by his opponent from Brighton.

Robin was surprised to be selected the following week for the fixture against Eastbourne. Although still nervous, he put up a far better performance and man-aged to halve his match. After that, he rarely missed a first-team fixture.

Although Robin began to take over many of his father's responsibilities at work, he never allowed busi-ness to interfere with his first love. On Mondays he would practise his driving, Wednesdays his bunker shots and on Fridays his putting. On Saturdays his brother Malcolm, who had recently completed his apprenticeship with the firm, kept a watchful eye on the shop while Robin kept his eye on the ball, until it had finally sunk into the eighteenth hole.

On Sundays, after attending church – his mother still wielded some influence over him – Robin would head for the club and play nine holes before lunch.

He wasn't sure which gave him more satisfaction: his father asking him to take over the business on his retirement, or Southend Golf Club inviting him to be the youngest captain in the club's history.

The following Christmas, his father sat at the head of the table as usual, puffing away on his cigar, but it was Robin who presented the annual report. He didn't rub in the fact that the profits had almost doubled during his first year as manager, and nor did he mention that at the same time he'd become a scratch player. This happy state of affairs might have continued without interruption, and indeed this story would never have been written, had it not been for an unexpected invitation landing on the club captain's desk.

◄○►

When the Royal Jersey Golf Club wrote to enquire if Southend would care for a fixture, Robin jumped at the opportunity to visit the birthplace of Harry Vardon and play on the course that had made him so famous.

Six weeks later Robin and his team took a train to Weymouth before boarding the ferry for St Helier. Robin had planned that they should arrive in Jersey the day before the match so they would have enough time to become acquainted with a course none of them had played before. Unfortunately, he hadn't planned for a storm breaking out during the crossing. The ancient vessel somehow managed to sway from side to side while at the same time bobbing up and down as it made its slow progress to Jersey. During the crossing, most of the team were to be found, a pale shade of green, leaning over the side being violently sick, while Robin, oblivious to their malady, strolled up and down the deck, enjoying the sea air. One or two of his fellow passengers looked at him with envy, while others just stared in disbelief.

When the ferry finally docked at St Helier, the rest of the team, several pounds lighter, made their way straight to their hotel where they quickly checked into their rooms and were not to be seen again before breakfast the following morning. Robin took a taxi in the opposite direction, and instructed the driver to take him to the Jersey Royal Golf Club.

'Royal Jersey,' corrected the cabbie politely. 'Jersey Royal is a potato,' he explained with a chuckle.

When the taxi came to a halt outside the main entrance of the magnificent clubhouse, Robin didn't budge. He stared at the Members Only sign, and if the driver hadn't said, 'That'll be two shillings, guv', he might not have moved. He settled the fare, got out of the cab and walked hesitantly across the gravel towards the clubhouse. He tentatively opened the large double door and stepped into an imposing marble entrance hall to be greeted by two full-length oil portraits facing each other on opposite walls. Robin immediately recognized Harry Vardon, dressed in plus fours and a Fair Isle cardigan, and carrying a niblick in his left hand. He gave him a slight bow before turning his attention to the other picture, but he did not recognize the elderly, chisel-faced gentleman wearing a long black frock-coat and grey pinstriped trousers.

Robin suddenly became aware of a young man looking at him quizzically. 'My name's Robin Chapman,' he said uncertainly, 'I'm—'

'– the captain of the Southend Golf Club,' the young man said. 'And I'm Nigel Forsyth, captain of the Royal Jersey. Care to join me for a drink, old fellow?'

'Thank you,' said Robin. He and his opposite number strolled through the hall to a thickly carpeted room furnished with comfortable leather chairs. Nigel pointed to a seat in a bay window overlooking the eighteenth hole, and went over to the bar. Robin wanted to look out of the window and study the course, but forced himself not to.

Nigel returned carrying two half-pints of shandy and placed one on the table in front of his guest. As he sat down he raised his own glass. 'Are you a one-man team, by any chance?' he asked.

Robin laughed. 'No, the rest of my lot are probably tucked up in bed,' he said, 'their rooms still tossing around.'

'Ah, you must have come over on the Weymouth Packet.'

'Yes,' said Robin, 'but we'll get our revenge on the return fixture.'

'Not a hope,' said Nigel. 'Whenever we travel to the mainland we always go via Southampton. That route has modern vessels fitted with stabilizers. Perhaps I should have mentioned that in my letter,' he added with a grin. 'Care for a round before it gets dark?'

Once they were out on the course, it soon became clear to Robin why so many old timers were always recalling rounds they had played at the Royal Jersey. The course was the finest he'd ever played, and the thought that he was walking in Harry Vardon's footsteps only added to his enjoyment.

When Robin's ball landed on the eighteenth green some five feet from the hole, Nigel volunteered, 'If the rest of your team are as good as you, Robin, we'll have one hell of a game on our hands tomorrow.'

'They're far better,' said Robin, not missing a beat as they walked off the green and made their way back to the clubhouse.

'Same again?' asked Nigel as they headed towards the bar.

'No, this one's on me,' insisted Robin.

'Sorry, old fellow, guests are not allowed to pay for a drink. Strict rule of the club.'

Robin came to a halt once again in front of the large portrait of the elderly gentleman. Nigel answered his unasked question. 'That's our president, Lord Trent. He's not half as frightening as he looks, as you'll discover tomorrow evening when he joins us for dinner. Have a seat while I go and fetch those drinks.'

Nigel was standing at the bar when a young woman came in. She walked briskly across and whispered something in his ear. He nodded, and she left as quickly as she'd arrived.

From the moment she entered the room to the moment she left, Robin had been unable to take his eyes off her. 'You didn't tell me you had a goddess on the island,' he said when Nigel handed him another half-pint of shandy.

'Ah, you must be referring to Diana,' he said as the young lady disappeared.

'An appropriate name for a goddess,' said Robin. 'And how enlightened of you to allow women members.'

'Certainly not,' said Nigel, grinning. 'She's Lord Trent's secretary.' He took a sip of his drink before adding, 'But I think she's attending the dinner tomorrow night, so you'll have a chance to meet your goddess.'

When Robin returned to the hotel later that evening, only one other member of the team felt able to join him for dinner. Robin wondered whether the rest would have recovered sufficiently to be standing on the first tee by ten o'clock the following morning. Though in truth, he was already thinking more about tomorrow evening.

◄○►

Southend somehow managed a full turnout by the time the chief steward asked the two captains to tee up at the first hole.

As the visiting captain, Robin struck the first ball. Five hours later the score board showed that the Royal Jersey had beaten Southend Golf Club by four and a half matches to three and a half. Not a bad result, Robin considered, given the circumstances, but then he'd never played a better round in his life, which may have been because Diana seemed to be following Nigel around the course. Another home advantage.

After a few drinks in the clubhouse, with no sign of Diana, the Southend team returned to their hotel to change for dinner. Robin was the first one waiting in the foyer. Nervously he touched his bow tie after he'd checked with the receptionist that three taxis had been ordered for seven o'clock.

Robin didn't speak on the journey back to the Royal Jersey, and when he led his team into the dining room, Nigel was waiting to greet him. Diana was standing by his side. Lucky man, thought Robin.

'Good to see you again, old fellow,' Nigel said, and turning to Diana, he added, 'I don't believe you've met my sister.'

◄○►

'You're going to do what?' said his father.

'I'm going to move to Jersey, where I intend to open a branch of Chapman's Cleaning Services.'

'But I always thought you planned to open a second branch in Southend, while I took over the main shop,' said Malcolm, sounding equally bemused by his brother's news.

'You'll still be taking over the main shop, Malcolm, while I open our first overseas branch.'

Robin's father seemed to be momentarily struck dumb, so his mother took advantage of this rare occurrence. 'What's the real reason you want to go back to Jersey?' she asked, looking her son in the eye.

'I've found the finest golf course on earth, Mother, and if they'll have me, I intend to become a member and play on it for the rest of my life.'

'No,' said his mother quietly, 'I asked for the real reason.' The rest of the family remained silent as they waited for Robin's reply.

'I've found the most beautiful woman on earth, and if she'll have me, I'd like her to become my wife.'

◄◊►

Robin boarded the boat back to Jersey the following Friday, despite having failed to answer his mother's third question: 'Has this young lady agreed to be your wife?'

The only thing Diana had agreed to was to join him on the dance floor for a quickstep, but during those three minutes Robin knew he wanted to hold on to this woman for the rest of his life. 'I'll be coming back next weekend,' he told her.

'But the team are playing away at Wentworth next Saturday,' she remarked innocently.

◄◊►

Robin was surprised to find Diana standing on the quayside when the ferry sailed into the harbour the following Saturday. Whom had she come to meet, he wondered, and only hoped it wasn't another man.

When he stepped off the gangway, Diana gave him the same warm smile that had remained in his mind for the past week.

'I wasn't sure you believed me when I said I'd be coming back,' he said shyly as they shook hands.

'I wasn't sure you would,' admitted Diana, 'but then I thought, if the poor man is willing to give up a weekend's golf just to spend some time with me, the least I can do is meet him off the boat.'

Robin smiled at the thought that he couldn't even remember who Southend were playing that day, and took Diana's hand as they walked along the causeway.

If you had asked him how they spent the weekend, all he could remember was reluctantly climbing back on the ferry on Sunday evening, after kissing her for the first time.

'See you same time next Saturday, Diana,' he shouted down as he leaned over the railings, but the boat's foghorn drowned his words.

Diana was standing on the quayside the following Saturday, and every Saturday until Robin stopped taking the ferry back to Weymouth.

During the week, Robin would book a trunk call so they could speak to each other every evening. Diana spent her spare time looking at properties in St Helier that might meet his requirements. She finally found a shop on the high street whose lease was about to expire, with a hotel across the road that needed to change its bed linen and towels every day, and several restaurants that believed in spotless napkins and fresh tablecloths.

Robin agreed that it was the ideal location to open a branch of Chapman's Cleaning Services.

The following Saturday he signed a three-year renewable lease, and immediately moved into the flat above the shop. If he hadn't won Diana's hand by the end of the lease, and also become a member of the Royal Jersey Golf Club, he would have to admit defeat, return to the mainland and open a second branch of Chapman's in Southend.

Although he was confident that, given time, both challenges would be surmounted, becoming a member of the RJGC turned out to be a far more difficult proposition than getting Diana to agree to be his wife.

It didn't take long for Robin to qualify as a playing member of the Royal Jersey, and he was delighted when Nigel invited him to represent the club in the hotly contested local derby against Guernsey. Robin won his match, and proposed to Diana that night.

'What if you hadn't been picked for the team?' she asked, unable to take her eyes off the small, sparkling diamond on the third finger of her left hand.

'I'd have whisked you off to England and sunk the Weymouth ferry,' said Robin without hesitation.

Diana laughed. 'So, what are my champion's plans for conquering the old guard who make up the committee of the Royal Jersey?'

'They've granted me an interview next month,' he told her, 'so we'll soon find out if we're going to spend the rest of our lives in St Helier or Southend-on-Sea.'

'Don't forget that only one in three people who apply for full membership even get on to the waiting list,' Diana reminded him.

Robin smiled. 'Possibly so, but with Lord Trent as my proposer, and your brother as my seconder, I must have a better than one-in-three chance.'

'So that's why you asked me to marry you,' Diana said, still staring at her ring.

When the appointed hour came for Robin to appear before the committee, he admitted to Diana that he had never been so nervous, even though everyone seated on the other side of the table seemed to smile whenever he answered their undemanding questions, and nods of approval greeted the Englishman's detailed knowledge of the life of Harry Vardon.

Ten days later, Robin received a letter from the club secretary to say that his application had been successful and his name would be placed on the waiting list.

'The waiting list?' said Robin in frustration. 'How long do they expect me to hang about before I become a member?'

'My brother warned me,' said Diana, 'that if you weren't born on the island, it usually takes ten to fifteen years.'

'Ten to fifteen years?' repeated Robin in disgust, before adding, 'Lord Trent wasn't born on the island.'

'True,' said Diana, 'but at the time the committee was looking for a new president, preferably with a title, so they made him an honorary life member.'

'And are there any other honorary life members?'

'Only Harry Vardon,' replied Diana.

'Well, I'm no Harry Vardon,' said Robin.

'There's one other way you could automatically become a life member,' said Diana.

'And what's that?' said Robin eagerly.

'Win the President's Cup.'

'But I was knocked out in the second round last year,' Robin reminded her. 'In any case, your brother's in a different class to me.'

'Just make sure you get to the final this year,' said Diana. 'I'll fix my brother.'

◄◦►

Robin and Diana were married at the local parish church later that summer. The vicar agreed to conduct the ceremony on a Sunday, but only because the Royal Jersey had a crucial match against Rye on the Saturday.

Robin's father, mother and brother had travelled over on the ferry from Southampton earlier in the week, and they spent a happy few days getting to know Diana. Long before the day of the wedding, Sybil fully understood why her son had wanted to return to Jersey after one dance. When the bride walked down the aisle, she found that the ceremony was so well attended that extra chairs had been placed at the back of the church.

Mr and Mrs Chapman left the parish church of St Helier as man and wife, to be greeted with a shower of confetti thrown by Diana's friends, while two rows of young men in RJGC blazers held up golf clubs to form an arch all the way to their waiting car.

The reception was held at the Royal Jersey, where Malcolm delivered such an accomplished best-man's speech that it came as no surprise to Robin that Chapman's of Southend continued to flourish in his absence.

Lord Trent rose to reply on behalf of the guests. He let slip the worst-kept secret on the island when he told everyone that the newly-weds would be sailing around the French coast on his yacht for their honeymoon, but only for ten days, because Robin needed to be back in time for the first round of the President's Cup. Diana couldn't be sure if he was joking.

When Mr and Mrs Chapman sailed into St Helier ten days later, the skipper informed Lord Trent that

148

Robin had turned out to be such a good sailor that he had allowed him to take the wheel whenever he needed a break.

The following day, Robin was knocked out in the first round of the President's Cup.

◄o►

Robin and Diana quickly settled into their new home on the seafront, and for the first time since he'd arrived in Jersey, Robin had to walk to work. Eleven months later, Diana gave birth to a boy whom they christened Harry.

'Will you do anything to become a member of that damned club?' Diana asked her husband as she sat in the hospital bed surrounded by flowers and cards from well-wishers.

'Anything,' replied Robin, picking up the sleeping baby.

'Well, I have one piece of information that might speed up the process,' said Diana, smiling.

'And what's that?' asked Robin, handing the suddenly screaming infant back to its mother.

'My brother tells me that the St Helier lifeboat is looking for a new crew member, and as you spent more time at the helm of Lord Trent's yacht than you did in our cabin, you must be an obvious candidate.'

'And how will that help me get elected to the Royal Jersey?' enquired Robin.

'Guess who's president of the RNLI?' said Diana coyly.

The day after Robin failed to make the third round of that year's President's Cup, he filled in an application form to join the crew of the lifeboat.

◄o►

Robin's interview for a place in the lifeboat turned out to be not so much a meeting as an endurance test. John Poynton, the coxswain, put all the applicants through a series of rigorous trials to make sure only the most resilient would want to return a week later.

Robin couldn't wait to get home and tell Diana how much he'd enjoyed the whole experience, the camaraderie of the crew, the chance to learn new skills and, most important, the opportunity to do something worthwhile. He only hoped the coxswain would take his application seriously, despite his lack of experience.

When the time came for Mr Poynton to select his new crew member, he unhesitatingly placed a tick by one name, telling his bosun that young Chapman was such a natural he wouldn't be surprised if the man could walk on water.

As the weeks passed, Robin found himself enjoying being tested by the rigorous drills the crew were put through on the high seas. Whenever the klaxon sounded, the crew were expected to drop everything and report to the boathouse within ten minutes. Robin could never be sure if it would be just another dry run, or if this time they would be going to the aid of someone who was genuinely in distress. The coxswain regularly reminded his crew that all the hours of hard work would prove worthwhile when someone called for their assistance, and only then would they discover which of them could handle the pressure.

◄○►

It was the middle of the night when the klaxon sounded, waking everyone within a mile of the boathouse. Robin leapt out of bed in the middle of a dream, just as he was taking a putt to win the President's Cup. He switched on the light and quickly got dressed.

'Off to see your other girlfriend?' enquired Diana, turning over.

'All eight of them,' Robin replied. 'But let's hope I'll be back in time for breakfast.'

'You'll be back,' said Diana. 'After all, it's the final of the President's Cup on Saturday, and as you're playing my brother, you may never have a better chance of winning.'

'I beat him in my dream,' said Robin as he picked up his bicycle clips.

'In your dreams,' said Diana, smiling.

Robin was pedalling frantically through the empty streets when the klaxon sounded a second time. He pedalled even harder.

He was among the first to arrive at the boathouse, and the look on the coxswain's face left him in no doubt that he was about to experience his first distress call.

'We've had an SOS from a small sailing boat that's capsized just off the Arden Rock,' the coxswain told his crew as they pulled on their oilskins and sea boots. 'It seems a young couple thought it would be fun to sail around the bay after midnight,' he grunted. 'I'll be launching in a couple of minutes.' None of the crew spoke as they climbed on board and carefully checked their stations.

'Knock her out!' the coxswain called to the head launcher once the last crew member had given a thumbs-up.

Robin felt a rush of adrenaline pump through his body as the lifeboat made its way across the lapping waves inside the harbour. Once they had passed the breakwater, the boat reared up and down in the open sea. None of the crew showed any sign of fear, which gave Robin confidence. They had only one thing on their minds as they each carried out their separate duties.

The lookout was the first to spot the capsized yacht. He pointed and bellowed against the high wind, 'Nor' nor'west, skipper, about three hundred yards.'

Robin felt exhilarated as they edged slowly towards the capsized vessel. All the drills they had practised during the past months were about to be put to the test. As they came alongside, Robin stared into the eyes of a terrified young couple, who couldn't believe there were eight people on that little island who were willing to risk their lives to rescue them. But however much the coxswain shouted at them to catch hold of one of the grab lines, they kept clinging to the keel of their sinking yacht. Robin began to feel that nothing would make either of them let go, and, if anything, the boy looked even more terrified than his girlfriend. The waves refused to let up, making Robin wonder how long it would be before the coxswain decided his own crew was in just as much danger as the yacht. They tried one more time to manoeuvre the lifeboat alongside the stricken vessel.

When the boat was at its highest point in the water, Robin wondered if he dare risk it. It was not something to spend much time thinking about. When the bow of the boat plunged into the next wave, he leapt into the sea and with all the strength he could muster managed to grab on to the side of the yacht. He waited for the wave to rise again before he pulled himself up on to what was left of the floating wreck. With the help of the next wave he hauled himself up on to the keel and somehow managed to smile at the two disbelieving faces.

'Take my hand!' he hollered to the girl. After a moment's hesitation, she released her grip on the keel and clung on to Robin's outstretched arm. For a moment he feared she might panic and push him back into the sea.

'You'll have to jump when I give you the signal,' screamed Robin above the noise of the wind. The girl didn't look convinced. 'Are you ready?' he cried as the next wave headed towards them. As the lifeboat reared into the air like a startled horse, Robin shouted, 'Now!' and pushed her off the yacht with all the strength left in his body.

Two arms grabbed her as she landed in the water by the side of the lifeboat and hauled her unceremoniously on board. Robin waited for the next wave before the young man obeyed the same instruction. He was not as lucky as his companion, and cracked his head on the gunnel before he was finally dragged on to the boat. Robin could see blood pouring from his forehead. He knew there was a first-aid kit in the cockpit but no one would be able to open it, let alone administer any succour, during such a storm.

Robin felt the yacht sinking beneath him and his thoughts switched from the young man's problems to his own survival. He would only have one chance before the boat disappeared below the waves.

He hunched up in a ball as he waited for the lifeboat to arch on the peak of the wave, then propelled himself towards it like an athlete bursting out of the blocks. But it turned out to be a false start because he missed the grab line by several feet and found himself floundering in the sea. His last thoughts as he sank below the unforgiving waves were of Diana and his son Harry, but then he bobbed up in a trough and a hand grabbed his hair while another clung to a shoulder and dragged him inch by inch, wave by wave, towards the boat. But the sea still refused to give him up, and when the next wave hurled him against the side of the lifeboat, he felt his arm snap. As he was dragged on to the deck he screamed, but no one heard him above the storm. He would have thanked the coxswain, but all he could manage was to unload a stomach full of seawater all over him. At least Poynton had the grace to laugh.

Robin couldn't recall much of the journey back to port, except for the excruciating pain in his right arm and the looks of relief on the faces of the young couple he'd rescued.

'We'll be back in time for breakfast,' said the coxswain as they passed the lighthouse and sailed into the relative calm of the harbour. When the crew finally disembarked, they were greeted by a cheering crowd.

Diana was standing on the quay, her eyes frantically searching for her husband. Robin smiled and waved at her with the arm that wasn't broken.

It wasn't until she read a full report in the *Jersey Echo* the following day that she realized just how close she'd been to becoming a widow. John Poynton described Robin's decision to leave the boat to rescue the stranded couple, who undoubtedly owed their lives to him, as an act of selfless courage in the face of overwhelming odds. He had told Robin privately that he thought he was mad, and then shook him by the hand. It was the wrong hand, and Robin screamed again.

All Robin had to say while he sat propped up in a hospital bed, one arm in plaster, the other attempting to handle a spoon and a bowl of cornflakes, was, 'I won't be able to play in the final of the President's Cup.'

—◇—

A year later, Diana gave birth to a girl whom they christened Kate, and Robin fell in love for a second time.

Chapman's Cleaning Services continued to flourish, not least because Robin had become such a popular member of the community, with some of the residents now treating him as if he were a local and not a newcomer.

The following year, he was elected a vice-president of the local rotary club, and when the head launcher stepped down, the RNLI committee voted unanimously to invite Robin to take his place. Despite these minor honours being bestowed upon him, he reminded his wife that he was no nearer to becoming a full member of the Royal Jersey, and as his handicap had begun to move in the wrong direction, he'd probably missed his one chance to win the President's Cup and automatically become a life member.

'You could always join another club,' Diana suggested innocently. 'After all, the Royal Jersey's not the only golf club on the island.'

'If I were to join another club, the committee would strike me off the waiting list without a second thought. No, I'm just going to have to be patient. After all, it should only be about another eight years before they get round to me,' he said, not attempting to hide the sarcasm in his voice.

Diana would have laughed if the klaxon hadn't sounded for the ninth time that year. Robin dropped his paper and leapt up from the table without a second thought. Diana wondered if her husband had any idea of the anxiety she experienced every time he was away at sea. It hadn't helped when a few weeks earlier one of the crew had been swept overboard during an abortive rescue attempt.

Robin kissed his wife before leaving her with the familiar parting words, 'See you when I see you, my darling.'

When he returned, four hours later, he crept quietly into bed, not wanting to wake Diana. She wasn't asleep.

◄◦►

Robin smiled after he'd read the letter a second time. It was just a short note from the club secretary, nothing official, of course, but he was confident that it wouldn't be too much longer before the committee was able to ratify his membership of the RJGC. What did 'too much longer' mean? Robin wondered. In theory he still had another four years to wait, and he was well aware that there were several other names ahead of his on the waiting list. However, Diana had told him that several members felt he should have been elected after he'd broken his arm and been forced to withdraw from the final of the President's Cup.

Robin's spell as head launcher on the lifeboat was coming to an end, as the job required a younger man. Diana couldn't wait for the day when her husband would become more preoccupied with propelling a little white ball towards a distant hole than with rescuing helpless bodies from a merciless sea.

The following year, Robin opened a second shop in St Brêlade, and was considering a third, on Guernsey. He felt a little guilty because his brother Malcolm was now running four establishments on the mainland, and contributing far more to the company's bottom line, while at the same time keeping an eye on his two children, who were at prep school on the mainland.

Robin was a contented man, and on his thirty-sixth birthday he promised Diana that he would serve only one more year as head launcher, even if he wasn't

156

elected to the Royal Jersey. He raised his glass. 'To the future,' he said.

Diana raised her glass and smiled. 'To the future,' she repeated, unaware that another man on the far side of Europe had other plans for Robin Chapman's future.

~<o>~

When Britain declared war on Germany on 3 September 1939, Robin's first instinct was to return to England and sign up, especially as several younger members of his crew had already found their way to Portsmouth and joined the Royal Navy. Diana talked him out of the idea, convincing him that he was too old, and in any case his expertise would be needed on Jersey.

They decided to leave the children at school in England, and Malcolm and his wife unhesitatingly agreed to look after them during the holidays.

When the German army goose-stepped down the Champs-Élysées nine months later, Robin knew it could only be a matter of weeks before Hitler decided to invade the Channel Islands. Thirty thousand islanders had been evacuated to Britain, including his own children, and German bombs had fallen on St Helier and St Peter Port on Guernsey.

'I'll have to stay on as head launcher,' Robin told Diana. 'With so few young men available, they'll never find a replacement before the war is over.'

Diana reluctantly agreed to what she imagined to be the lesser of two evils.

~<o>~

When Lord Trent phoned Robin at home and asked if they could have a private meeting at the club, he assumed the old man was at last going to confirm his membership of the Royal Jersey.

Robin arrived a few minutes early and the club steward ushered him straight into Lord Trent's study. The look on the President's face was not one that suggested glad tidings. Lord Trent rose from behind his desk, indicated that they should sit in the more comfortable leather chairs by the fire, and poured two large brandies.

'I need to ask you a special favour, Robin,' he said once he'd settled in his chair.

'Of course, sir,' said Robin. 'How can I help?'

'As you know, the ferries from Weymouth and Southampton have been requisitioned by the Government as part of the war effort, and although I thoroughly approve this decision, it presents me with something of a problem, as the Prime Minister has asked me to return to England at the first possible opportunity.'

Before Robin could ask why, Trent took a telegram from an inside pocket and handed it to him. Robin's heart missed a beat when he saw the address: 'No.10 Downing Street, London, SW1'. Trent waited until he had finished reading the telegram from Winston Churchill.

'The Prime Minister may well wish to see me urgently,' said Trent, 'but he seems to have forgotten that I have no way of getting off this island.' He took another sip of his brandy. 'I rather hoped you might feel able to take Mary and me across to the mainland in the lifeboat.'

Robin knew that the lifeboat was never meant to leave the harbour unless it was answering a distress call, but a direct request from the Prime Minister surely allowed him to tear up the rule book. Robin considered the request for some time before he responded. 'We'd have to slip out after nightfall, then I could be back before sunrise and no one need be any the wiser.'

'Whatever you say,' said Trent, command changing hands.

'Would tomorrow night suit you, sir?'

The old man nodded. 'Thank you, Robin.'

Robin rose from his place. 'Then I'll see you and Lady Trent on the quayside at nine tomorrow night, sir.' He left without another word, his brandy untouched.

◄○►

Robin was assisted by two young crew members who also wanted to reach the mainland, as they wished to join up. He was surprised by how uneventful the Channel crossing turned out to be. It was a full moon that night and the sea was remarkably calm for October, although Lady Trent proved to be a far better sailor than his lordship, who never opened his mouth during the entire voyage except when he leaned over the side.

When the lifeboat entered Weymouth harbour, a patrol boat escorted them to the dockside, where a Rolls-Royce was waiting to whisk the Trents off to London. Robin shook hands with the old man for the last time.

After a bacon sandwich and half a pint of Courage in a dockside pub, he wished his two crew members good luck before they boarded a train for Portsmouth, and he set off on the return voyage to Jersey. Robin checked his watch and reckoned he should be back in time to join Diana for breakfast.

Robin slipped back into St Helier before first light. He had just stepped on to the dock when the fist landed in his stomach, causing him to double up in pain and collapse on to his knees. He was about to protest when he realized that the two uniformed men who were now pinning him to the ground were not speaking English.

He didn't waste any time protesting as they marched him down the High Street and into the nearest police station. There was no friendly desk sergeant on duty to greet him. He was pushed roughly down a flight of stone steps before being flung into a cell. He felt sick when he saw Diana seated on a bench against the wall. She jumped up and ran to him as the cell door slammed behind them.

'Are they safe?' she whispered as he held her in his arms.

'Yes,' he replied. 'But a spell in prison isn't going to help my membership application for the Royal Jersey,' he remarked, trying to lighten the mood. Diana didn't laugh.

They didn't have long to wait before the heavy iron door was pulled open once again. Two young soldiers marched in, grabbed Robin by the elbows and dragged him back out. They led him up the stairs and out on to an empty street. There were no locals to be seen in any direction as a curfew had been imposed. Robin assumed that he was about to be shot, but they continued to march him up the high street, and didn't stop until they reached the Bailiff's Chambers.

Robin had visited the seat of local government many times in the past, as each new bailiff required his dress robes to be spotless on inauguration day, a ceremony he and Diana always attended. But on this occasion Robin was led into the front office, where he found a German officer seated in the Bailiff's chair. One look at his crisp uniform suggested that he wasn't going to enquire about Chapman's services.

'Mr Chapman,' the officer said with no trace of an accent, 'my name is Colonel Kruger, I am the new commandant for the Channel Islands. Perhaps you could start by telling me why you took Lord Trent back to England?'

Robin didn't reply.

'No doubt Lord and Lady Trent are enjoying breakfast at the Ritz Hotel while you languish in jail for your troubles.' The officer rose and walked across the room, coming to a halt when the two men were standing face to face. 'If you feel unable to assist me, Mr Chapman, you and your wife will remain in jail until there is space on a ship to transport you to the Fatherland.'

'But my wife was not involved,' Robin protested.

'In normal circumstances, I would be willing to accept your word, Mr Chapman, but as your wife was Lord Trent's secretary . . .' Robin said nothing. 'You will be sent to one of our less well-appointed camps, unless, of course, one of you decides to enlighten me on the reason Lord Trent needed to rush back to England.'

◄○►

Robin and Diana remained in their tiny cell for nineteen days. They were fed on bread and water, which until then Robin had always assumed was a Dickensian myth. He began to wonder if the authorities had forgotten about them.

He managed to pick up snippets of information from those islanders who had been forced to work at the police station, but the only thing of any consequence he was able to find out was that German ships were docking at St Helier regularly to unload more soldiers, arms and ammunition.

On the twentieth morning, one of their informants told them that a ship would be arriving from Hamburg the following day, and that he had seen their names on the embarkation log for its return journey. Diana wept. Robin never slept while his wife was awake.

In the middle of the night, when they were both sleeping fitfully, the cell door was pulled open without warning. Two German soldiers stood in the doorway. One of them asked politely if Mr Chapman would join them. Robin was puzzled by the officer's courteous manner, and wondered if this was how German soldiers behaved just before they shot you.

He accompanied the soldiers up the stairs. Was he being escorted to the ship? Surely not, or they would have taken Diana as well. Once again he was taken down the street in the direction of the Bailiff's Chambers, but this time the soldiers walked by his side, making no attempt to hold on to him.

When he entered the Bailiff's office, Colonel Kruger looked up from behind his desk, an anxious look on his face. He didn't waste his words. 'The ship that was meant to transport prisoners to Hamburg has struck a rock just outside the harbour.' Robin wondered which brave islander had managed to remove the warning lights. 'It's sinking fast,' continued the colonel. 'The lives of all those on board will be lost, including several civilians, unless the lifeboat is sent out to rescue them.' He avoided saying 'my countrymen'.

'Why are you telling me this, Colonel?' asked Robin. 'The lifeboat crew is refusing to cast off without their head launcher, so I am asking you – ' he paused – 'begging you, to join them before it's too late.'

Strange, the things that pass through one's mind when faced with a moral dilemma, Robin thought. He knew the directive by heart. It is the duty of every member of the RNLI to go to the aid of anyone in distress on the high seas, irrespective of their nationality, colour or creed, even if they are at war with Britain. He nodded curtly at the colonel.

Out on the street a car was waiting, its door open, to take him to the harbour. Fifteen minutes later they cast off.

Robin and the rest of the crew returned to Arden Rock several times that night. In all, they rescued 73 passengers, including 11 German officers and 37 crew members. The remainder were civilians who had been selected to assist in the administration of the island. A cargo of arms, ammunition and transport vehicles was resting on the bottom of the ocean.

When Robin carried the last of the survivors back to the safety of the island, two German officers were waiting for him as he stepped off the lifeboat. They handcuffed him and escorted him back to the police station. As he walked into the cell, Diana smiled for the first time in days.

◄○►

When the cell door was opened the following morning, two plates of bacon and eggs, along with cups of hot tea, were laid before them by a young German corporal.

'Last breakfast before they execute us,' suggested Robin as the guard slammed the cell door behind him.

'It wouldn't be hard to guess what your final request will be,' said Diana, smiling.

A few minutes after they'd devoured their unexpected feast, another soldier appeared and told them he was taking them to the commandant's headquarters.

'I shall be happy to accompany you to the Bailiff's Chambers,' said Robin defiantly.

'We're not going to the Connétable,' said the soldier. 'The commandant has requisitioned the golf club as his new headquarters.'

'Your final wish has been granted,' said Diana as she and Robin settled into the back seat of a staff car, which brought a puzzled expression to the young German's face.

When they arrived at the club, they were taken to Lord Trent's office. Colonel Kruger stood up and offered them both a seat. Diana sat down, but Robin remained standing.

'This morning,' the colonel said, 'I rescinded the order that you were to be shipped to prison in Germany, and issued a new directive, releasing you immediately. You will therefore be allowed to return to your home. Should you be foolish enough to break the law a second time, Mr Chapman, you will both be aboard the next ship that sails for Germany. Think of it as what's called, in your country, a suspended sentence.'

The commandant once again rose from behind his desk. 'You are a remarkable man, Mr Chapman. If your fellow countrymen are forged from the same steel, your nation may not prove quite as easy to defeat.'

'Perhaps you should read *Henry V*,' suggested Robin.

'I have,' replied the commandant. He paused and looked out of the window towards the weed-covered eighteenth green before adding, 'But I'm not sure the Führer has.'

◄◦►

The remainder of Robin's war turned out to be something of an anticlimax, except for those occasions when the klaxon sounded and he had to pedal furiously along the seafront to join his crew at the boathouse. He stayed on as the lifeboat's head launcher while the Germans remained on the island.

During the occupation, members of the Royal Jersey were not permitted to enter the clubhouse, let alone play a round of golf. As the years passed, the finely tended course became so overgrown with weeds and nettles you couldn't tell where the rough ended and the fairways began. Clubs rusted in the store-room, and there were only tattered flags fluttering on the ends of their poles to show where the greens had been.

◄○►

On 9 May 1945, the day after VE day, an advance party of English troops landed on Jersey and the German commandant on the Channel Islands surrendered.

Once the thirty-six thousand intruders had finally departed, the locals quickly did everything in their power to restore the old order. This didn't prove easy, as the Germans had destroyed many of the island's records, including applications for membership of the Royal Jersey Golf Club.

Other forms of life did return to normal. Robin and Diana were standing on the dockside waiting to welcome the first ferry from Weymouth when she sailed into St Helier on 12 July.

'Oh my goodness!' cried Diana the moment she saw her children. 'How they've grown.'

'It's been more than five years since we last saw them, darling,' Robin was reminding her as a young man accompanied by his teenage sister stepped on to the quayside.

The Chapman family spent six happy weeks together before Harry reluctantly returned to the mainland to take up his place at Durham University, and Kate went back to Weybridge to begin her final year at St Mary's;

both were looking forward to returning to Jersey at Christmas.

◄○►

Robin was reading the morning paper when he heard a knock on the door.

'I have a recorded delivery for you, Mr Chapman,' said the postman. 'I'll need a signature.'

Robin signed on the dotted line, recognizing the crest of the Royal Jersey Golf Club stamped in the top left-hand corner of the envelope. He ripped it open and read the letter as he returned to the kitchen, and read it a second time before he handed it across to Diana.

THE ROYAL JERSEY GOLF CLUB

St Helier, Jersey

9 September 1946

Dear Sir,

We have reason to believe that at some time in the past you applied to become a member of the Royal Jersey Golf Club, but unfortunately all our records were destroyed during the German occupation.

If you still wish to be considered for membership of the club, it will be necessary for you to go through the application process once again and we will be happy to arrange an interview.

Should your application prove successful, your name will be placed on the waiting list.

Yours sincerely,

J. L. Tindall
(Secretary)

Robin swore for the first time since the Germans had left the island.

Diana could do nothing to console him, despite the fact that his brother was coming across from the mainland to spend his first weekend with them since the end of the war.

Robin was standing on the dockside when Malcolm stepped off the Southampton ferry. Malcolm was able to lift his older brother's spirits when he told him and Diana all the news about the company's expansion plans, as well as delivering several messages from their children.

'Kate has a boyfriend,' he told them, 'and—'

'Oh, God,' said Robin. 'Am I that old?'

'Yes,' said Diana, smiling.

'I'm thinking of opening a fourth branch of Chapman's in Brighton,' Malcolm announced over dinner that night. 'With so many factories springing up in the area, they're sure to be in need of our services.'

'Not looking for a manager are you, by any chance?' asked Robin.

'Why, are you available?' replied Malcolm, looking genuinely surprised.

'No, he isn't,' said Diana firmly.

━◦━

By the time Malcolm took the boat back home to Southend the following Monday, Robin had perked up considerably. He even felt able to joke about attending the interview at the Royal Jersey. However, when the day came for him to face the committee, Diana had to escort him to the car, drive him to the club and deposit him at the entrance to the clubhouse.

'Good luck,' she said, kissing him on the cheek. Robin grunted. 'And don't even hint at how angry you are. It's not their fault that the Germans destroyed all the club's records.'

'I shall tell them they can stick my application form up their jumpers,' said Robin. They both burst out laughing at the latest expression they'd picked up from the mainland. 'Do they have any idea how old I'll be in fifteen years' time?' he added as he stepped out of the car.

Robin checked his watch. He was five minutes early. He straightened his tie before walking slowly across the gravel to the clubhouse. So many memories came flooding back: the first time he had seen Diana, when she had walked into the bar to speak to her brother; the day he was appointed captain of the club – the first Englishman to be so honoured; that missed putt on the eighteenth that would have won him the President's Cup; not being able to play in the final the following year because he'd broken his arm; the evening Lord Trent had asked him to sail him to the mainland because the Prime Minister needed his services; the day a German officer had shown him respect and compassion after he had saved the lives of his countrymen. And now, today . . . he opened the newly painted door and stepped inside.

He looked up at the portrait of Harry Vardon and gave him a respectful bow, then turned his attention to Lord Trent, who had died the previous year, having served his country during the war as the Minister for Food.

'The committee will see you now, Mr Chapman,' said the club steward, interrupting his thoughts.

Diana had decided to wait in the car, as she assumed the interview wouldn't take long. After all, every member of the committee had known Robin for over twenty years. But after half an hour she began to glance at her watch every few minutes, and couldn't believe that Robin still hadn't appeared an hour later. She had just decided to go in and ask the steward what was holding her husband up when the clubhouse door swung open and Robin marched out, a grim look on his face. She jumped out of the car and ran towards him.

'Anyone who wishes to reapply for membership cannot hope to be elected for at least another fifteen years,' he said, walking straight past her.

'Are there no exceptions?' asked Diana, chasing after him.

'Only for the new president,' said Robin, 'who will be made an honorary life member. The rules don't seem to apply to him.'

'But that really is so unfair,' said Diana, bursting into tears. 'I shall personally complain to the new president.'

'I'm sure you will, my dear,' said Robin, taking his wife in his arms. 'But that doesn't mean I'll take any notice.'

THE UNDIPLOMATIC
DIPLOMAT *

10

PERCIVAL ARTHUR Clarence Forsdyke – his mother called him Percival, while the few friends he had called him Percy – was born into a family which had played its part in ensuring that the sun never set on the British Empire.

Percy's grandfather, Lord Clarence Forsdyke, had been Governor General of the Sudan, while his father, Sir Arthur Forsdyke KCMG, had been our man in Mesopotamia. So, naturally, great things were expected of young Percy.

Within hours of entering this world, he had been put down for the Dragon prep school, Winchester College and Trinity, Cambridge, establishments at which four generations of Forsdykes had been educated.

After Cambridge, it was assumed that Percy would follow his illustrious forebears into the Foreign Office, where he would be expected at least to equal and possibly even to surpass their achievements. All might have gone to plan had it not been for one small problem: Percy was far too clever for his own good. He won a scholarship to the Dragon at the age of eight, an election to Winchester College before his eleventh birthday, and the Anderson Classics Prize to Trinity while he was still in short trousers. After leaving Cambridge with a double first in Classics, he sat the Civil Service exam, and frankly no one was surprised when he came top in his year.

Percy was welcomed into the Foreign and Commonwealth Office with open arms, but that was when his problems began. Or, to be more accurate, when the Foreign Office's problems began.

The mandarins at the FCO, who are expected to identify high flyers worthy of being fast-tracked, came to the reluctant conclusion that, despite Forsdyke's academic achievements, the young man lacked common sense, possessed few social skills and cared little for the diplomatic niceties required when representing your country abroad – something of a disadvantage if you wish to pursue a career in the Foreign Office.

During his first posting, to Nigeria, Percy told the Minister of Finance that he had no grasp of economics. The problem was that the minister *didn't* have any grasp of economics, so Percy had to be dispatched back to England on the first available boat.

After a couple of years in administration, Percy was given a second chance, and sent to Paris as an assistant secretary. He might have survived this posting had he not told the French President's wife at a government reception that the world was overpopulated, and she wasn't helping matters by producing so many children. Percy had a point, as the lady in question had seven offspring and was pregnant at the time, but he was still to be found packing his bags before lunch the following day. A further spell in admin followed before he was given his third, and final, chance.

On this occasion he was dispatched to one of Her Majesty's smaller colonies in Central Africa as a deputy consul. Within six months he had managed to cause an altercation between two tribes who had lived in harmony for over a century. The following morning Percy was escorted on to a British Airways plane clutching a one-way ticket to London, and was never offered a foreign posting again.

—◄o►—

On returning to London, Percy was appointed as an archives clerk (no one gets the sack at the FCO), and allocated a small office in the basement.

As few people at the FCO ever found any reason to visit the basement, Percy flourished. Within weeks he had instigated a new procedure for cataloguing statements, speeches, memoranda and treaties, and within months he could locate any document, however obscure, required by even the most demanding minister. By the end of the year he could offer an opinion on any FCO demand, based on historic precedent, often without having to refer to a file.

No one was surprised when Percy was appointed Senior Archivist after his boss unexpectedly took early retirement. However, Percy still yearned to follow in his father's footsteps and become our man in some foreign field, to be addressed by all and sundry as 'Your Excellency'. Sadly, it was not to be, because Percy was not allowed out of the basement for the next thirty years, and only then when he retired at the age of sixty.

At Percy's leaving party, held in the India Room of the FCO, the Foreign Secretary described him in his tribute speech as a man with an unrivalled encyclopaedic memory who could probably recite every agreement and treaty Britain had ever entered into. This was followed by laughter and loud applause. No one heard Percy mutter under his breath, 'Not every one, Minister.'

Six months after his retirement, the name of Percival Arthur Clarence Forsdyke appeared on the New Year's

175

Honours List. Percy had been awarded the CBE for services to the Foreign and Commonwealth Office.

He read the citation without any satisfaction. In fact, he felt he was a failure and had let the family down. After all, his grandfather had been a peer of the realm, his father a Knight Commander of St Michael and St George, whereas he ended up a mere Commander of a lower order.

However, Percy had a plan to rectify the situation, and to rectify it quickly.

◄◦►

Once he had left the FCO, Percy did not head straight for the British Library to begin work on his memoirs, as he felt he had achieved nothing worthy of historic record, nor did he retire to his country home to tend his roses, possibly because he didn't have a country home, or any roses. However, he did heed the Foreign Secretary's words, and decided to make use of his unrivalled encyclopaedic memory.

Deep in the recesses of his remarkable mind, Percy recalled an ancient British law which had been passed by an Act of Parliament in 1762, during the reign of King George III. It took Percy some considerable time to double-check, in fact, triple-check, that the Act had not been repealed at any time in the past two hundred years. He was delighted to discover that, far from being repealed, it had been enshrined in the Treaty of Versailles in 1919, and again in the Charter of the United Nations in 1945. Clearly neither organization had someone of Percy's calibre tucked away in its basement. Having read the Act several times, Percy decided to visit the Royal Geographical Society on Kensington Gore, where he spent hours poring over charts that detailed the coastal waters surrounding the British Isles.

After completing his research at the RGS, Percy was satisfied that everything was in place for him to comply with clause 7, addendum 3, of the Territories Settlement Act of 1762.

He returned to his home in Pimlico and locked himself away in his study for three weeks – with only Horatio, his three-legged, one-eyed cat, for company – while he put the final touches to a detailed memorandum that would reveal the real significance of the Territories Settlement Act of 1762, and its relevance for Great Britain in the year 2009.

Once he'd completed his task, he placed the nineteen-page handwritten document, along with a copy of the 1762 Act showing one particular clause highlighted, in a large white envelope which he addressed to Sir Nigel Henderson KCMG, Permanent Secretary to the Foreign and Commonwealth Office, King Charles Street, Whitehall, London SW1A 2AH. He then put the unsealed envelope in the top drawer of his desk, where it would remain for the next three months while he disappeared off the face of the earth. Horatio purred.

◄◦►

On 22 June 2009, Percy took a taxi to Euston station, where he boarded the overnight sleeper for Inverness. His luggage consisted of an overnight bag and his old school trunk, while inside his jacket pocket was a wallet containing two thousand pounds in cash.

On arrival in Inverness, Percy changed platforms and, an hour later, boarded a train that would take him even further north. The five-carriage shuttle stopped at every station on its long and relentless journey up the north-east coast of Scotland, until it finally came to a halt at the remote harbour town of Wick.

When Percy left the station, he commandeered the

only taxi, which took him to the only hotel, where he booked into the only available room. After a one-course meal – the menu being fairly limited, and the kitchen staff having all left at nine o'clock – Percy retired to his room and read *Robinson Crusoe* before falling asleep.

The following morning he rose before the sun, as do most of the natives of the outer reaches of Scotland. He feasted on a large bowl of porridge oats and a pair of kippers that would have graced the Savoy, but rejected an offer of the *Scotsman* in favour of studying a long list of the items that would have to be acquired before the sun had set that afternoon.

Percy spent the first hour after breakfast walking up and down the high street, trying to identify the shops he would have to patronize if his trunk was to be filled by the time he left the following morning.

The first establishment he entered was Mac-Pherson's Camping Store. 'Everything a hiker needs when trekking in the Highlands' was stencilled boldly on the window. After much bending over, lying down and crawling in and out, Percy purchased an easy-to-erect, all-weather tent that the proprietor assured him would still be standing after a desert storm or a mountain gale.

By the time Percy had left the store he had filled four large brown carrier bags with his tent, a primus stove, a kettle, a goose-down sleeping bag with an inflatable pillow, a Swiss army knife (he had checked that it had a tin opener), a pair of Wellington boots, a fishing rod, a camera, a compass and a portable telescope.

Mr MacPherson directed Percy towards the Mac-Pherson General Store on the other side of the road, assuring him that his brother Sandy would be happy to fulfil any other requirements he might still have.

The second Mr MacPherson supplied Percy with a shovel, a plastic mug, plate, knife, fork and spoon, a dozen boxes of matches (Swan Vesta), a Roberts radio, three dozen Eveready batteries, four dozen candles and a first-aid kit, which filled three more carrier bags. Once Percy had established that there wasn't a third Mac-Pherson brother to assist him, he settled for Menzies, where he was able to place several more ticks against items on his long list – a copy of the *Radio Times*, the *Complete Works of Shakespeare* (paperback), a day-to-day 2009 diary (half price) and an Ordnance Survey map showing the outlying islands in the North Sea.

Percy took a taxi back to his hotel, accompanied by nine carrier bags, which he dragged in relays up to his room on the second floor. After a light lunch of fish pie and peas, he set off once again for the high street.

He spent most of the afternoon pushing a trolley up and down the aisles of the local supermarket, stocking up with enough provisions to ensure he could survive for ninety days. Once he was back in his hotel room, he sat on the end of the bed and checked his list once again. He still required one essential item; in fact, he couldn't leave Wick without it.

Although Percy had failed to find what he wanted in any of the shops in town, he had spotted a perfect second-hand example on the roof of the hotel. He approached the proprietor, who was surprised by the guest's request but, noticing his desperation, drove a hard bargain, insisting on seventy pounds for the family heirloom.

'But it's old, battered and torn,' said Percy.

'If it's nae guid enough fur ye, sur,' said the owner loftily, 'ah feel sure y'll bi able tae find a superior wan in Inverness.' Percy gave in, having discovered the true meaning of the word *canny*, and handed over seven ten-pound notes. The proprietor promised that he would have it taken down from the roof before Percy left the following morning.

After such an exhausting day, Percy felt he had earned a rest, but he still had one more task to fulfil before he could retire to bed.

At supper in the three-table dining room, the head waiter (the only waiter) told Percy the name of the man who could solve his final problem, and exactly where he would be located at that time of night. After cleaning his teeth (he always cleaned his teeth after a meal), Percy made his way down to the harbour in search of the Fisherman's Arms. He tapped his jacket pocket to check he hadn't forgotten his wallet and the all-important map.

When Percy entered the pub he received some curious stares from the locals, who didn't approve of stray Englishmen invading their territory. He spotted the man he was looking for seated in a far corner, playing dominoes with three younger men, and made his way slowly across the room, every eye following him, until he came to a halt in front of a squat, bearded man dressed in a thick blue sweater and salt-encrusted jeans.

The man looked up and gave the stranger who had dared to interrupt his game an unwelcoming gaze.

'Are you Captain Campbell?' Percy enquired.

'Who wants tae ken?' asked the bearded man suspiciously.

'My name is Forsdyke,' said Percy, and then, to the astonishment of everyone in the pub, delivered a short, well-rehearsed speech at the top of his voice.

When Percy came to the end, the bearded man placed his double four reluctantly back on the table and, in a brogue that Percy could just about decipher, asked, 'An wur exactly dae ye expect mi tae tak' ye?'

Percy opened his map and spread it out on the table, propelling dominoes in every direction. He then placed a finger in the middle of the North Sea. Four pairs of eyes looked down in disbelief. The captain shook his head, repeating the words 'Nae possible' several times, until Percy mentioned the figure of five hundred pounds. All four of the men seated around the table suddenly took a far greater interest in the Englishman's preposterous proposal. Captain Campbell then began a conversation with his colleagues that no one south of Inverness would have been able to follow without a translator. He finally looked up and said, 'Ah want a hundred pound up front, noo, an' the ether four hundred afore ah let ye oan ma boat.'

Percy extracted five twenty-pound notes from his wallet and handed them across to the captain, who smiled for the first time since they'd met. 'Bi stannin' on the dockside ae *Bonnie Belle* at five tamorra moarnin',' said Campbell as he distributed the cash among his mates. 'Once I have the ether four hundred, I'll tak' ye to your island.'

—◦—

Percy was standing on the quayside long before five the following morning, an overnight bag, his battered old school trunk and a ten-foot pole at his feet. He was dressed in a three-piece suit, white shirt, his old school tie, and was carrying a rolled umbrella. Standard FCO kit when one is posted to some foreign field. He braced himself against the biting wind as he waited for the captain to appear. He felt both exhilarated and terrified at the same time.

He turned his attention to the little fishing vessel he'd chartered for this expedition, and wondered if it had ever ventured outside territorial waters, let alone into the middle of the North Sea. For a moment he considered returning to his hotel and abandoning the whole exercise, but the vision of his father and grand-father standing on the dock beside him strengthened his resolve.

The captain and his three mates appeared out of the early morning mist at one minute to five. All four of them were dressed in exactly the same clothes they had been wearing the night before, making Percy wonder if they'd come straight from the Fisherman's Arms. Was it a seafarer's gait they displayed as they strolled towards him, or had they spent his hundred pounds on what the Scots are most celebrated for?

The captain gave Percy a mock salute, and thrust out his hand. Percy was about to shake it, when he realized that it was being held palm upwards. He handed over four hundred pounds, and Captain Camp-bell ordered his crew to carry Percy's luggage on board. Two of the young men were clearly surprised by how heavy the trunk was. Percy followed them up the gangway, clinging on to the pole which never left his side, even when he joined the captain on the bridge.

The captain studied several oceanographic charts before confirming the exact location at which Percy had asked to be abandoned and then gave the order to cast off. 'Ah think it'll tak' us at least a day an' a night afore wi reach oor destination,' said the captain, 'so perhaps, laddie, it might bi wise fur ye tae lay doon. The waves cin bi a wee bit choppy wance wi leave the shelter ae the harbour.'

They had only just passed Wick lighthouse when Percy began to appreciate the true meaning of Captain Campbell's words, and to regret having had a second helping of porridge that morning. He spent most of the day leaning over the railing, depositing what he'd eaten the previous day into the waves. It wasn't much different during the night, except that it was dark and the crew couldn't see him. He declined the captain's offer to join them for a supper of fish stew.

After thirty hours of Percy wishing the ship would sink, or someone would throw him overboard, the first mate pointed through the mist and hollered, 'Land ahoy!' But it was some time before the blurred dot on the horizon finally turned into a piece of land that might just have been described by an assiduous cartographer as an island.

Percy wanted to cheer, but his voice became muffled as the little vessel continued to circle the island in a valiant attempt to find a landing place. All they could see ahead of them were treacherous rocks and unassailable cliffs that didn't require a 'no entry' sign to warn them off. Percy sank down on to the deck, feeling that the whole exercise simply mirrored his career and would end in failure. He bowed his head in despair, so didn't see the captain pointing to a cove that boasted a small beach.

The crew were experienced at landing far more slippery objects than Percy, and an hour later they left him on the beach along with all his worldly goods. His parting words to the skipper as he climbed back into his small dinghy were, 'If you return in ninety-one days and take me back to the mainland, I'll pay you a further thousand pounds.'

He had anticipated the captain's response, and without waiting to be asked handed over two hundred pounds in cash; but not before he had confirmed the exact date on which the *Bonnie Belle* was to return.

'If you turn up even one hour before the ninety-first day,' he said without explanation, 'you will not be paid another penny.'

Captain Campbell shrugged his shoulders, as he was past trying to understand the eccentric Englishman, but he did manage another salute once he'd pocketed the cash. The crew then rowed him back to his little fishing vessel so they could go about their normal business on the high seas, though not until they were back within the 150-mile legal limit.

Percy placed his feet wide apart and tried to steady himself, but after thirty hours on the *Bonnie Belle* it felt as if the whole island was swaying from side to side. He didn't move until his former companions were out of sight.

He then dragged his belongings up the beach on to higher ground before he went in search of a suitable piece of land on which to pitch his tent. The relentless wind and squalls of rain did not assist his progress.

The flattest piece of land Percy came across during his initial recce turned out to be the highest point on the island, while the most sheltered spot was a large cave nestled in a cliff on the west side. It took him the rest of the day to move all his belongings from the beach to his new home.

After devouring a can of baked beans and a carton of long-life milk, he climbed into his sleeping bag and spent his first night on Forsdyke Island. He missed Horatio.

◄○►

Most people would find trying to survive for three months on a small, uninhabited island in the North Sea somewhat daunting, but having spent thirty years in the basement of the Foreign and Commonwealth Office, Percy Forsdyke was equal to the task. Moreover, he knew that his father and grandfather would regard it as nothing more than character building.

Percy spent his first full day on the island unpacking his trunk and making his new home as comfortable as possible. He stacked all the food at the coldest end of the cave and placed his equipment neatly along the sides.

For some weeks Percy had been planning the routine he'd follow on the island. He would begin the day with a bowl of cornflakes, a boiled egg (until he could bear them no more) and a mug of tea while listening to the *Today Programme* on Radio Four. This would be followed by a session of digging on the highest point of the island, weather permitting. Lunch, usually spam and baked beans, would be followed by a siesta. Not that Percy was avoiding the heat of the sun, you understand; he was just tired. When he woke, Percy would spend the rest of the afternoon exploring the island until he was familiar with every nook and cranny of his kingdom. Once the sun had set, which was very late at that time of year, he would prepare his dinner: more spam and baked beans. It didn't take long for Percy to regret his lack of culinary imagination.

After listening to the ten o'clock news and reading some Shakespeare by candlelight, he would climb into his sleeping bag and carry out the last ritual of the day, bringing his diary up to date. He would detail everything he'd done that day, as it would be part of the evidence he would eventually present to the Foreign Office.

◄○►

Percy had selected his ninety days of isolation carefully. He was able to follow the ball-by-ball commentary of all five Test matches against Australia, as well as the seven One Day Internationals. He also enjoyed thirteen plays of the week, and sixty-four episodes of *The Archers*, but he stopped listening to *Gardeners' Question Time* when he realized it didn't provide many useful tips for someone living on a small island in the North Sea.

If Percy had one regret, it was that he hadn't been able to bring his ginger cat with him. Not that Horatio would have appreciated exchanging his warm kitchen for a cold cave. He had left clear instructions with his housekeeper that she should feed him every morning, and before she left at night.

Percy had more than enough food and drink to survive for ninety days, and was determined to revisit the *Complete Works of Shakespeare*, all 37 plays and 154 sonnets, by the time he returned to the mainland.

By the end of the first month, Percy felt he was well qualified to appear on *Desert Island Discs*, even though that nice Mr Plomley was no longer in charge.

On a more practical level, Percy learned to catch a fish with a sharpened stick. To be accurate, he speared his first fish on the thirty-ninth day, by which time he considered himself a fully domiciled resident.

On the sixty-third day, he completed digging a five-foot hole at the highest point of the island. One of the problems Percy hadn't anticipated was that whenever he visited his hole each morning, it would be full of water, as hardly a day went by when it didn't rain. It took Percy about an hour to scoop out yesterday's water with his plastic mug before he could start digging again, sometimes longer, if it was still raining. He then roamed the island searching for large stones which he lugged back and deposited by the side of the hole.

On the morning of the eighty-ninth day, Percy dragged his pole slowly up to the summit of the island, some 227 feet above sea level, and dumped it unceremoniously by the hole. He then returned to the cave and listened to *Woman's Hour* on Radio Four before having lunch. He'd learned a great deal about women during the past three months. He spent the afternoon shining his shoes, washing his shirt and rehearsing the speech he would deliver on behalf of Her Majesty.

He retired to bed early, aware that he needed to be at his best for the ceremony he would be performing the following day.

◄○►

Percy rose with the sun on 23 September 2009, and ate a light breakfast consisting of a bowl of cornflakes and an apple while he listened to Jim Naughtie discuss with Mr Cameron whether the three party leaders should take part in a television debate before the election. Percy didn't care for the idea: not at all British.

At nine o'clock he shaved, cutting himself in several places, then put on a white shirt, now not quite so white, his three-piece suit, old school tie and shining black shoes, none of which he'd worn for the past three months.

When Percy emerged from the cave carrying his radio, he had a pleasant surprise awaiting him on this, the most important day of his life. The sun was shining brightly in a clear blue sky, and what a blue. When he reached the top of his hill, there was not a drop of water in the hole. God clearly was an Englishman.

He checked his watch: ten twenty-six. Too early to begin proceedings if he intended to keep to the letter of the law. He sat on the ground and recited his favourite speeches from *Henry V*, while checking his watch every few minutes.

At eleven o'clock, Percy lifted the flagpole on to his shoulder and lowered one end into the hole. He then spent forty minutes selecting the stones that would secure it firmly in place. Having completed the task he sat down on the ground, exhausted. Once he'd got his breath back he turned on the radio and still had to wait for some time before Big Ben struck twelve times and the sun reached its highest point. At one minute past twelve, Percy stood to attention, slowly raised the Union Jack up the flagpole and delivered the exact words required by the Territories Settlement Act of 1762: 'I claim this sovereign territory in the name of Her Majesty Queen Elizabeth II, to whom I swear my allegiance.' He then sang the 'National Anthem', and ended with three rousing cheers.

The ceremony completed, Percy fell to his knees and thanked God, and all his ancestors, that like them he had been able to serve the British Empire.

He then picked up his telescope and began to search the high seas for a bobbing fishing vessel. As each hour passed, he became more and more anxious as to where the *Bonnie Belle*, Captain Campbell and his three shipmates might be. He feared they were in the Fisherman's Arms, spending his money.

Once the sun had set on this part of the British Empire, Percy restricted himself to half-rations before spending a sleepless night wondering if he was destined to spend the rest of his days on Forsdyke Island, having fulfilled his mission, but without anyone realizing what he had achieved.

He rose early the following morning, skipped breakfast, missed the *Today Programme* and climbed back up to the highest point on the island, where he was delighted to see the Union Jack still fluttering in the breeze.

He picked up his telescope, swung it slowly through 180 degrees, and there she was, ploughing determinedly, if slowly, through the waves. Not usually a demonstrative man, Percy leapt up and down, shouting with joy. He ran back to his cave, packed his overnight bag with all the evidence he needed to support his claim, then made his way down to the beach. He left everything else in the cave, including his trunk, in case anyone should require more proof that he really had been a resident for ninety days.

Percy waited patiently on the beach, but it was another three hours before the little dinghy came ashore to collect the unappointed ambassador who wished to be transported back to the mainland, having served his tour of duty.

Captain Campbell showed no interest in why Mr Forsdyke had wished to spend ninety-one days on a deserted island, and left him in his cabin to rest. Although Percy was just as sick on the voyage back to Wick as he had been on the way to Forsdyke Island, his heart was full of joy.

Once the captain, the three crew members and their passenger had disembarked from the *Bonnie Belle* they all went to the nearest bank, where Percy withdrew eight hundred pounds. But he didn't hand over the cash until Captain Campbell and his first mate had signed a one-page document confirming that they had taken him to Forsdyke Island on 25 June 2009, and hadn't picked him up again until 24 September 2009, when they had accompanied him back to the mainland. The local bank manager witnessed both signatures.

A taxi took Percy to Wick station, from where he began the slow journey back along the coast to Inverness before boarding the overnight train to London. He found his first-class bunk bed uncomfortable, while the clattering wheels kept him awake most of the night, and the fish served for breakfast had unquestionably left the North Sea some days before he had. He arrived at Euston more tired and hungry than he'd been for the past three months, and then had to hang about in a long taxi queue before he was driven back to his home in Pimlico.

Once he'd let himself in he went straight to his study, unlocked the centre drawer of his desk and retrieved the unsealed envelope containing his detailed memorandum and the copy of the 1762 Territories Settlement Act. He placed Captain Campbell's sworn affidavit in the envelope along with two maps and a diary, then sealed the envelope and wrote on the front, in capital letters, FOR YOUR EYES ONLY.

Despite his impatience to fulfil his dream, Percy didn't leave the house until he'd checked that his one-eyed, three-legged cat was sound asleep on the kitchen boiler. 'I did it, Horatio, I did it,' whispered Percy as he left the kitchen. Once he'd locked the front door, he hailed a passing taxi.

'The Foreign Office,' said Percy as he climbed into the back seat.

When the taxi drew up outside the King Charles Street entrance, Percy said, 'Please wait, cabbie, I'll only be a minute.'

The security guard at the FCO was about to prevent the dishevelled tramp from entering the building when he realized it was Mr Forsdyke.

'Please deliver this to Sir Nigel Henderson immediately,' said Percy, handing over the bulky envelope.

'Yes, Mr Forsdyke,' said the duty clerk, giving him a salute.

Percy sat in the cab on the way back home chanting the 'Nunc Dimittis'.

The first thing Percy did on returning to Pimlico was to feed the cat. He then fed himself and watched the early evening news on television. It was too early for any announcement about his triumph, although he did wonder if it would be the Foreign Secretary or perhaps even the Prime Minister who would be standing at the dispatch box in the House of Commons to deliver an unscheduled announcement. He climbed into bed at ten, and quickly fell into a deep sleep.

◄o►

Percy wasn't surprised to receive a call from Sir Nigel the following afternoon, but he was surprised by the Permanent Secretary's request. 'Good afternoon, Percy,' said Sir Nigel. 'The Foreign Secretary wonders if you could spare the time to drop in and have a chat with him at your earliest convenience.'

'Of course,' said Percy.

'Good,' said Sir Nigel. 'Would eleven tomorrow morning suit you?'

'Of course,' repeated Percy.

'Excellent. I'll send a car. And Percy, can I just check that no one else has seen any of the documents you sent me?'

'That is correct, Sir Nigel. You'll note that everything is handwritten, so you are in possession of the only copies.'

'I'm glad to hear that,' said Sir Nigel without explanation, and the phone went dead.

◄o►

A staff car picked up Percy at ten-thirty the following morning, and drove him to the Foreign Office in Whitehall. He was dressed in his only other Savile Row suit, a fresh white shirt and a new, old school tie, in anticipation of his triumph.

Percy always enjoyed entering the FCO, but even he was flattered to find a clerk waiting to escort him to the Foreign Secretary's office. He savoured every

191

moment as they walked slowly up the broad marble staircase, past the full-length portraits of Castlereagh, Canning, Palmerston, Salisbury and Curzon, before continuing down a long, wide corridor where photographs of Stewart, Douglas-Home, Callaghan, Carrington, Hurd and Cook adorned the walls.

When they reached the Foreign Secretary's office, the clerk tapped lightly on the door before opening it. Percy was ushered into a room large enough to hold a ball, to find the Foreign Secretary and the head of the Foreign Service awaiting him at the far end.

'Welcome back, Percy,' said the Foreign Secretary as if he were greeting an old chum, although he had only met him once before, at his retirement party. 'Come and join myself and Sir Nigel by the fire. There are one or two things I think we need to have a chat about. Didn't we do well to win the Ashes?' he added as he sat down. 'Although I suppose you missed the entire series, remembering that—'

'I was able to follow the ball-by-ball commentary on Radio Four,' Percy assured the Foreign Secretary, 'and it was indeed a magnificent series.' Percy relaxed back in his chair, and was served with a coffee.

'That must have helped kill the time,' said Sir Nigel, who waited until the coffee lady had left the room before he addressed the subject that was on all their minds.

'I read your report yesterday morning, Percy. Quite brilliant,' said Sir Nigel. 'And I must congratulate you on identifying an anomaly in the 1762 Act that we'd all previously overlooked.'

'For well over two hundred years,' chipped in the Foreign Secretary. 'After Sir Nigel had read your memorandum, he phoned me at home and briefed me. I went straight to Number Ten and had a private meeting with the PM, at which I was able to tell him what you've been up to since leaving the FCO. He was most impressed. Most impressed,' repeated the Foreign Secretary. Percy beamed with delight. 'He asked me to send you his congratulations, and best wishes.'

'Thank you,' said Percy, and only just stopped himself from saying, 'And please return mine.'

'The PM also asked me to let him know,' continued the Foreign Secretary, 'what decision you'd come to.'

'What decision I'd come to?' repeated Percy, no longer sounding quite so relaxed.

'Yes,' said Sir Nigel. 'You see, a problem has arisen that we felt we ought to share with you.'

Percy was prepared to answer any queries relating to treaty rights, sovereign status or the relevance of the Territories Settlement Act of 1762.

'Percy,' continued Sir Nigel, giving his former colleague a warm smile, 'you'll be pleased to know that the Lord Chancellor has confirmed that your claim on behalf of the Sovereign is valid, and would stand up in any international court.' Percy began to relax again. 'And indeed, should you press your suit, Forsdyke Island would become part of Her Majesty's Overseas Territories. You were quite correct in your assessment that if you occupied the island for ninety days, without any other person or government making a claim on it, it would become the sole possession of the occupier, and would be governed by the laws of whichever country the occupier is a citizen of, as long as that claim is ratified within six months – if I remember the words of the 1762 Act correctly?'

Almost word perfect, thought Percy. 'Which means,' he said, turning to the Foreign Secretary, 'that we can lay claim not only to the fishing rights, but also to the oil reserves within a radius of one hundred and fifty miles, not to mention the obvious strategic advantage its location gives to our defence forces.'

'And thereby hangs a tale,' said the Permanent Secretary.

Percy wondered which of four possible Shakespeare plays Sir Nigel was quoting from, but decided this wasn't the time to enquire. 'I am also confident,' continued Percy, 'that should you present our case to a plenary session of the United Nations, it would have no choice but to ratify my claim on behalf of the British Government.'

'I'm sure you're right, Percy,' said Sir Nigel, 'but it is the responsibility of the Foreign Office to look at the wider picture and consider all the implications.' As if on cue, both men rose from their places. Percy followed them to the centre of the room, where they halted before a vast globe.

Sir Nigel gave the globe a spin. When it stopped, he pointed to a tiny speck in the Pacific Ocean. 'If the Russians were to lay claim to that island, it could turn out to be a bigger problem for the Americans than Cuba.'

He spun the globe again and when it stopped he pointed to another apparently unnamed island, this time in the middle of the South China Sea. 'If either country laid claim to this, you could end up with a war between Japan and China.'

He spun the globe a third time and, when it stopped, he placed a finger on the Dead Sea. 'Let us pray that the Israelis never get to hear about the Territories Settlement Act of 1762, because that would be the end of any Middle East peace process.'

Percy was speechless. All he had wanted was to prove himself worthy of his father and grandfather, and emulate the contribution they had made to the Foreign

Office but, once again, all he'd achieved was to bring embarrassment to the family name and to the country he loved more than life itself.

The Foreign Secretary placed his arm round Percy's shoulder. 'If you felt able to allow us to file your submission in the archives, and to leave this meeting unrecorded, I know that the PM, and I suspect Her Majesty, would be eternally grateful.'

'Of course, Foreign Secretary,' said Percy, his head bowed.

He slipped out of the Foreign Office a few minutes later, and never mentioned the subject of Forsdyke Island again to anyone other than Horatio. But should anyone ever find themselves lost in the North Sea and come across a fluttering Union Jack . . .

◄o►

On 1 January 2010, among the knighthoods listed in the New Year's Honours, was that of Sir Percival Arthur Clarence Forsdyke, awarded the KCMG for further services to the Foreign and Commonwealth Office.

THE LUCK OF THE IRISH *

11

No one would believe this tale unless they were told that an Irishman was involved.

Liam Casey was born in Cork, the son of a tinker. One of many things he learned from his shrewd father was that while a wise man can spend all day making a few bob, a foolish one can lose them in a few minutes.

During Liam's lifetime, he made over a hundred million 'few bobs', but despite his father's advice, he still managed to lose them all in a few minutes.

After Liam left school, he didn't consider going to university, explaining to his friends that he wanted to join the real world. Liam quickly discovered that you also had to graduate from the University of Life before you could place your foot on the first rung of the ladder to fortune. After a few false starts, as a petrol pump attendant, bus conductor and door-to-door *Encyclopaedia Britannica* salesman, Liam ended up as a trainee with Hamptons, an established English estate agent that had branches all over Ireland.

He spent the next three years learning about the value of property, commercial and residential, the setting and collecting of rents, and how to close a deal on terms that ensured you made a profit but didn't lose a customer. The average person will move house five times during their lifetime, the English manager informed Liam, so you need to retain their confidence.

'I wish I'd been James Joyce's estate agent,' was all Liam had to say on the subject.

'Why?' asked the Englishman, sounding puzzled.

'He moved house over a hundred times during his lifetime.' It was about the only thing Liam could remember about James Joyce.

Working for an English company, Liam quickly discovered that if you have a gentle Irish brogue and are graced with enough charm, the invaders have a tendency to underestimate you – a mistake the English have made for over a thousand years.

Another important lesson he learned, and one they certainly don't teach you at any university, was that the only difference between a tinker and a merchant banker is the sum of money that changes hands. However, Liam couldn't work out how to take advantage of this knowledge until he met Maggie McBride.

Maggie didn't consider the tinker's son from Cork to be much of a catch, even if he was good-looking and fun to be with, but when he invited her to join him for a holiday in Majorca, she began to show a little more interest.

Liam's current account at the Allied Irish Bank was just enough in credit for him to be able to afford a package holiday to Magaluf, a resort on the south-west coast of the island, which for three months of every year is taken over by the British.

Maggie was not impressed when they booked into a one-star hotel and were shown to a room with a double bed. She made it absolutely clear that she might have agreed to come on holiday with Liam, but that didn't mean they would be sleeping together. Liam booked himself into a separate room, which he knew would stretch his budget to the limit. Another lesson learned. Before you sign a contract, check the small print.

The next day Liam was lying next to Maggie on an

overcrowded beach in a pair of tight-fitting swimming trunks, becoming redder and redder by the minute. His mother had once told him that the Irish have the greenest grass and the whitest skins on earth, but he had not, until then, realized the significance of the second part of her statement.

On the second day, Liam, still having failed to make any progress with Maggie, was beginning to wonder why he'd bothered to take her on holiday in the first place. But then he discovered that the thousand Englishwomen walking up and down the beach had only one thing on their minds – and a handsome young Irishman who would be disappearing back to Cork in two weeks' time ticked most of their boxes.

Liam was telling a girl from Doncaster how he'd discovered Riverdance when she said, 'You're getting very red.' So red that he had to lie on his stomach all night, quite unable to move, which was not at all what the girl from Doncaster had planned.

The next morning Liam smothered himself with factor thirty suncream, put on a long-sleeved shirt and long trousers, ignored the signs to the beach and took a bus into Palma, wondering if it would turn out to be just another Magaluf.

The medieval capital took him by surprise, with its wide streets lined with palm trees and flower baskets, and the narrow alleys with picturesque pavement restaurants and stylish boutiques. He could have been in a different country.

As he strolled down the Paseo Maritimo, Liam found himself stopping to look in the estate agents' windows. He was surprised how cheap the houses were compared to Cork, and even more surprised to discover that the banks were offering 80, sometimes even 90 per cent mortgages.

He considered entering one of the estate agents' offices, as he had a hundred questions he wanted answering, but as he couldn't speak a word of Spanish, he satisfied himself with looking in the windows and admiring the large colour photographs of properties described as *deseable*, *asequible*, *sensational*. He was thinking of returning to Magaluf when he spotted a familiar green, white and orange flag flapping in the wind outside a shopfront with a sign which announced, 'Patrick O'Donovan, International Real Estate Co.'

Liam pushed open the front door without bothering to look in the window. As he stepped into the office, a smartly dressed woman looked up, and an older man, unshaven and wearing soiled jeans and a T-shirt, swung his feet off a desk and smiled.

'I was just wondering—' began Liam.

'A fellow Irishman!' exclaimed the man, leaping up. 'Allow me to introduce myself. I'm Patrick O'Donovan.'

'Liam Casey,' said Liam, shaking him by the hand.

'Is it to be business or pleasure, Liam?' asked O'Donovan.

'I'm not quite sure,' Liam replied, 'but as I'm here on holiday—'

'Then it's pleasure,' said O'Donovan. 'So let's begin our relationship as any self-respecting Irishmen should. Maria, if anyone calls, my friend and I can be found at the Flanagan Arms.'

Without another word, O'Donovan led Liam out of the office, across the road and into a side alley where they entered a pub few tourists would ever come across. The next words O'Donovan uttered were, 'Two pints of Guinness', without asking his new-found friend what he would like.

Liam was able to get through most of his questions while O'Donovan was still sober. He learned that Patrick had been living on the island for over thirty years, and was convinced that Majorca was about to take off like California at the time of the gold rush. O'Donovan went on to tell Liam that the island was attracting a record number of tourists but, more important, it had recently become the most popular destination for Brits who wanted to spend their retirement years abroad.

'When I set up my agency,' he told Liam between gulps of his third Guinness, 'it was long before Majorca became fashionable. In those days there were only a dozen of us in the business; now, everybody on the island thinks they're an estate agent. I've done well, can't complain, but I only wish I was your age.'

'Why?' asked Liam innocently.

'We're about to enter a boom period,' said O'Donovan. 'An ageing population with disposable incomes and an awareness of their own mortality are migrating here like a flock of starlings searching for warmer climes.'

By the fifth Guinness, Liam had only one or two more questions left to ask. Not that it mattered, as O'Donovan was no longer capable of answering them.

◄o►

The next morning, and every morning for the following week, Liam did not join Maggie on the overcrowded beaches but took the bus that was heading into Palma. He had some serious research to carry out before he met up with Patrick O'Donovan again.

During the day, he made appointments with several estate agents to view apartments and other properties. What he was shown confirmed O'Donovan's opinion – Majorca was about to enter a period of rapid growth.

On the final morning of his holiday, having not once returned to the beach in the past ten days, even though his red Majorca skin had faded back to Irish white, Liam boarded the bus to Palma for the last time.

Once he'd been dropped off in the city centre, he headed straight for the Paseo Maritimo and didn't stop walking until he reached the offices of Patrick O'Donovan, International Real Estate Co. He had only one more question to ask his fellow countryman. 'Would you consider taking me on as a junior partner?'

'Certainly not,' said O'Donovan. 'But I would consider taking you on as a partner.'

Maggie McBride flew back to Ireland, *virgo intacta*, while the tinker from Cork remained in Majorca.

‐◁◦▷‐

Liam's first year in Majorca didn't turn out to be quite the bonanza his new partner had promised, despite his working night and day and making full use of the skills he'd honed in Cork. While he spent most of his days in the office or showing clients around properties, O'Donovan spent more and more of his time in the Flanagan Arms, drinking away the company's dwindling profits.

By the end of his second year, Liam was considering returning to Ireland, which was experiencing its own economic boom, fuelled by massive grants from the European Union. And then, without warning, the decision was taken out of his hands. O'Donovan failed to return to work after the pub had closed for the afternoon siesta. He'd dropped dead in the street a hundred yards from the office.

Liam organized Patrick's funeral, held a wake at the Flanagan Arms and was the last to leave the pub that night. By the time he crawled into bed at three in the morning, he'd made a decision.

The first person he called after arriving at the office

the next day was a sign-writer he'd found in the Yellow Pages. By twelve o'clock, the name above the door read 'Casey & Co, International Estate Agents'.

The second phone call Liam made was to Pepe Miro, a young man who worked for a rival company and had beaten him to several deals in the past two years. They agreed to meet in a tapas bar that evening, and after another late night, during which a José Ferrer L. Rosado replaced Guinness, Liam was able to convince Pepe they would both be better off working together as partners.

A month later, a Spanish flag was raised beside the Irish one, and the sign-writer returned. When he left, the name above the door read, 'Casey, Miro & Co.' While Pepe handled the natives, Liam took care of any foreign intruders; a genuine partnership.

The new company's profits grew slowly to begin with, but at least the graph was now heading in the right direction. But it wasn't until Pepe told his new partner about an old local custom that their fortunes began to change.

Majorca is a small island with a large, fertile, central plain where vineyards, almond and olive trees thrive. Traditionally, when a Majorcan farmer dies, he leaves any property in the fertile heartland to his eldest son, while any daughters end up with small pieces of craggy coastline. Liam's Irish charm and good looks did no harm when he advised these daughters how they could benefit from this chauvinistic injustice.

He purchased his first plot of land in 1991, from a middle-aged lady who was short of cash and boyfriends: a tiny strip of infertile coastline with uninterrupted views of the Mediterranean. A bulldozer levelled the ground, and within a few weeks, after a bunch of itinerant workers had cleaned up the site, a developer purchased the plot for almost double Liam's original outlay.

Liam bought his second piece of land from a grieving widow. It had splendid panoramic views all the way to Barcelona. Once again he flattened the plot, and this time he built a path wide enough to allow a car to reach it from the main road. On this occasion he made an even larger return, which he used to build a small house on a piece of land Pepe had purchased from a lady who spoke only Spanish. A year later they sold the property for triple their original investment.

By the time Liam had purchased their fourth piece of coastal land, which was large enough to divide into three plots, he realized he was no longer an estate agent but had unwittingly become a property developer. While Pepe continued to woo an endless stream of Spanish daughters and widows, Liam converted their scraggy inheritances into saleable properties. As time went by and the company's profits increased, it became clear to Liam that the only obstacle preventing him from progressing at an even more rapid pace was a lack of capital. He decided to make one of his rare trips back to Ireland.

The property manager of the Allied Irish Bank in Dublin – Liam avoided Cork – listened with interest to the proposals put forward by his fellow countryman, and eventually agreed to advance him a hundred thousand pounds with which to purchase two new sites. When Liam delivered a profit of over 40 per cent the following year, the bank agreed to double its investment.

Liam closed his first million-pound deal in 1997, and his success might have continued unabated, if only he'd recalled his father's sound advice. *While a wise man can spend all day making a few bob, a foolish one can lose them in a few minutes.*

◄○►

On the evening of 31 December 1999, Liam and Pepe held a party for their friends and clients at the Palace Hotel in Palma to celebrate their good fortune. As they were now both millionaires, they had every reason to look forward to the new millennium with confidence, especially as Pepe announced, just before the sun rose on 1 January 2000, that he had come across the deal of a lifetime. Liam had to wait two more days before Pepe had recovered sufficiently to tell him the details.

A Majorcan from one of the oldest families on the island had recently died intestate. After some considerable legal wrangling, the court had decided that his wife was entitled to inherit his entire estate – an area of land in Valldemossa that stretched for several kilometres, from the slopes of the Sierra de Tramuntana all the way down to the coast.

Liam spent a week in Dublin trying to convince the Allied Irish that it should put up the largest property loan in its history. Once the bank had agreed terms, which included personal guarantees from both Liam and Pepe, something Liam's tinker father would never have advised, he returned to Majorca and began to conduct negotiations with the widow. She finally agreed to sell her two-thousand-hectare site for twenty-three million euros.

Within days, Liam had hired a leading architect from Barcelona, a highly respected surveyor from Madrid and a well-connected lawyer in Palma, and began to prepare the necessary documents to ensure that outline planning permission would be granted by the local council. They divided the land into 360 individual plots that included roads with broad pavements, street lighting, electricity, drainage and sewerage, an eighteen-hole golf course, a shopping centre, a cinema, eleven restaurants and a sports complex. Every home would have its own swimming pool, while some of the larger plots would even have their own tennis courts. But the feature that made the development unique was that whichever house a customer purchased, from the top of the mountain all the way down to the coast, they were guaranteed an uninterrupted view of the ocean.

Liam and Pepe both accepted that because of the huge amount of work involved with the project, it would be years before they could consider taking on any other commitments.

Liam had a large-scale model of the site built, and commissioned a documentary film maker to produce a twenty-minute promotional video entitled *Valldemossa Vision*. The Allied Irish Bank clearly bought into this vision, and released an initial two point three million euros to Liam as a deposit on the land.

It was another year before Liam was ready to present his outline planning application to the Consell Insular de Mallorca. When Liam rose to make his speech to the Valldemossa council, every elected member was seated in his place. He took them slowly through his master plan, and when his presentation came to an end, he called for questions.

If only to persuade people they haven't fallen asleep, politicians always have well-prepared questions to hand. However, Liam's experts had spent hours anticipating each and every question they were asked, and others that hadn't even been thought of. When Liam finally sat down, he was greeted by warm applause from both main political parties.

The governor of the Balearics rose to congratulate Liam and his team on a splendid and imaginative scheme, while the Mayor of Valldemossa enthusiastically assured his colleagues that the project would undoubtedly attract wealthy residents, ensuring increased revenue for the council's coffers for many years to come.

No one was surprised when, six weeks later, the Consell Insular de Mallorca granted outline planning permission to Casey, Miro & Co. for its Valldemossa project, which the mayor described to the press as bold, imaginative and of civic importance. But Pepe had already warned Liam there was one more hurdle that had to be negotiated before they could return to the bank and ask for the remaining twenty point seven million euros of their advance. It was still necessary for the Supreme Court in Madrid to rubber-stamp the whole project before the first bulldozer would be allowed on the site, and the court was well known for rejecting projects at the last moment.

Three different sets of lawyers worked night and day in Madrid, Barcelona and Palma, and nine months later to everyone's relief the Supreme Court gave its imprimatur.

The following day Liam flew to Dublin, where even more lawyers were working on the documentation that would allow him to be able to draw on a rolling fifty-million-euro loan. Building costs only ever go in one direction.

Within minutes of the ink drying on the paper, four of the leading construction companies in Europe were driving their vehicles on to the site, followed by over a thousand workers who were looking forward to being employed for the next ten years.

◄○►

Liam had never taken a great deal of interest in Majorcan politics, and he made a point of not supporting either main party when it came to the local elections. He made it a policy to donate exactly the same amount to the campaign funds of both the major parties so he could continue to deal with whichever one was in power.

Over the years, it had always been a close-run thing between the Partido Socialista Obrero Español and the Partido Popular, with power changing hands every few years. But to everyone's surprise, when the election result was announced from the town hall steps later that year, the Green Party had captured three seats and, more important, held the balance of power, as the other two parties were evenly split with twenty-one seats each. Liam didn't give the result a great deal of thought, even when the *Mallorca Daily Bulletin* informed its readers that the Greens would join a coalition with whichever party was willing to support their ideological aims. The most important of which, as had been stated in their manifesto, was not to grant any future planning permission in Valldemossa.

This suited Liam as it would cut out any further rivals, making his the last project to be approved by the Supreme Court in Madrid. But once the resolution had been passed in council, with the backing of both main parties, the Greens, encouraged by their success, immediately announced that any projects currently underway should have their planning permission rescinded. This time Liam was concerned, because his lawyers warned him that even if the Supreme Court eventually overruled the council's decision, his project could be held up for years.

'Every day we're not working will cost us money,' Liam warned Pepe. He realized that if the Greens were

210

able to get either of the two main parties to support their proposal, he and Pepe would be bankrupt within weeks.

When the council met to take a vote on the Greens' resolution, Liam and his team sat nervously in the public gallery waiting to learn their fate. Passionate speeches were made from all sides of the chamber, and even after the last councillor had offered his opinion, no one could be sure how the numbers would fall.

The chief clerk called for the vote, and for the first time that evening the chamber fell silent. A few minutes later the Mayor solemnly announced that the Greens' proposal to rescind all current planning permissions had been carried by twenty-three votes to twenty-two.

Liam had lost all his few bobs in a few minutes.

Every one of his workers immediately deserted the site. Unfinished houses were left without doors or windows, cranes stood unmanned and expensive equipment and materials were left to rust. By the time Liam recalled his late father's wise advice, it was too late to turn the clock back.

The company's lawyers recommended an appeal. Liam reluctantly agreed, although, as they had pointed out to him, even if they were eventually able to overturn the council's decision, by then years would have passed and any possible profit would have been swallowed up by interest payments alone, not to mention lawyers' fees.

◄○►

The Allied Irish Bank quickly responded to the news from Valldemossa by placing an immediate stop order on all Liam's accounts. They also issued a directive instructing Casey, Miro & Co, and any of its associates, to repay the outstanding thirty-seven-million-euro loan at the first possible opportunity, although it must have known that neither Liam nor Pepe could any longer afford the airfare to Dublin.

Liam informed the bank that he intended to appeal against the council's decision, but *he* knew, and so did they, that even if he won, they still would have lost everything by the time the Supreme Court reached its verdict.

An appeal date was set for the Supreme Court of Madrid to sit in judgement on the Valldemossa project, but before then Liam and Pepe had been forced to sell their homes, as well as what was left of the company's assets, to pay lawyers' bills on both sides of the Irish Sea.

Liam returned to the Flanagan Arms for the first time in twenty-three years.

◄○►

When Liam and Pepe appeared before the Supreme Court two years later, the senior panel judge expressed considerable sympathy for Mr Casey and Mr Miro, as they had invested ten years of hard work, as well as their personal fortunes, in a project that both the Valldemossa council and the Supreme Court had considered to be bold, imaginative and of civic importance. However, the court did not have the authority to overturn the decision of an elected council, even when it was retrospective. Liam bowed his head.

'Nevertheless,' the judge continued, 'this court does have the authority to award compensation in full to the appellants, who carried out their business in good faith, and fulfilled every obligation required of them by the Valldemossa council. With that in mind, this court will appoint an independent arbitrator to assess the costs Mr Casey and Mr Miro have incurred, which will include any projected losses.'

As Spaniards were involved, it was another year before the arbitrator presented his findings to the Supreme Court, which necessitated a further six months of making some minor adjustments to the costs so that no one would be in any doubt about how seriously the court had taken their responsibilities.

The day after the senior judge announced the court's findings, *El Pais* suggested in its leader that the size of the award was a warning to all politicians not to consider making retrospective legislation in the future.

The Valldemossa Council was ordered to pay 121 million euros in compensation to Mr Liam Casey, Mr Pepe Miro and their associates.

At the local council election held six months later, the Green Party lost all three of its seats by overwhelming majorities.

Pepe took over the business in Majorca, while Liam retired to Cork, where he purchased a castle with a hundred acres of land. He tells me he has no intention of seeking planning permission, even for an outhouse.

Postscript

Observant readers who have followed the timescale during which this story took place might feel that even if the Green Party had failed to overturn Liam and Pepe's planning permission, they would have gone bankrupt anyway following the sudden downturn in the world's economy, and without being paid any compensation. But, as I said at the outset, no one would believe this tale unless they were told that an Irishman was involved.

POLITICALLY CORRECT

12

'Never judge a book by its cover,' Arnold's mother always used to tell him.

Despite this piece of sage advice, Arnold took against the man the moment he set eyes on him. The bank had taught him to be cautious when it came to dealing with potential customers. You can have nine successes out of ten and then one failure can ruin your balance sheet, as Arnold had found to his cost soon after he had joined the bank; he was still convinced that was why his promotion had been held up for so long.

Arnold Pennyworthy – he was fed up with being told by all and sundry, *That's an appropriate name for a banker* – had been deputy manager of the Vauxhall branch of the bank for the past ten years, but had recently been offered the chance to move to Bury St Edmunds as branch manager. Bury St Edmunds might have been one of the bank's smaller branches, but Arnold felt that if he could make a fist of it, he still had one more promotion left in him. In any case, he couldn't wait to get out of London, which seemed to him to have been over-run by foreigners who had changed the whole character of the city.

When Arnold's wife had left him without giving a reason – at least, that's what he told his mother – he had moved into Arcadia Mansions, a large block of flats which he liked to refer to as apartments. The rent was extortionate, but at least there was a hall porter. 'It gives the right impression whenever anyone visits me,' Arnold told his mother. Not that he had many visitors since his wife had walked out on him. Arcadia Mansions also had the advantage of being within walking distance of the bank, so the extra money he paid out on rent he clawed back on bus and train fares. The only real disadvantage was that the Victoria line ran directly below the building, so the only time you could be guaranteed any peace was between twelve-thirty and five-thirty in the morning.

The first time Arnold caught sight of his new neighbour was when they found themselves sharing a lift down to the ground floor. Arnold waited for him to speak, but he didn't even say good morning. Arnold wondered if the man even spoke English. He stood back to take a closer look at the most recent arrival. The man was a little shorter than Arnold, around five feet seven inches, solidly built but not overweight, with a square jaw and what Arnold later described to his mother as soulless eyes. His skin was dark, but not black, so Arnold couldn't be sure where he was from. The unkempt beard reminded him of another of his mother's homilies: 'Never trust a man with a beard. He's probably hiding something.'

Arnold decided to have a word with the porter. Dennis was the fount of all knowledge when it came to what took place in Arcadia Mansions and was certain to know all about the man. When the lift doors opened, Arnold stood back to allow the new resident to get out first. He waited until the man had left the building before strolling across to join Dennis at the reception desk.

'What do we know about him?' asked Arnold, nodding at the man as he disappeared into a black cab.

'Not a lot,' admitted Dennis. 'He's taken a short-term lease and says he won't be with us for long. But he did warn me that he'd be having visitors from time to time.'

'I don't like the sound of that,' said Arnold. 'Any idea where he comes from, or what he does for a living?'

'Not a clue,' said Dennis. 'But he certainly didn't get that tan holidaying in the South of France.'

'That's for sure,' said Arnold, laughing. 'Don't misunderstand me, Dennis, I'm not prejudiced. I've always liked Mr Zebari from the other end of my corridor. Keeps himself to himself, always respectful.'

'That's true,' said Dennis. 'But then you must remember that Mr Zebari is a radiologist.' Not that he was altogether sure what a radiologist was.

'Well, I must get a move on,' said Arnold. 'Can't afford to be late for work. Now that I'm going to be manager, I have to set an example to the junior staff. Keep your ear to the ground, Dennis,' he added, touching the side of his nose with a forefinger. 'Although our masters have decided it's not politically correct, I have to tell you I don't like the look of him.'

The porter gave a slight nod as Arnold pushed through the swing doors and headed off in the direction of the bank.

The next time Arnold came across the new resident was a few days later; he was returning from work when he saw him chatting to a young man dressed from head to toe in leather and sitting astride a motorbike. The moment the two of them spotted Arnold, the young man pulled down his visor, revved up and shot away. Arnold hurried into the building, relieved to find Dennis sitting behind the reception desk.

'Those two look a bit dodgy to me,' said Arnold.

'Not half as dodgy as some of the other young men

who've been visiting him at all hours of the night and day. There are times when I can't be sure if this is Albert Embankment or the Khyber Pass.'

'I know what you mean,' said Arnold as the lift door opened and Mr Zebari stepped out.

'Good evening, Mr Zebari,' said Dennis with a smile. 'On night duty again?'

'Afraid so, Dennis. No rest for the wicked when you work for the NHS,' he added as he left the building.

'A real gentleman, that Mr Zebari,' said Dennis. 'Sent my wife a bunch of flowers on her birthday.'

–◦–

It was a couple of weeks later, after arriving home late from work, that Arnold spotted the motorbike again. It was parked up against the railing but there was no sign of its owner. Arnold walked into the building, to find a couple of young men chatting loudly in a tongue he didn't recognize. They headed towards the lift, so he held back, as he had no desire to join them.

Dennis waited until the lift door had closed before saying, 'No prizes for guessing who they're visiting. God knows what they get up to behind closed doors.'

'I have my suspicions,' said Arnold, 'but I'm not going to say anything until I've got proof.'

When he got out of the lift at the fourth floor, Arnold could hear raised voices coming from the apartment opposite his. Noticing that the door was slightly ajar, he slowed down and casually glanced inside.

A man was lying flat on his back on the floor, his arms and legs pinned down by the two men he'd seen getting into the lift, while the youth he'd spotted on the motorbike was holding a kitchen knife above the man's head. All around the room were large blown-up photographs of the devastation caused by the 7/7 bus and tube bombings that had recently appeared on the front pages of every national newspaper. The moment the youth spotted Arnold staring at him, he walked quickly across the room and closed the door.

For a moment, Arnold just stood there shaking, unsure what to do next. Should he run downstairs and tell Dennis what he'd witnessed, or make a dash for the relative safety of his apartment and call the police?

Hearing what sounded like a roar of laughter coming from inside the apartment, Arnold ran across to his front door, fumbled for his keys and attempted to push his office Yale into the lock, while continually looking over his shoulder. When he eventually found the right key, he was so nervous he tried to force it in upside down and ended up dropping it on the floor. He picked it up and managed to open the door with his third attempt.

Once Arnold was inside he quickly double-bolted the door and put the safety chain in place, although he still didn't feel safe. When he'd caught his breath, he dragged the largest chair in the room across the floor and rammed it up against the door, then collapsed into it, trembling, as he tried to think what he should do next.

He thought again about phoning the police, but then became fearful that the man would discover who had reported him and the kitchen knife would end up hovering above his head. And when the police raided the building, a fight might break out in the corridor. How many innocent people would become involved? Mr Zebari would surely open his door to find out what was going on and come face to face with the terrorists. It was a risk Arnold wasn't willing to take.

Several minutes passed, and as he could hear nothing happening outside, Arnold nipped across to the sideboard and shakily poured himself a large whisky. He drank it down in two gulps, then poured himself another before slumping back into the chair, clinging on to the bottle. He took another gulp of whisky, more than he usually drank in a week, but his heart was still pounding. He sat there, his shirt saturated with sweat, terrified to move, until the sun had disappeared behind the highest building. He took another swig, and then another, until he finally passed out.

Arnold couldn't be sure how many hours he'd slept, but he woke with a start when the clickety-clack of the first tube could be heard rumbling below him. He saw the empty bottle of whisky lying on the floor by his feet and tried to sober up. In the cold, clear light of morning, he knew exactly what his mother would expect him to do.

When the time came for him to leave for work, he tentatively pulled the heavy chair back a few inches, then placed an ear against the door. Were the men standing outside in the corridor waiting for him to come out? He unlocked the door without making the slightest sound and slowly removed the safety chain. He waited for some time before gingerly opening the door an inch, and then another inch, before peeping into the corridor. He was greeted by silence and no sign of anyone.

Arnold took off his shoes, stepped out into the corridor, closed the door quietly behind him and tiptoed slowly towards the lift, never once taking his eyes off the door on the other side of the corridor. There was no sound coming from inside, and he wondered if they'd panicked and made a run for it. He jabbed at the lift button several times, and it seemed to take forever before the doors finally slid open. He jumped inside and pressed G, but even when the doors had closed, he didn't feel safe. By the time the lift reached the ground floor he'd put his shoes back on and tied the laces. When the doors slid open he ran out of the building, not even looking in Dennis's direction when he said, 'Good morning.' He didn't stop running until he had reached the bank. Arnold opened the front door with the correct key and quickly stepped inside, setting off the alarm. It was the first time he'd had to turn it off.

Arnold went straight to the lavatory, and when he looked at himself in the mirror two bleary red eyes in an unshaven face stared back at him. He tidied himself up as best he could before creeping into his office. He hoped that when the staff arrived, not too many of them would notice that he hadn't shaved and was wearing the same clothes as he had worn the day before.

He sat at his desk and began to write down everything he'd witnessed during the past month, going into particular detail when it came to what had taken place the night before. Once he'd finished, he sat staring into space for some time before he picked up the phone on his desk and dialled 999.

'Emergency services, which service do you require?' said a cool voice.

'Police please,' said Arnold, trying not to sound nervous. He heard a click, then another voice came on the line and said, 'Police service. What is the nature of your emergency?'

Arnold looked down at the pad in front of him, and read out the statement he had just prepared. 'My name is Arnold Pennyworthy. I need to speak to a senior police officer, as I have some important information concerning the possibility of a serious crime having been committed, in which terrorists may be involved.'

Another click, another voice, this time with a name. 'Control room. Inspector Newhouse.'

Arnold read his statement a second time, word for word.

'Could you be a little more specific, sir?' the inspector asked. Once Arnold had told him the details, the officer said, 'Hold on, please, sir. I'm going to put you through to a colleague at Scotland Yard.'

Another line, another voice, another name. 'Sergeant Roberts speaking. How can I help?'

Arnold repeated his prepared statement a third time.

'I think it may be wise, sir, if you didn't say too much more over the phone,' suggested Roberts. 'I'd prefer to come and see you so we can discuss it in person.'

Arnold didn't realize that this suggestion was used to get rid of crank callers and those who simply wanted to waste police time.

'That's fine by me,' he said, 'but I'd prefer it if you visited me at the bank rather than my apartment.'

'I quite understand, sir. I'll be with you as soon as I can.'

'But you don't know the address.'

'We know your address, sir,' said Sergeant Roberts without explanation.

Arnold didn't leave his office that morning, even to carry out his usual check on the tellers. Instead, he busied himself opening the post and checking his emails. There were several phone messages he should have responded to, but they could wait until the man from Scotland Yard had come and gone.

Arnold was pacing up and down in his office when there was a tap on the door.

'There's a Sergeant Roberts to see you,' said his surprised-looking secretary. 'Says he has an appointment.'

'Show him in, Diane,' said Arnold, 'and make sure that we're not disturbed.'

Arnold's secretary stood aside to allow a tall, smartly dressed young man to enter the office. She closed the door behind him.

The sergeant introduced himself and the two men shook hands before he produced his warrant card.

'Would you like a tea or coffee, Sergeant Roberts?' Arnold asked after he had carefully checked the card.

'No, thank you, sir,' the sergeant replied, sitting down opposite Arnold and opening a notebook.

'Where shall I start?' said Arnold.

'Why don't you take me through exactly what you saw taking place, Mr Pennyworthy. Don't spare me any details, however irrelevant you may consider they are.'

Arnold checked through his notes once again. He began by describing in great detail everything he'd seen during the past month, ending with a full account of what he'd witnessed in the flat opposite the previous night. When he finally came to the end, he poured himself a glass of water.

'What's your neighbour's name?' was the sergeant's first question.

'Good heavens,' said Arnold, 'I have no idea. But I can tell you that he's recently moved into the block, and has taken a short lease.'

'Which floor are you on, Mr Pennyworthy?'

'The fourth.'

'Thank you. That will be more than enough to be going on with,' said the sergeant, closing his notebook.

'So what happens next?' asked Arnold.

'We'll put a surveillance team on the building immediately, keep an eye on the suspect for a few days and try to find out what he's up to. It could all be completely innocent, of course, but should we come up with anything, Mr Pennyworthy, be assured we'll keep you informed.'

'I hope it won't turn out to be a waste of your time,' said Arnold, suddenly feeling a little foolish.

'We'll find out soon enough,' said the young detective with a smile. 'Let me assure you, Mr Pennyworthy, I only wish there were more members of the public who were as vigilant. It would make my job much easier. Good luck with your new job,' he added as he stood to leave.

As soon as the policeman had left, Arnold picked up the phone on his desk and called his mother. 'Can I come and stay with you for a few days, Mother, before I move to Bury St Edmunds?'

'Yes, of course, dear,' she replied. 'Nothing wrong, I hope?'

'Nothing for you to worry about, Mother.'

◄◦►

Once Arnold had moved to Bury St Edmunds, running the branch took up most of his time, and as the weeks passed and he heard nothing from Sergeant Roberts, the incident at Arcadia Mansions began to fade in his memory.

From time to time he read reports in the *Daily Telegraph* about police raids on terrorist cells in Leeds, Birmingham and Bradford. He always studied the photos of the suspects being led away by the police, and on one occasion he could have sworn that. . .

Arnold had just finished interviewing a customer about a mortgage application when the phone on his desk rang.

'There's a Sergeant Roberts on the line,' said his secretary.

'Just give me a moment,' said Arnold. He could feel

his heart racing as he bustled the customer out of his office and closed the door behind him.

'Good morning, Sergeant.'

'Good morning, sir,' came back a voice he recognized. 'I was wondering if you were planning to be in London during the next few days. It's just that I'd like to bring you up to date on what our surveillance team has come up with.' Arnold began to thumb through his diary. 'If that's not convenient,' the sergeant continued, 'I'd be happy to visit you in Bury St Edmunds.'

'No, no,' said Arnold, 'I'll be coming up to London on Friday evening. It's my sister's birthday, and I'm taking her to see *The Sound of Music* at the London Palladium.'

'Good, then I wonder if you could spare the time to pop in to Scotland Yard, say around five o'clock, because I know that Commander Harrison is very keen to have a word with you.'

'That will be fine,' said Arnold, looking down at the blank page. He made a note in his diary, not that he was likely to forget.

'Good,' said the sergeant. 'I'll meet you in reception at five o'clock on Friday.'

As the week went by, Arnold couldn't help thinking that he was looking forward to meeting Commander Harrison more than he was to seeing *The Sound of Music*.

◄○►

Arnold left the office just after lunch on Friday, explaining to his secretary that he had an important appointment in London. When he arrived at Liverpool Street station he went straight to the taxi rank, as he didn't want to be late for the meeting.

The taxi swung into the forecourt of Scotland Yard

a few minutes before five, and Arnold was pleased to see Sergeant Roberts standing by the reception desk waiting for him.

'Good to see you again, Mr Pennyworthy,' said Roberts. They shook hands, and the sergeant guided Arnold towards a bank of lifts. He chatted about *The Sound of Music*, which he'd taken his wife to see at Christmas, while they waited for the lift, and about the parlous state of English rugby while they were in the lift. He hadn't even hinted why Commander Harrison wanted to see Arnold by the time the lift doors opened on the sixth floor.

Roberts led Arnold to a door at the far end of the corridor, which displayed the name Commander Mark Harrison OBE. He gave a gentle tap, waited for a moment, then opened the door and walked in.

The commander immediately rose from behind his desk and gave Arnold a warm smile before shaking hands with him. 'Good to meet you at last,' he said. 'Can I offer you a drink?'

'No, thank you,' said Arnold, now even more desperate to discover why such a senior officer wanted to see him.

'I know you're going to the theatre this evening, Mr Pennyworthy, so I'll get straight to the point,' said the commander, waving Arnold to a seat. 'I must explain from the outset,' he continued, 'that the case I'm going to discuss with you is due to begin at the Old Bailey next week, so there will be some details I'm not at liberty to disclose, although I feel sure I can rely on your complete discretion, Mr Pennyworthy.'

'I fully understand,' said Arnold.

'Let me begin by saying how grateful we all are at the Yard for the information you supplied. I think I can say without exaggeration that you have been responsible for uncovering one of the most active terrorist cells in this country. In fact, it's hard to quantify just how many lives you may have been responsible for saving.'

'I did no more than what I considered to be my duty,' said Arnold.

'You did far more, believe me,' said the commander. 'Because of the information you supplied, Mr Penny-worthy, we've been able to arrest fifteen terrorist suspects, one of whom, the man who rented the flat on your corridor, was undoubtedly the cell chief. At a house in Birmingham which he led us to, we discovered explosive devices, bomb-making equipment and detailed plans of buildings, along with the names of high-profile individuals the group planned to target, including a member of the royal family. Frankly, Mr Pennyworthy, you contacted us just in time.'

Arnold beamed as the commander continued, 'I only wish we could make your contribution public, but you will understand the restrictions we're under in such cases, not least when it comes to your own safety.'

'Yes, of course,' said Arnold, trying not to sound disappointed.

'But when you read the press reports of the case next week, you can take some satisfaction from knowing the role you played in bringing this group of violent criminals to justice.'

'Couldn't agree more, sir,' chipped in the sergeant.

Arnold didn't know what to say.

'I won't keep you any longer, Mr Pennyworthy,' said the commander. 'I wouldn't want you to be late for the theatre. But be assured that the Yard will remain in your debt, and my door will always be open.'

Arnold bowed his head and tried to look suitably humble.

The commander shook hands with Arnold and

thanked him once again, before Sergeant Roberts escorted him out of the room. 'And may I add my personal thanks, Mr Pennyworthy,' Roberts said as they walked down the corridor, 'because on the first of the month, I'm to be promoted to Inspector.'

'Many congratulations,' said Arnold. 'Well deserved, I feel sure.'

Arnold walked out of the building and made his way down Whitehall. He held his head high as he strolled past Downing Street, wondering how much he could tell his sister about the meeting that had just taken place. He checked his watch and decided to hail another taxi. After all, it was a special day.

'Where to, guv?' asked the taxi driver.

'The Palladium,' said Arnold as he climbed into the back seat.

Arnold thought about his meeting with the commander as the taxi made its slow progress into the West End. He played the conversation over and over again in his mind as if he was pressing the repeat button on a tape recorder. The cab came to a halt on Great Marlborough Street, a police cordon preventing them from going any further.

'What's the problem?' Arnold asked the driver.

'There must be a member of the royal family or some foreign head of state going to the show tonight. I'm afraid you'll have to walk the last hundred yards.'

'Not a problem,' said Arnold, handing over a ten-pound note and not waiting for any change.

He made his way past the large crowd of people pressing against the safety barriers hoping to discover who was causing so much interest. When he reached the theatre entrance, his ticket was carefully checked before he was allowed to enter the foyer. He walked up the wide red-carpeted steps and looked around for his sister. A few moments later he spotted a programme being waved energetically. Janet was never late for anything.

Arnold gave his sister a kiss on both cheeks, wished her a happy birthday and asked her if she'd like a glass of champagne before the curtain went up.

'Certainly not,' said Janet. 'Let's go and find our seats. A member of the royal family is expected in tonight, and I want to see who it is.'

'Please take your seats,' said a voice over the tannoy. 'The performance will begin in five minutes.'

'I've been looking forward to this for weeks,' said Janet as an usher tore their tickets in half and said, 'Halfway down on the left-hand side.'

'What wonderful seats, Arnold,' said Janet when they reached row G.

'Well, you're not forty every day,' said Arnold, giving her arm a squeeze.

'I wish,' she said as they made their way to the centre of the row, trying not to tread on anyone's toes but causing several people to have to stand.

'I thought we'd go to Cipriani afterwards,' said Arnold once they'd settled down.

'Isn't that a bit extravagant?' said Janet.

'Not on my sister's birthday, it isn't. In any case, it's turned out to be a rather special day for me as well.'

'And why's that?' asked Janet as she handed him a programme. 'Not another promotion?'

'No, more important than that—' began Arnold as people around him began to rise and start clapping as the Princess Royal entered the royal box. She gave the audience a wave before taking her seat. Janet waved back.

'She's always been one of my favourites,' Janet said as the audience sat back down. 'But do tell me, Arnold, why it's such a special day for you?'

'Well, it all began when he moved into our block—'

'Who are you talking about?' interrupted Janet as the lights went down.

'I must confess, I had my doubts about him from the start . . .' Arnold whispered as the conductor raised his baton. 'I'll tell you all about it over dinner,' he added as the orchestra began to play a melody most of the audience knew off by heart.

Arnold enjoyed the first half of the musical, and when the curtain fell for the interval, it was clear from the rapturous applause that he was not alone.

Several members of the audience rose and peered up at the royal box, where Princess Anne was chatting to her husband. Suddenly the door at the back of the box opened, and a man whose face Arnold could never forget walked in, dressed in a scruffy dinner jacket, one hand in his pocket.

'Oh my God,' said Arnold, 'it's him!'

'It's who?' said Janet, her eyes not straying from the royal box.

'The man I was telling you about,' said Arnold. 'He's a terrorist, and somehow he's managed to escape and get into the royal box.' Arnold didn't wait to hear his sister's next question. He knew his duty, and quickly squeezed past the people in his row, not caring whose toes he trod on while ignoring a barrage of angry protests. When he reached the aisle he began to run towards the exit, pushing aside anyone who got in his way. Once he was in the foyer he quickly looked around then charged up the sweeping staircase that led to the dress circle, while the majority of theatregoers were making their way slowly down to the crush bar on the ground floor. Several people stopped and stared at the ill-mannered man going so rudely against the tide. Arnold ignored them, as well as several caustic comments addressed directly at him. At the top of the stairs he set off in the direction of the royal box, but when he came to a red rope barrier, two burly police officers stepped forward and blocked his path.

'Can I help you, sir?' one of them asked politely.

'There's a dangerous terrorist in the royal box,' shouted Arnold. 'The princess's life is in danger.'

'Please calm down, sir,' said the officer. 'The only guest in the royal box this evening is Professor Naresh Khan, the distinguished American orthopaedic surgeon who is over here to give a series of lectures on the problems he encountered following 9/11.'

'Yes, that's him,' said Arnold. 'He may be posing as a famous surgeon, but I assure you, he's an escaped terrorist.'

'Why don't you show this gentleman back to his seat,' said the officer, turning to his colleague.

'And why don't you call Commander Harrison at Scotland Yard,' said Arnold. 'He'll confirm my story. My name is Arnold Pennyworthy.'

The two officers looked at each other for a moment, and then more closely at Arnold. The senior officer dialled a number on his mobile phone.

'Put me through to the Yard.' A few moments passed, too long for Arnold, who was becoming more frantic by the second.

'I need to speak to Commander Harrison, urgently,' the officer said.

After what seemed an eternity to Arnold, the commander came on the line.

'Good evening, sir, my name is Bolton, Royal Protection team, currently on duty at the London Palladium.

233

A member of the public – a Mr Pennyworthy – is convinced there's a terrorist in the royal box, and he says you'll confirm his story.' Arnold hoped they would still be in time to save her life. 'I'll put him on, sir.' The officer handed the phone to Arnold, who tried to remain calm.

'That man we discussed this afternoon, Commander, he must have escaped, because I've just seen him in the royal box.'

'I can assure you, Mr Pennyworthy,' said the commander calmly, 'that's not possible. The man we spoke about this afternoon is locked up in a high-security prison from which he's unlikely to be released in your lifetime.'

'But I've just seen him in the royal box!' shouted Arnold desperately. 'You must tell your men to arrest him before it's too late.'

'I don't know whom you've just seen in the royal box, sir,' said the commander, 'but I can assure you that it isn't Mr Zebari.'

BETTER THE DEVIL
YOU KNOW

13

THE CHAIRMAN CLIMBED OUT of the back of his car and strode into the bank.

'Good morning, Chairman,' said Rod, the young man standing behind the reception desk.

The chairman walked straight past without acknowledging him and headed towards a lift that had just opened. A group of people who'd been expecting to take it stood aside. None of them would have considered sharing a lift with the chairman, not if they wanted to keep their jobs.

The lift whisked him up to the top floor and he marched into his office. Four separate piles of market reports, telephone messages, press clippings and emails had been placed neatly on his desk by his secretary, but today they could wait. He checked his diary, although he knew he didn't have any appointments before his check-up with the company's doctor at twelve o'clock.

He walked across to the window and looked out over the City. The Bank of England, the Guildhall, the Tower, Lloyd's of London and St Paul's dominated the skyline. But his bank, the bank he'd built up to such prominence over the past thirty years, looked down on all of them, and now they wanted to take it away from him.

There had been rumours circulating in the City for some time. Not everyone approved of his methods, or some of the tactics he resorted to just before closing a deal. 'Brings the very reputation of the City into question,' one of his directors had dared to suggest at a recent board meeting. The chairman had made sure the man was replaced a few weeks later, but his departure had caused even more unease not only amongst the rest of the board but also as far as the inner reaches of Threadneedle Street.

Perhaps he'd bent the rules a little over the years, possibly a few people had suffered on the way, but the bank had thrived and those who'd remained loyal to him had benefited, while he had built one of the largest personal fortunes in the City.

The chairman was well aware that some of his colleagues hoped he would retire on his sixtieth birthday, but they didn't have the guts to put the knife in and hasten his departure. At least, not until a story appeared in one of the gossip columns hinting that he'd been seen paying regular visits to a clinic in Harley Street. They still didn't make a move until the same story appeared on the front page of the *Financial Times*.

When the chairman was asked at the next board meeting to confirm or deny the reports, he procrastinated, but one of his colleagues, someone he should have got rid of years ago, called his bluff and insisted on an independent medical report so that the rumours could be scotched. The chairman called for a vote and didn't get the result he'd anticipated. The board decided by eleven votes to nine that the company's doctor, not the chairman's personal physician, should carry out a full medical examination and make his findings known to the board. The chairman knew it would be pointless to protest. It was exactly the same procedure he insisted on for all his staff when they had their annual checkups. In fact, over the years, he'd found it a convenient way to rid himself of any incompetent or overzealous executives who'd dared to question his judgement. Now they intended to use the same tactic to get rid of him.

The company's doctor was not a man who could be bought, so the board would find out the truth. He had cancer, and although his personal physician said he could live for another two years, possibly three, he knew that once the medical report was made public, the bank's shares would collapse, with no hope of recovering until he'd resigned and a new chairman had been appointed in his place.

He'd known for some time that he was dying, but he'd always beaten the odds in the past, often at the last moment, and he believed he could do it once again. He'd have given anything, anything for a second chance . . .

'Anything?' said a voice from behind him.

The chairman continued to stare out of the window, as no one was allowed to enter his office without an appointment, even the deputy chairman. Then he heard the voice again. 'Anything?' it repeated.

He swung round to see a man dressed in a smartly tailored dark suit, white silk shirt and thin black tie.

'Who the hell are you?'

'My name is Mr De Ath,' the man said, 'and I represent a lower authority.'

'How did you get into my office?'

'Your secretary can't see or hear me.'

'Get out, before I call security,' said the chairman, pressing a button under his desk several times.

A moment later the door opened and his secretary came rushing in. 'You called, Chairman?' she said, a notepad open in her hand, a pen poised.

'I want to know how this man got into my office without an appointment,' he said, pointing at the intruder.

'You don't have any appointments this morning, Chairman,' said his secretary, looking uncertainly around the room, 'other than with the company doctor at twelve o'clock.'

'As I told you,' said Mr De Ath, 'she can't see or hear me. I can only be seen by those approaching death.'

The chairman looked at his secretary and said sharply, 'I don't want to be disturbed again unless I call.'

'Of course, Chairman,' she said and quickly left the room.

'Now that we've established my credentials,' said Mr De Ath, 'allow me to ask you again. When you said you'd do anything to be given a second chance, did you mean anything?'

'Even if I did say it, we both know that's impossible.'

'For me, anything is possible. After all, that's how I knew what you were thinking at the time, and at this very moment I know you're asking yourself, "Is he for real? And if he is, have I found a way out?"'

'How do you know that?'

'It's my job. I visit those who'll do anything to be given a second chance. In Hell, we take the long view.'

'So what's the deal?' asked the chairman, folding his arms and looking at Mr De Ath defiantly.

'I have the authority to allow you to change places with anyone you choose. For example, the young man working on the front desk in reception. Even though you're scarcely aware of his existence and probably don't even know his name.'

'And what does he get, if I agree to change places with him?' asked the chairman.

'He becomes you.'

'That's not a very good deal for him.'

'You've closed many deals like that in the past and it's never concerned you before. But if it will ease what passes for your conscience, when he dies, he will go up,' said De Ath, pointing towards the ceiling. 'Whereas if you agree to my terms, you will eventually be coming down, to join me.'

'But he's just a clerk on the front desk.'

'Just as you were forty years ago, although you rarely admit as much to anyone nowadays.'

'But he doesn't have my brain—'

'Or your character.'

'And I know nothing about his life, or his background,' said the chairman.

'Once the change has taken place, he'll be supplied with your memory, and you with his.'

'But will I keep my brain, or be saddled with his?'

'You'll still have your own brain, and he'll keep his.'

'And when he dies, he goes to Heaven.'

'And when you die, you'll join me in Hell. That is, if you sign the contract.'

Mr De Ath took the chairman by the elbow and led him across to the window, where they looked down on the City of London. 'If you sign up with me, all this could be yours.'

'Where do I sign?' asked the chairman, taking the top off his pen.

'Before you even consider signing,' said Mr De Ath, 'my inferiors have insisted that because of your past record when it comes to honouring the words "legal and binding", I'm obliged to point out all the finer points should you decide to accept our terms. It's part of the lower authority's new regulations to make sure you can't escape the final judgement.' The chairman put his pen down. 'Under the terms of this agreement, you will exchange your life for the clerk at the reception desk.

When he dies, he'll go to Heaven. When you die, you'll join me in Hell.'

'You've already explained all that,' said the chairman.

'Yes, but I have to warn you that there are no break clauses. You don't even get a period in Purgatory with a chance to redeem yourself. There are no buy-back options, no due diligence to enable you to get off the hook at the last moment, as you've done so often in the past. You must understand that if you sign the contract, it's for eternity.'

'But if I sign, I get the boy's life, and he gets mine?'

'Yes, but my inferiors have also decreed that before you put pen to paper, I must honestly answer any questions you might wish to put to me.'

'What's the boy's name?' asked the chairman.

'Rod.'

'And how old is he?'

'Twenty-five next March.'

'Then I only have one more question. What's his life expectancy?'

'He's just been put through one of those rigorous medical examinations all your staff are required to undertake, and he came out with a triple A rating. He plays football for his local club, goes to the gym twice a week and plans to run the London Marathon for charity next April. He doesn't smoke, and drinks only in moderation. He's what life assurance companies call an actuary's dream.'

'It's a no-brainer,' said the chairman. 'Where do I sign?'

Mr De Ath produced several sheets of thick parchment. He turned them over until he had reached the last page of the contract, where his name was written in what looked a lot like blood. The chairman didn't bother to read the small print – he usually left that to his team of lawyers and in-house advisors, none of whom was available on this occasion.

He signed the document with a flourish and handed the pen to Mr De Ath, who topped and tailed it on behalf of a lower authority.

'What happens now?' asked the chairman.

◄○►

'You can get dressed,' said the doctor.

The chairman put on his shirt as the doctor examined the X-rays. 'For the moment the cancer seems to be in remission,' he said. 'So, with a bit of luck, you could live for another five, even ten years.'

'That's the best news I've heard in months,' said the chairman. 'When do you think you'll need to see me again?'

'I think it would be wise for you to continue with your usual six-monthly check-ups, if for no other reason than to keep your colleagues happy. I'll write up my report and have it biked over to your office later today, and I shall make it clear that I can't see any reason why you shouldn't continue as chairman for a couple more years.'

'Thank you, Doctor, that's a great relief.'

'Mind you, I do think a holiday might be in order,' said the doctor as he accompanied his patient to the door.

'I certainly can't remember when I last had one,' said the chairman, 'so I may well take your advice.' He shook the doctor warmly by the hand. 'Thank you. Thank you very much.'

Later that afternoon a large brown box was delivered to the surgery.

'What's this?' the doctor asked his assistant.

'A gift from the chairman.'

'Two surprises in one day,' said the doctor, examining the label on the box. 'A dozen bottles of a 1994 Côtes du Rhône. How very generous of him.' He didn't add until his assistant had closed the door, 'And how out of character.'

The chairman sat in the front seat of his car and chatted to his chauffeur as he was driven back to the bank. He hadn't realized that, like him, Fred was an Arsenal supporter.

When the car drew up outside the bank, he leapt out. The doorman saluted and held the door open for him.

'Good morning, Sam,' said the chairman, then walked across reception to the lift which a young man was holding open for him.

'Good morning, Chairman,' said the young man. 'Would it be possible to have a word with you?'

'Yes, of course. By the way, what's your name?'

'Rod, sir,' said the young man.

'Well, Rod, what can I do for you?'

'There's a vacancy coming up on the Commodities floor, and I wondered if I might be considered for it.'

'Of course, Rod. Why not?'

'Well, sir, I don't have any formal qualifications.'

'Neither did I when I was your age,' said the chairman. 'So why don't you go for it?'

'I hope you know what you're up to,' said the senior clerk when Rod returned to his place behind the reception desk.

'I sure do. I can tell you I don't intend to spend the rest of my life on the ground floor like you.'

The chairman held open the lift doors to allow two women to join him. 'Which floor?' he asked as the doors closed.

'The fifth please, sir,' one of them said nervously.

He pressed the button, then asked, 'Which department do you work in?'

'We're cleaners,' said one of the girls.

'Well, I've wanted to have a word with you for some time,' said the chairman.

The girls looked anxiously at each other.

'Yours must be a thankless task at times, but I can tell you, these are the cleanest offices in the City. You should be very proud of yourselves.'

The lift came to a halt at the fifth floor.

'Thank you, Chairman,' the girls both said as they stepped out. They could only wonder if their colleagues would believe them when they told them what had just happened.

When the lift reached the top floor, the chairman strolled into his secretary's office. 'Good morning, Sally,' he said, and sat down in the seat next to her desk. She leapt up. He waved her back down with a smile.

'How did the medical go?' she asked nervously.

'Far better than I'd expected,' said the chairman. 'It seems the cancer is in remission, and I could be around for another ten years.'

'That is good news,' said Sally. 'So there's no longer any reason for you to resign?'

'That's what the doctor said, but perhaps the time has come for me to accept the fact that I'm not immortal. So there are going to be a few changes around here.'

'What exactly did you have in mind?' the secretary asked anxiously.

'To start with, I'm going to accept the board's generous retirement package and stay on as non-executive director, but not before I've taken a proper holiday.'

'But will that be enough for you, Chairman?' asked his secretary, not certain she was hearing him correctly.

'More than enough, Sally. Perhaps the time has come for me to do some voluntary work. I could start by helping my local football club. They need some new changing rooms. You know, when I was a youngster, that club was the only thing that kept me off the streets, and who knows, maybe they even need a new chairman?'

His secretary couldn't think what to say.

'And there's something else I must do before I go, Sally.'

She picked up her notepad as the chairman removed a chequebook from an inside pocket.

'How many years have you been working for me?'

'It will be twenty-seven at the end of this month, Chairman.'

He wrote out a cheque for twenty-seven thousand pounds and passed it across to her. 'Perhaps you should take a holiday as well. Heaven knows, I can't have been the easiest of bosses.'

Sally fainted.

◄○►

'Well, I'm off for lunch,' said Rod, checking his watch.

'Where have you got in mind?' asked Sam. 'The Savoy Grill?'

'All in good time,' said Rod. 'But for now I'll have to be satisfied with the Garter Arms because the time has come for me to get to know my future colleagues in Commodities.'

'Aren't you getting a bit above yourself, lad?'

'No, Sam, just keep your eyes open. It won't be long before I'm their boss, because this is just the first step on my way to becoming chairman.'

'Not in my lifetime,' said Sam as he unwrapped his sandwiches.

'Don't be so sure about that, Sam,' said Rod, taking off his long blue porter's coat and replacing it with a smart sports jacket. He strolled across the foyer, pushed his way through the swing doors and out on to the pavement. He glanced across the road at the Garter Arms, looking forward to taking his first step on the corporate ladder.

Rod checked to his right as a double-decker bus came to a halt and disgorged several passengers. He spotted a gap in the traffic and stepped out into the road just as a motorcycle courier overtook the bus. The biker threw on his brakes the moment he saw Rod, swerved and tried to avoid him, but he was a fraction of a second too late. The bike hit Rod side-on, dragging him along the road until it finally came to a halt on top of him.

Rod opened his eyes and stared at a package marked URGENT, which had landed in the road by his side: *The Chairman's Medical Report.* He looked up to see a man dressed in a smartly tailored dark suit, white silk shirt and thin black tie looking down at him.

'If only you'd asked me how long the young man had to live, and not what his life expectancy was,' were the last words Rod heard before departing from this world.

NO ROOM AT THE INN

14

RICHARD EDMISTON climbed off the bus feeling tired and hungry. It had been a long day, and he was looking forward to a meal and a bath, although he wasn't sure if he could afford both.

He was coming to the end of his holiday, which was a good thing because he was also coming to the end of his money. In fact, he had less than a hundred euros left in his wallet, along with a return train ticket to London.

But he wasn't complaining. He'd spent an idyllic month in Tuscany, even though Melanie had dropped out at the last minute without offering any explanation. He would have cancelled the whole trip but he'd already bought his ticket and put a deposit down at several small *pensioni* dotted around the Italian countryside. In any case, he'd been looking forward to exploring northern Italy for the past year, ever since he'd read an article in *Time* magazine by Robert Hughes which said that half the world's treasures were to be found in one country. He was finally persuaded to go after he and Melanie had attended a lecture given by John Julius Norwich at the Courtauld, at which the celebrated historian ended with the words, 'If you were given two lives, you'd spend one of them in Italy.'

Richard may well be ending his holiday penniless, tired and hungry, but he'd quickly discovered just how accurate Hughes and Norwich were after he'd visited

Florence, San Gimignano, Cortona, Arezzo, Siena and Lucca, each of which contained masterpieces that in any other country would have been worthy of several pages in the national tourist guides, whereas in Italy were often no more than a footnote.

Richard needed to leave for England the following day because he would start his first job on Monday, as an English teacher at a large comprehensive in the East End of London. His old headmaster at Marlborough had offered him the chance to return and teach English to the lower fifth, but what could he hope to learn by going back to his old school and simply repeating his experiences as a child, even if he did exchange his blazer for a graduates gown?

He adjusted his rucksack and began to trudge slowly up the winding path that led to the ancient village of Monterchi, perched on top of the hill. He'd saved Monterchi until last because it possessed the Madonna del Parto, a fresco of the pregnant Virgin Mary and two angels by Piero della Francesca. It was considered by scholars to be one of the artist's finest works, which was why many pilgrims and lovers of the Renaissance period came from all parts of the world to admire it.

Richard's rucksack felt heavier with each step he took, while the view of the valley below became more spectacular, dominated by the River Arno winding its way through vineyards, olive groves and green-sculpted hills. But even this paled into insignificance when he reached the top of the hill and saw Monterchi in all its glory for the first time.

The fourteenth-century village had been stranded in a backwater of history and clearly did not approve of anything modern. There were no traffic lights, no sign-posts, no double yellow lines and not a McDonald's in sight. As Richard strolled into the market square, the town hall clock struck nine times. Despite the hour, the evening was warm enough to allow the natives and an occasional interloper to dine al fresco. Richard spotted a restaurant shaded by ancient olive trees and walked across to study the menu. He reluctantly accepted that it might have suited his palate, but sadly not his purse, unless he was willing to sleep in a field that night before walking the ninety kilometres back to Florence.

He noticed a smaller establishment tucked away on the far side of the square, where the tables didn't have spotless white cloths and the waiters weren't wearing smart linen jackets. He took a seat in the corner and thought about Melanie, who should have been sitting opposite him. He'd planned to spend a month with her so they could finally decide if they should move in together once they'd both settled in London, she as a barrister, he as a teacher. Melanie clearly hadn't felt she needed another month to make up her mind.

For the past couple of weeks, whenever Richard had studied a menu, he'd always checked the prices rather than the dishes before he came to a decision. He selected the one dish he could afford before rummaging around in his rucksack and pulling out the book of short stories that had been recommended to him by his tutor. He'd advised Richard to ignore the sacred cows of Indian literature and instead enjoy the genius of R. K. Narayan. Richard soon became so engrossed by the problems of a tax collector living in a small village on the other side of the world that he didn't notice when a waitress appeared with a pitcher of water in one hand, and a basket of freshly baked bread and a small bowl of olives in the other. She placed them on the table and asked if he was ready to order.

'*Spaghetti all' Amatriciana*,' he said, looking up, '*e un bicchiere di vino rosso.*' He wondered how many kilos he'd put on since crossing the Channel; not that it mattered, because once he began the new job he would return to his old routine of running five miles a day, which he'd managed even when he was taking his exams.

He'd only read a few more pages of *Malgudi Days* when the waitress reappeared and placed a large bowl of spaghetti and a glass of red wine in front of him.

'*Grazie*,' he said, looking up briefly from his book.

He became so involved in the story that he continued to read as he forked up his food until he suddenly realized his plate was empty. He put the book down and mopped up the remains of the thick tomato sauce with his last piece of bread, before devouring what remained of the olives. The waitress returned and removed his empty plate before handing him the menu.

'Would you like anything else?' she asked in English.

'I can't afford anything else,' he admitted without guile, not even opening the menu for fear it might tempt him. '*Il conto, per favore*,' he added, giving her a warm smile.

He was preparing to leave when the waitress reappeared carrying a large portion of tiramisu and an espresso. 'But I didn't order—' he began, but she put a finger to her lips and hurried away before he could thank her. Melanie had once told him it was his boyish charm which made women want to mother him – a charm which clearly no longer worked on Melanie.

The tiramisu was delicious, and Richard even put his book down so he could fully appreciate the delicate flavours. As he sipped his coffee, he began to think about where he would spend the night. His thoughts were interrupted when the waitress returned with the bill. As he checked it, he realized she hadn't charged him for the glass of house red. Should he draw her attention to the omission? Her smile suggested he shouldn't.

He handed her a ten-euro note and asked if she could recommend somewhere he might spend the night.

'There are only two hotels in the village,' she told him. 'And La Contessina – ' she hesitated – 'might be . . .'

'Out of my price range?' suggested Richard.

'But the other one is not expensive, if a little basic.'

'Sounds like my kind of place,' said Richard. 'Is it far?'

'Nothing is far in Monterchi,' she said. 'Walk to the end of the via dei Medici, turn right and you'll find the Albergo Piero on your left.'

Richard stood up, leaned over and kissed her on the cheek. She blushed and hurried away, bringing to his mind Harry Chapin's sad lyrics in the ballad, 'A Better Place to Be'. He threw his rucksack over his shoulder and began to walk down via dei Medici. At the end he turned right and, as the waitress had promised, the hotel was on his left.

He stood outside, uncertain if he could still afford a room now he was down to his last eighty-six euros. Through the glass door he could see a receptionist, head down, checking the register. She looked up, handed a waiting couple a large key, and a porter picked up their bags and led them to the lift.

When he saw her for the first time, he didn't dare take his eyes off her, for fear the mirage might disappear. She had flawless olive skin, long dark hair that curled up as it touched her slim, graceful shoulders and large brown eyes that lit up when she smiled. Her dark tailored suit and white blouse had an elegance that Italian men take for granted and English women spend a fortune trying to emulate. She must have been around thirty, perhaps thirty-five, but she was graced with the kind of ageless beauty that made Richard wish he hadn't only just graduated.

Even if he couldn't afford a room, nothing was going to stop him speaking to her. He pushed open the door, walked up to the counter and smiled. She returned the compliment, which made her look even more radiant.

'*Vorrei una camera per la notte,*' he said.

She looked down at the register. 'I'm sorry,' she replied in English, revealing only the slightest accent, 'but we're fully booked. In fact, the last room was taken just a few moments ago.'

Richard glanced across at a row of keys dangling on hooks behind her. 'Are you sure you don't have any-thing?' he asked. 'I don't care how small the room is,' he added as he peered over the counter at a short list of upside-down names.

Once again, she glanced down at the guest register. 'No, I'm sorry,' she repeated. 'One or two guests haven't checked in yet, but I can't release their rooms because they've paid in advance. Have you tried La Contessina? They may still have a room.'

'Not one that I can afford,' said Richard.

She nodded understandingly. 'There's an old lady who runs a guest house at the bottom of the hill, but you'll have to hurry because she locks her door at eleven.'

'Would you be kind enough to call her and ask if she has a room?'

'She doesn't have a phone.'

'Perhaps I could spend the night in the lounge?' said Richard hopefully. 'Would anyone notice?' He tried out the boyish grin Melanie had once assured him was irresistible.

The receptionist frowned for the first time. 'If the manageress were to discover you were sleeping in the lounge, not only would she throw you out, but I'd probably lose my job.'

'So it will have to be the nearest field,' he said.

She looked at Richard more closely, leaned across the counter and whispered, 'Take the lift to the top floor and wait there. If any of the bookings don't show up before midnight, you can have their room.'

'Thank you,' said Richard, wanting to give her a hug.

'You'd better leave your bag in reception,' she added without explanation.

He took off his rucksack and she quickly placed it under the counter. 'Thank you,' he repeated, before making his way across to the lift. When the door opened, the porter stepped out and stood to one side, giving Richard a warm smile as he entered it.

The little lift whirred its way slowly up to the top floor and when he stepped out into a dark corridor that was lit by a single, uncovered bulb, Richard couldn't believe he was still in the same hotel. As there wasn't a chair to be seen, he hunched down on the well-trodden carpet, his back against the wall, already regretting that he hadn't taken the book out of his rucksack. For a moment he considered returning to the lobby to retrieve it, but the thought of coming face to face with the manageress and being thrown out onto the street was enough to convince him to stay put.

After a few minutes he stood up and began to pace restlessly up and down the corridor, frequently checking his watch.

When midnight struck on the town hall clock, he decided he'd rather sleep in the open air than hang around in that corridor a moment longer. He walked across to the lift, pressed the button and waited. When the doors finally opened, she was standing there, looking even more seductive in the half-light. She stepped out of the lift, took him by the hand and led him along the corridor until they reached a door with no number. She placed a key in the lock, opened the door and pulled him inside.

Richard looked around a room that wasn't much larger than his college study, and was almost completely taken up by a bed that was neither a single nor quite a double. The family photographs dotted around the walls suggested that this was where she lived. As there was only one small chair, he wondered where she expected him to sleep.

'I won't be a moment,' she said, and gave him that disarming smile again before disappearing into the bathroom. Richard sat down on the wooden chair and waited for her to reappear, not certain what he should do next. When he heard a shower being turned on, a hundred thoughts began to race through his head. He was thinking about Melanie, his first real girlfriend, when the bathroom door swung open. He hadn't looked at another woman for the past two years. She stepped out, dressed in a bathrobe, the cord undone.

'You look as if you need a shower,' she said, leaving the door open as she brushed past him.

'Thank you,' he replied, and disappeared inside, closing the door behind him. Richard enjoyed the feeling of the warm water cascading down on him, and with the assistance of a bar of soap he slowly removed the dirt and grime of a long, hot, sweaty day. After he'd dried himself, he once again regretted leaving his rucksack downstairs, as he didn't want to put his dirty clothes back on. He looked around the room and spotted another hotel bathrobe hanging on the back of the door. He was surprised how well it fitted.

Richard turned out the bathroom light and tentatively opened the door. The room was dark, but he could see the outline of her lithe body under a single sheet. As he stood there, a hand pulled the sheet back. He tiptoed across the room and sat upright on the edge of the bed. She pulled the sheet further back, but didn't speak. He lay down on the bed, his back to her.

A moment later, he felt a hand undo the cord of his bathrobe, while the other hand tried to take it off. He was thinking about Melanie when the receptionist finally pulled off his robe, threw it on the floor and slid her naked body up against his back. When she began to kiss the nape of his neck, Melanie evaporated. Richard didn't move a muscle as she began to explore his body, first his neck, then his back, with one hand, while the other moved slowly up the inside of his thigh. He turned over and took her in his arms. She felt so enticing that he wanted to switch the light back on and enjoy the sight of her naked body. When he kissed her, he felt a desire he'd never experienced with any other woman, and when they made love, it was as if it were the first time. As she lay back, Richard still held her in his arms, not wanting to fall asleep.

He woke when he felt her hand moving gently up the inside of his leg. This time he made love slowly and with more confidence, and she made no attempt to disguise her feelings. He couldn't be sure how many times they made love before the morning sun came streaming into the room, and he saw, for the first time, just how beautiful she was.

When the town hall clock struck eight, she whispered, 'You'll have to leave, *amore mio*. I'm expected back on duty at nine.'

Richard kissed her gently on the lips, slipped out of bed and went into the bathroom. After a quick shower, he put on his old clothes. When he returned to the bedroom she was standing by the window. He walked across, took her in his arms and looked hopefully down at the bed.

'Time for you to go,' she whispered after giving him one last kiss.

'I'll never forget you,' he told her. She smiled wistfully.

She pushed the window up and pointed silently to the fire escape. Richard climbed out and began to tiptoe down the iron staircase, trying not to make too much noise. When his feet touched the ground, he looked up and caught a final glimpse of her naked body. She blew him a kiss, making him wish it was the first day of his holiday and not the last.

He crept stealthily around some flower pots and down a gravel pathway that led to a trellised gate. He opened the gate and found himself back on the street. He made his way to the front of the hotel, and once again looked through the glass door. The beautiful vision of last night had been replaced by an overweight middle-aged woman, who could only have been the manager.

Richard checked his watch. He needed to collect his rucksack and be on his way if he hoped to see the fresco of the Madonna del Parto and still leave himself enough time to catch the train for Florence.

He walked into the hotel more confidently this time, and strolled up to the counter. The manager raised her head, but didn't smile. '*Buongiorno*,' said Richard.

'*Buongiorno*,' she replied, taking a closer look at him. 'How can I help you?'

'I left my rucksack here last night and I've come back to collect it.'

'Do you know anything about this, Demetrio?' she asked, not taking her eyes off Richard.

'*Si, signora,*' the porter replied, removing the rucksack from behind his desk and placing it on the counter. 'This one, if I remember, sir,' he said, giving Richard a wink.

'Thank you,' said Richard, who would have liked to give him a tip, but . . . he pulled the rucksack over his shoulder and turned to leave.

'Did you stay with us last night?' asked the manager just as he reached the door.

'No I didn't,' said Richard, turning round. 'Unfortunately, I arrived a little too late, and you didn't have a room.'

The manager glanced down at the register and frowned. 'You say you tried to get a room last night?'

'Yes, but you were fully booked.'

'That's strange,' she said, 'because there were several rooms available last night.'

Richard couldn't think of a suitable reply.

'Demetrio,' she said, turning to the porter, 'who was on duty last night?'

'Carlotta, *signora.*'

Richard smiled. Such a pretty name.

'Carlotta,' the manager repeated, shaking her head. 'I'll need to have a word with the girl. When is she back on?'

Nine o'clock, Richard almost blurted out.

'Nine o'clock, *signora,*' said the porter.

The manager turned back towards Richard. 'I must apologize, *signor*. I hope you were not inconvenienced.'

'Not at all,' said Richard as he opened the door, but he didn't look back for fear that she might see the smile on his face.

The manager waited until the door was closed before she turned to the porter and said, 'You know, Demetrio, it's not the first time she's done that.'

CASTE-OFF ★

15

THE DRIVER OF the open-top red Porsche touched his brakes, slipped the gear lever into neutral and brought the car to a halt at the lights before checking his watch. He was running a few minutes late for his lunch appointment. As he waited for the light to turn green, he noticed several men admiring his car, while the women smiled at him.

Jamwal gently touched the accelerator. The engine purred like a tiger and the smiles became even broader. Far more men than usual seemed to be looking in his direction. As the light turned green, he heard an engine revving up to his left. He glanced across to see a Ferrari accelerate away before dodging in and out of the morning traffic. He put his foot down and chased after the man who had dared to steal his thunder.

The Ferrari screeched to a halt at the next set of lights, only just avoiding a cow that was sitting in the middle of the road like a traffic bollard. Jamwal drew up by the side of his challenger, and couldn't believe his eyes. The young woman seated behind the wheel didn't give him so much as a glance, although he couldn't take his eyes off her.

When the light turned green, she accelerated away and left him standing again. Jamwal threw the gear lever into first and chased after her, searching for even the hint of a gap in the traffic that might allow him to overtake her. For the next minute, he kept one hand on the steering wheel and the other on the horn as he swerved from lane to lane, narrowly missing bicycles, rickshaws, taxis, buses and trucks that had no intention of moving aside for him. She matched him yard for yard, and he only just managed to catch her up by the time she came to a reluctant halt at the next traffic lights.

Jamwal drew up by her side and took a closer look. She was wearing an elegant cream silk dress that, like her car, could only have been designed by an Italian, although his mother certainly wouldn't have approved of the way the hemline rose high enough for him to admire her shapely legs. His eyes returned to her face as she once again accelerated away, leaving him in her slipstream. When he caught up with her at the next intersection, she turned and graced him with a smile that lit up her whole face.

When the lights changed this time, Jamwal was ready to pounce, and they took off together, matching each other cyclist for cyclist, cow for cow, rickshaw for rickshaw, until they both had to throw on their brakes and screech to a halt when a traffic cop held up an insistent arm.

When the policeman waved them on, Jamwal took off like a greyhound out of the slips and shot into the lead for the first time. But his smile of triumph turned to a frown when he glanced in his rear-view mirror to see her slowing down and driving into the entrance of the Taj Mahal Hotel. He cursed, threw on his brakes and executed a U-turn that resulted in a cacophony of horns, shaking fists and crude expletives as he tried not to lose sight of her.

He glided up to the front of the hotel, where he watched as she stepped out of her car and handed the keys to a valet. Jamwal leapt out of his Porsche without bothering to open the door, threw his keys to the valet, ran up the steps and followed her into the hotel. As he entered the lobby, she was disappearing into a lift. He waited to see which floor she would get out on. First stop was the mezzanine: fashionable shops, a hair salon and a French bistro. Would it be minutes or hours before she reappeared? Jamwal walked over to the reception desk. 'Did you see that girl?' he asked the clerk.

'I think every man in the lobby saw her, sahib.'

Jamwal grinned. 'Do you know who she is?'

'Yes, sir, she is Miss Chowdhury.'

'The daughter of Shyam Chowdhury?'

'I believe so.'

Jamwal smiled again. A few phone calls and he would know everything he needed to about Shyam Chowdhury's daughter. By the time they next met, he would already be in first gear. The only thing that surprised him was that he hadn't come across her before. He picked up the guest phone and dialled a local number.

'Hi, Sunita. I've been held up at the office, someone needed to see me urgently. Let's try and catch up this evening. Yes, of course I remembered,' he said, keeping a watchful eye on the bank of lifts. 'Yes, yes. We're having dinner tonight. I'll be with you around eight,' he promised.

The lift door opened and she stepped out carrying a Ferragamo bag. 'Got to rush,' he said. 'Can't keep my next appointment waiting.' He put the phone down, just as she walked past him, and quickly caught up with her.

'I didn't want to bother you . . .' he began.

She turned and smiled sweetly, but did not stop walking. 'It's no bother, but I'm not looking for a chauffeur at the moment.'

'How about a boyfriend?' he said, not missing a beat.

'Thank you but no. I don't think you could handle the pace.'

'Well, why don't we try and find out over dinner tonight?'

'How kind of you to ask,' she said, still not slackening her pace, 'but I already have a dinner date tonight.'

'Then how about tomorrow?'

'Not tomorrow, and tomorrow, and tomorrow.'

'Creeps in this petty pace from day to day,' he quoted back at her.

'Sorry,' she said, as an attendant opened the door for her, 'but I don't have a day free before the last syllable of recorded time.'

'How about a coffee?' said Jamwal. 'I'm free right now.'

'I feel sure you are,' she said, finally coming to a halt and looking at him more closely. 'You've clearly forgotten, Jamwal, what happened the last time we met.'

'The last time we met?' said Jamwal, unusually lost for words.

'Yes. You tied my pigtails together.'

'That bad?'

'Worse. You tied them round a lamp post.'

'Is there no end to my infamy?'

'No, there isn't, because not satisfied with tying me up, you then left me.'

'I don't remember that. Are you sure it was me?' he added, refusing to give up.

'I can assure you, Jamwal, it's not something I'd be likely to forget.'

'I'm flattered that you still remember my name.'

'And I'm equally touched,' she said, giving him the same sweet smile, 'that you clearly don't remember mine.'

'But how long ago was that?' he protested as she stepped into her car.

'Certainly long enough for you to have forgotten me.'

'But perhaps I've changed since—'

'You know, Jamwal,' she said as she switched on the ignition, 'I was beginning to wonder if you could possibly have grown up after all these years.' Jamwal looked hopeful. 'And had you bothered to open the car door for me, I might have been persuaded. But you are so clearly the same arrogant, self-satisfied child who imagines every girl is available, simply because you're the son of a maharaja.' She put the car into first gear and accelerated away.

Jamwal stood and watched as she eased her Ferrari into the afternoon traffic. What he couldn't see was how often she checked in her rear-view mirror to make sure he didn't move until she was out of sight.

Jamwal drove slowly back to his office on Bay Street. Within an hour he'd found out all he needed to know about Nisha Chowdhury. His secretary had carried out similar tasks for him on several occasions in the past. Nisha was the daughter of Shyam Chowdhury, one of the nation's leading industrialists. She had been educated in Paris, before going on to Stanford University to study fashion design. She would graduate in the summer and was hoping to join one of the leading couture houses when she returned to Delhi.

Such gaps as Jamwal's secretary hadn't been able to fill in, the gossip columns supplied. Nisha was currently to be seen on the arm of a well-known racing driver, which answered two more of his questions. She had also been offered several modelling assignments in the past, and even a part in a Bollywood film, but had turned them all down as she was determined to complete her course at Stanford.

Jamwal had already accepted that Nisha Chowdhury was going to be more of a challenge than some of the girls he'd been dating recently. Sunita Desai, who he was meant to be having lunch with, was the latest in a long line of escorts who had already survived far longer than he'd expected, but that would rapidly change now that he'd identified her successor.

Jamwal wasn't all that concerned who he slept with. He didn't care what race, colour or creed his girlfriends were. Such matters were of little importance once the light was switched off. The only thing he would not consider was sleeping with a girl from his own Rajput caste, for fear that she might think there was a chance, however slim, of ending up as his wife. That decision would ultimately be made by his parents, and the one thing they would insist on was that Jamwal married a virgin.

As for those who had ideas above their station, Jamwal had a well-prepared exit line when he felt the time had come to move on: 'You do realize that there's absolutely no possibility of us having a long-term relationship, because you simply wouldn't be acceptable to my parents.'

This line was delivered with devastating effect, often when he was dressing to leave in the morning. Nine out of ten girls never spoke to him again. One in ten remained in his phone book, with an asterisk by their names which indicated 'available at any time'.

Jamwal intended to continue this very satisfactory way of life until his parents decided the time had come for him to settle down with the bride they had chosen for him. He would then start a family, which must include at least two boys, so he could fulfil the traditional requirement of siring an heir and a spare.

As Jamwal was only months away from his thirtieth

birthday, he suspected his mother had already drawn up a list of families whose daughters would be interviewed to see if they would make suitable brides for the second son of a maharaja.

Once a shortlist had been agreed upon, Jamwal would be introduced to the candidates, and if his parents were not of one mind, he might even be allowed to offer an opinion. If by chance one of the contenders was endowed with intelligence or beauty, that would be considered a bonus, but not one of real significance. As for love, that could always follow some time later, and if it didn't, Jamwal could return to his old way of life, albeit a little more discreetly. He had never fallen in love, and he assumed he never would.

Jamwal picked up the phone on his desk, dialled a number he didn't need to look up, and ordered a bunch of red roses to be sent to Nisha the following morning – hello flowers; and a bunch of lilies to be sent to Sunita at the same time – farewell flowers.

—◦—

Jamwal arrived a few minutes late for his date with Sunita that evening, something no one complains about in Delhi, where the traffic has a mind of its own.

The door was opened by a servant even before Jamwal had reached the top step, and as he walked into the house, Sunita came out of the drawing room to greet him.

'What a beautiful dress,' said Jamwal, who had taken it off several times.

'Thank you,' said Sunita as he kissed her on both cheeks. 'A couple of friends are joining us for dinner,' she continued as they linked arms and began walking towards the drawing room. 'I think you'll find them amusing.'

'I was sorry to have to cancel our lunch date at the last moment,' he said, 'but I became embroiled in a takeover bid.'

'And were you successful?'

'I'm still working on it,' Jamwal replied as they entered the drawing room together.

She turned to face him, and the second impression was just as devastating as the first.

'Do you know my old school friend, Nisha Chowdhury?' asked Sunita.

'We bumped into each other quite recently,' said Jamwal, 'but were not properly introduced.' He tried not to stare into her eyes as they shook hands.

'And Sanjay Promit.'

'Only by reputation,' said Jamwal, turning to the other guest. 'But of course I'm a great admirer.'

Sunita handed Jamwal a glass of champagne, but didn't let go of his arm.

'Where are we dining?' Nisha asked.

'I've booked a table at the Silk Orchid,' said Sunita. 'So I hope you all like Thai food.'

Jamwal could never remember the details of their first date, as Nisha so often described it, except that during dinner he couldn't take his eyes off her. The moment the band struck up, he asked her if she would like to dance. To the undisguised annoyance of both their partners, they didn't return to the table again until the band took a break. When the evening came to an end, Jamwal and Nisha reluctantly parted.

As Jamwal drove Sunita home, neither of them spoke. There was nothing to say. When she stepped out of the car, she didn't bother to kiss him goodbye. All she said was, 'You're a shit, Jamwal,' which meant that at least he could cancel the farewell flowers.

The following morning Jamwal sent a handwritten

note with Nisha's red roses, inviting her to lunch. Every time the phone on his desk rang, he picked it up hoping to hear her voice saying, 'Thank you for the beautiful flowers, where shall we meet for lunch?' But it was never Nisha on the end of the line.

At twelve o'clock he decided to call her at home, just to make sure the flowers had been delivered.

'Oh, yes,' said the houseman who answered the phone, 'but Miss Chowdhury was already on her way to the airport by the time they arrived, so I'm afraid she never saw them.'

'The airport?' said Jamwal.

'She took the early morning flight to Los Angeles. Miss Chowdhury begins her final term at Stanford on Monday,' the houseman explained.

Jamwal thanked him, put the phone down and pressed a button on his intercom. 'Get me on the next plane to Los Angeles,' he said to his secretary. He then called home and asked his manservant to pack a suitcase, as he would be going away.

'For how long, sahib?'

'I've no idea,' Jamwal replied.

–◆–

Jamwal had visited San Francisco many times over the years, but had never been to Stanford. After Oxford he had completed his education on the Eastern seaboard, finishing up at Harvard Business School.

Although the gossip columns regularly described Jamwal Rameshwar Singh as a millionaire playboy, the implied suggestion was far from the mark. Jamwal was indeed a prince, the second son of a maharaja, but the family wealth had been steadily eroding over the years, which was the reason the palace had become the Palace Hotel. And when he had left Harvard to return to

273

Delhi, the only extra baggage he carried with him was the Parker Medal for Mathematics, along with a citation recording the fact that he had been in the top ten students of his year, which now hung proudly on the wall of the guest toilet. However, Jamwal did nothing to dispel the gossip columnists' raffish image of him, as it helped to attract exactly the type of girl he liked to spend his evenings with, and often the rest of the night.

On returning to his homeland, Jamwal had applied for a position as a management trainee with the Raj Group, where he was quickly identified as a rising star. Despite rumours to the contrary, he was often the first to arrive in the office in the morning, and he could still be found at his desk long after most of his colleagues had returned home.

But once he had left the office, Jamwal entered another world, to which he devoted the same energy and enthusiasm that he applied to his work.

The phone on his desk rang. 'There's a car waiting for you at the front door, sir.'

◄○►

Jamwal had rarely been known to cross the dance floor for a woman, let alone an ocean.

When the 747 touched down at San Francisco International Airport at five forty-five the following morning, Jamwal took the first available cab and headed for the Palo Alto Hotel.

Some discreet enquiries at the concierge's desk, accompanied by a ten-dollar bill, produced the information he required. After a quick shower, shave and change of clothes, another cab drove him across to the university campus.

When the smartly dressed young man wearing a Harvard tie walked into the registrar's office and asked

274

where he might find Miss Nisha Chowdhury, the woman behind the counter smiled and directed him to the north block, room forty-three.

As Jamwal strolled across the campus, few students were to be seen, other than early morning joggers or those returning from very late-night parties. It brought back memories of Harvard.

When he reached the north block, he made no attempt to enter the building, fearing he might find her with another man. He took a seat on a bench facing the front door and waited. He checked his watch every few minutes, and began to wonder if she had already gone to breakfast. A dozen thoughts flashed through his mind while he waited. What would he do if she appeared on Sanjay Promit's arm? He'd slink back to Delhi on the next flight, lick his wounds and move on to the next girl. But what if she was away for the weekend and didn't plan to return until Monday morning, when term began? He had several pressing appointments on Monday, none of whom would be impressed to learn that Jamwal was on the other side of the world chasing a girl he'd only met twice – well, three times if you counted the pigtail incident.

When she came through the swing doors, he immediately knew why he'd circled half the globe to sit on a wooden bench at eight o'clock in the morning.

Nisha walked straight past him. She wasn't ignoring Jamwal this time, but simply hadn't registered who it was sitting on the bench. Even when he rose to greet her, she didn't immediately recognize him, perhaps because he was the last person on earth she expected to see. Suddenly her whole face lit up, and it seemed only natural that he should take her in his arms.

'What brings you to Stanford, Jamwal?' she asked once he'd released her.

'You,' he replied simply.

'But why—' she began.

'I'm just trying to make up for tying you to a lamp post.'

'I could still be there for all you cared,' she said, grinning. 'So tell me, Jamwal, have you already had breakfast with another woman?'

'I wouldn't be here if there was another woman,' he said.

'I was only teasing,' she said softly, surprised that he had risen so easily to her bait. Not at all his reputation. She took his hand as they walked across the lawn together.

Jamwal could always recall exactly how they had spent the rest of that day. They ate breakfast in the refectory with five hundred chattering students; walked hand-in-hand around the lake – several times; lunched at Benny's diner in a corner booth, and only left when they became aware that they were the last customers. They talked about going to the theatre, a film, perhaps a concert, and even checked what was playing at the Globe, but in the end they just walked and talked.

When he took Nisha back to the north block just after midnight, he kissed her for the first time, but made no attempt to cross the threshold. The gossip columnists had got that wrong as well, at least that was something his mother would approve of. His final words before they parted were, 'You do realize that we're going to spend the rest of our lives together?'

◄◦►

Jamwal couldn't sleep on the long flight back to Delhi as he thought about how he would break the news to his parents that he had fallen in love. Within moments of landing, he was on the phone to Nisha to let her know what he'd decided to do.

'I'm going to fly up to Jaipur during the week and tell my parents that I've found the woman I want to spend the rest of my life with, and ask for their blessing.'

'No, my darling,' she pleaded. 'I don't think it would be wise to do that while I'm stuck here on the other side of the world. Perhaps we should wait until I return.'

'Does that mean you're having second thoughts?' he asked in a subdued voice.

'No, I'm not,' she replied calmly, 'but I also have to think about how I break the news to *my* parents, and I'd prefer not to do it over the phone. After all, my father may be just as opposed to the marriage as yours.'

Jamwal reluctantly agreed that they should do nothing until Nisha had graduated and returned to Delhi. He thought about visiting his brother in Chennai and asking him to act as an intermediary, but just as quickly dismissed the idea, only too aware that in time he would have to face up to his father. He would have discussed the problem with his sister Shilpa, but however much she might have wanted to keep his secret, within days she would have shared it with their mother.

In the end Jamwal didn't even tell his closest friends why he boarded a flight to San Francisco every Friday afternoon, and why his phone bill had recently tripled.

As each week went by, he became more certain that he'd found the only woman he would ever love. He also accepted that he couldn't put off telling his parents for much longer.

Every Saturday morning Nisha would be standing by the arrivals gate at San Francisco International airport waiting for him to appear. On Sunday evening, he would be among the last passengers to have their passports checked before boarding the overnight flight to Delhi.

◄○►

When Nisha walked up on to the stage to be awarded her degree by the President of Stanford, two proud parents were sitting in the fifth row warmly applauding their daughter.

A young man was standing at the back of the hall, applauding just as enthusiastically. But when Nisha stepped down from the stage to join her parents for the reception, Jamwal decided the time had come to slip away. When he arrived back at his hotel, the concierge handed him a message:

> *Jamwal,*
> *Why don't you join us for dinner at the Bel Air?*
> *Shyam Chowdhury*

It became clear to Jamwal within moments of meeting Nisha's parents that they had known about the relationship for some time, and they left him in no doubt that they were delighted to have a double cause for celebration: their daughter's graduation from Stanford, and meeting the man there she'd fallen in love with.

The dinner lasted long into the night, and Jamwal found it easy to relax in the company of Nisha's parents. He only wished . . .

'A toast to my daughter on her graduation day,' said Shyam Chowdhury, raising his glass.

'Daddy, you've already proposed that toast at least six times,' said Nisha.

'Is that right?' he said, raising his glass a seventh time. 'Then let's toast Jamwal's graduation day.'

'I'm afraid that was several years ago, sir,' said Jamwal.

Nisha's father laughed, and turning to his prospective son-in-law, said, 'If you plan to marry my daughter, young man, then the time has come for me to ask you about your future.'

'That may well depend, sir, on whether my father decides to cut me off, or simply sacrifice me to the gods,' he replied. Nobody laughed.

'You have to remember, Jamwal,' said Nisha's father, placing his glass back on the table, 'that you are the son of a maharaja, a Rajput, whereas Nisha is the daughter of a—'

'I don't give a damn about that,' said Jamwal.

'I feel sure you don't,' said Shyam Chowdhury. 'But I have no doubt that your father does, and that he always will. He is a proud man, steeped in the Hindi tradition. So if you decide to go ahead and marry my daughter against his wishes, you must be prepared to face the consequences.'

'I appreciate what you are saying, sir,' said Jamwal, now calmer. 'I love my parents, and will always respect their traditions. But I have made my choice and I will stand by it.'

'It is not only you who will have to stand by it, Jamwal,' said Mr Chowdhury. 'If you decide to defy the wishes of your father, Nisha will have to spend the rest of her life proving that she is worthy of you.'

'Your daughter has nothing to prove to me, sir,' said Jamwal.

'It isn't you I am worried about.'

◄o►

Nisha returned to Delhi a few days later and moved back into her parents' home in Chanakyapuri. Jamwal wanted them to be married as soon as possible, but Nisha was more cautious, only because she wanted him to be certain before he took such an irrevocable step.

Jamwal had never been more certain about anything in his life. He worked harder than ever by day, buoyed up by the knowledge that he would be spending the evening with the woman he adored. He no longer had any desire to visit the fleshpots of the young. The fashionable clubs and fast cars had been replaced by visits to the theatre and cinema, followed by quiet dinners in restaurants that cared more about their cuisine than about which Bollywood star was sitting next to which model at which table. Each night after he'd driven her home he always left her with the same words: 'How much longer do I have to wait before you will agree to be my wife?'

Nisha was about to tell him that she could see no reason why they should wait any longer, when the decision was taken out of her hands.

—◁o▷—

One evening, just as Jamwal had finished work and was leaving to join Nisha for dinner, the phone on his desk rang.

'Jamwal, it's your mother. I'm so glad to catch you.' He could feel his heart beating faster as he anticipated her next sentence. 'I was hoping you might be able to come up to Jaipur for the weekend. There's a young lady your father and I are keen for you to meet.'

After he had put the phone down, Jamwal didn't call Nisha. He knew that he would have to explain to her face to face why there had been a change of plan. Jamwal drove slowly over to her home in Chanakyapuri, relieved that her parents were away for the weekend visiting relatives in Hyderabad.

When Nisha opened the front door, she only had to look into his eyes to realize what must have happened. She was about to speak, when he said, 'I'll be flying up to Jaipur this weekend to visit my parents, but before I leave, there's something I have to ask you.'

Nisha had prepared herself for this moment, and if they were to part, as she had always feared they might, she was determined not to break down in front of him. That could come later, but not until he'd left. She dug her fingernails into the palms of her hands – something she'd always done as a child when she didn't want her parents to realize she was trembling – before looking up at the man she loved.

'I want you to try to understand why I'm flying to Jaipur,' he said. Nisha dug her nails deeper into the palms of her hands, but it was Jamwal who was trembling. 'Before I see my father, I need to know if you still want to be my wife, because if you do not, I have nothing to live for.'

—◇—

'Jamwal, welcome home,' said his mother as she greeted her son with a kiss. 'I'm so glad you were able to join us for the weekend.'

'It's wonderful to be back,' said Jamwal, giving her a warm hug.

'Now, there's no time to waste,' she said as they walked into the hall. 'You must go and change for dinner. Your father and I have something very important to discuss with you before our guests arrive.'

Jamwal remained at the bottom of the sweeping marble staircase while a servant took his bags up to his room. 'And I have something very important to discuss with you,' he said quietly.

'Nothing that can't wait, I'm sure,' said his mother

smiling up at her son, 'because among our guests tonight is someone who I know is very much looking forward to meeting you.'

How Jamwal wished it was he who was saying those same words because he was about to introduce his mother to Nisha. But he doubted if petals would ever be strewn at the entrance of this home to welcome his bride on their wedding day.

'Mother, what I have to tell you can't wait,' he said. 'It's something that has to be discussed before we sit down for dinner.' His mother was about to respond when Jamwal's father came out of his study, a broad smile on his face.

'How are you, my boy?' he asked, shaking hands with his son as if he'd just returned from prep school.

'I'm well, thank you, Father,' Jamwal replied, giving him a traditional bow, 'as I hope you are.'

'Never better. And I hear great things about your progress at work. Most impressive.'

'Thank you, Father.'

'No doubt your mother has already warned you that we have a little surprise for you this evening.'

'And I have one for you, Father,' he said quietly.

'Another promotion in the pipeline?'

'No, Father. Something far more important than that.'

'That sounds ominous, my boy. Shall we retire to my study for a few moments while your mother changes for dinner?'

'I would like Mother to be present when I tell you my news.'

The Maharaja looked apprehensive, but stood aside to allow his wife and son to enter the study. Both men remained standing until the Maharani had taken her seat.

Once the Maharani had sat down, Jamwal turned to his mother and said in a gentle voice, 'Mother, I have fallen in love with the most wonderful young woman, and I want you to know that I have asked her to be my wife.'

The Maharani bowed her head.

Jamwal turned to face his father, who was gripping the arms of his chair, ashen-faced, but before Jamwal could continue, the Maharaja said, 'I have never concerned myself with the way you conduct your life in Delhi, even when those activities have been reported in the gutter press. Heaven knows, I was young myself once. But I have always assumed that you were aware of your duties to this family, and that in time would marry a young woman not only from your own background, but who also met with the approval of your mother and myself.'

'Nisha and I are from the same background, Father, so let's be frank, it's not her background we're discussing, but my caste.'

'No,' said his father, 'what we are discussing is your responsibility to the family that raised you, and bestowed on you all the privileges you have taken for granted since the day you were born.'

'Father,' said Jamwal quietly, 'I didn't fall in love simply to annoy you. What has happened between Nisha and me is something rare and beautiful, and a cause for celebration, not anger. That is why I returned home in the hope of receiving your blessing.'

'You will never have my blessing,' said his father. 'And if you are foolish enough to go ahead with this unacceptable union, you will not be welcome in this house again.'

Jamwal looked towards his mother, but her head remained bowed and she didn't speak.

'Father,' Jamwal said, turning back to face him, 'won't you even meet Nisha before you make your decision?'

'Not only will I never meet this young woman, but also no member of this family will ever be permitted to come into contact with her. Your grandmother must go to her grave unaware of this misalliance, and your brother, who married wisely, will now become not only my successor, but also my sole heir, while your sister will enjoy all the privileges that were once to be bestowed on you.'

'If it was a lack of wisdom that caused me to fall in love, Father, so be it, because the woman I have asked to be my wife and the mother of my children is a beautiful, intelligent and remarkable human being, with whom I intend to spend the rest of my life.'

'But she is not a Rajput,' said his father defiantly.

'That was not her choice,' replied Jamwal, 'as it was not mine.'

'It is clear to me,' said his father, 'that there is no point in continuing with this conversation. You have obviously made up your mind, and chosen to bring dishonour on this house and humiliation to the family we have invited to share our name.'

'And if I were not to marry Nisha, having given her my word, Father, I would bring dishonour on the woman I love and humiliation to the family whose name she bears.'

The Maharaja rose slowly from his chair and glowered defiantly at his youngest child. Jamwal had never seen such anger in those eyes. He stood to face his wrath, but his father didn't speak for some time, as if he needed to measure his words.

'As it appears to me that you are determined to marry this young woman against the wishes of your family, and that nothing I can say will prevent this inappropriate and distasteful union, I now tell you, in the presence of your mother, that you are no longer my son.'

—◦—

Nisha had been standing by the barrier for over an hour before Jamwal's plane was due to land, painfully aware that as he was returning on the same day, it could not be good news. She did not want him to see that she'd been crying. While he was away she had resolved that if his father demanded he must choose between her and his family, she would release him from any obligation he felt to her.

When Jamwal strode into the arrivals hall, he looked grim-faced but resolute. He took Nisha firmly by the hand and, without saying a word, led her out on to the concourse, clearly unwilling to tell her what had happened in front of strangers. She feared the worst, but said nothing.

At the taxi rank, Jamwal opened the door for Nisha before climbing in beside her.

'Where to, sahib?' asked the driver cheerfully.

'The District Court,' Jamwal said without emotion.

'Why are we going to the District Court?' asked Nisha.

'To get married,' Jamwal replied.

—◦—

Nisha's mother and father held a more formal ceremony on the lawn of their home in Chanakyapuri a few days later to celebrate their daughter's marriage. The festivities had gone on for several days, and culminated in a large party that was attended by over a thousand guests, although not a single member of Jamwal's family attended the ceremony.

After completing the seven pheras of the sacred flame, the final confirmation of their wedding vows, the newly married couple strolled around the grounds, speaking to as many of their guests as possible.

'So where are you spending your honeymoon, dare I ask?' said Noel Kumar.

'We're flying to Goa, to spend a few days at the Raj,' said Jamwal.

'I can't think of a more beautiful place to spend your first few days as man and wife,' said Noel.

'A wedding gift from your uncle,' said Nisha. 'So generous of him.'

'Just be sure you have him back in time for the board meeting on Monday week, young lady, because one of the items under discussion is a new project that I know the chairman wants Jamwal to mastermind.'

'Any clues?' asked Jamwal.

'Certainly not,' said Noel. 'You just go away and enjoy your honeymoon. Nothing's so important that it can't wait until you're back.'

'And if we hang around here any longer,' said Nisha, taking her husband by the hand, 'we might miss our plane.'

A large crowd gathered by the entrance to the house and threw marigold petals in their path and waved as the couple were driven away.

When Mr and Mrs Rameshwar Singh drove on to the airport's private runway forty minutes later, the company's Gulfstream jet awaited them, door open, steps down.

'I do wish someone from your family had attended the wedding,' said Nisha as she fastened her seat belt. 'I was hoping that perhaps your brother or sister might have turned up unannounced.'

'If either of them had,' said Jamwal, 'they would

have suffered the same fate as me.' Nisha felt the first moment of sadness that day.

Two and a half hours later the plane touched down at Goa's Dabolim airport, where another car was waiting to whisk them off to their hotel. They had planned to have a quiet supper in the hotel dining room, but that was before they were shown around the bridal suite, where they immediately started undressing each other. The bellboy left hurriedly and placed a 'Do not disturb' sign on the door. In fact, they missed dinner, and breakfast, only surfacing in time for lunch the following day.

'Let's have a swim before breakfast,' said Jamwal as he placed his feet on the thick carpet.

'I think you mean lunch, my darling,' said Nisha as she slipped out of bed and disappeared into the bathroom.

Jamwal pulled on a pair of swimming trunks and sat on the end of the bed waiting for Nisha to return. She emerged from the bathroom a few minutes later wearing a turquoise swimsuit that made Jamwal think about skipping lunch.

'Come on, Jamwal, it's a perfect day,' Nisha said as she drew the curtains and opened the French windows that led on to a freshly cut lawn surrounded by a luxuriant tropical garden of deep red frangipani, orange dahlias and fragrant hibiscus.

They were walking hand in hand towards the beach when Jamwal spotted the large swimming pool at the far end of the lawn. 'Did I ever tell you, my darling, that when I was at school I won a gold medal for diving?'

'No, you didn't,' Nisha replied. 'It must have been some other woman you were showing off to,' she added with a grin.

'You'll live to regret those words,' he said, releasing her hand and beginning to run towards the pool. When he reached the edge of the pool he took off and leapt high into the air before executing a perfect dive, entering the water so smoothly he hardly left a ripple on the surface.

Nisha ran towards the pool laughing. 'Not bad,' she called out. 'I bet the other girl was impressed.'

She stood at the edge of the pool for a moment before falling to her knees and peering down into the shallow water. When she saw the blood slowly rising to the surface, she screamed.

◄o►

I have a passion, almost an obsession, about not being late, and it's always severely tested whenever I visit India. And however much I cajoled, remonstrated with and simply shouted at my poor driver, I was still several minutes late that night for a dinner being held in my honour.

I ran into the dining room of the Raj and apologized profusely to my host, who wasn't at all put out, although the rest of the party were already seated. He introduced me to some old friends, some recent acquaintances and a couple I'd never met before.

What followed was one of those evenings you just don't want to end: that rare combination of good food, vintage wine and sparkling conversation which was emphasized by the fact that we were the last people to leave the dining room, long after midnight.

One of the guests I hadn't met before was seated opposite me. He was a handsome man, with the type of build that left you in no doubt he must have been a fine athlete in his youth. His conversation was witty and well informed, and he had an opinion on most things, from

Sachin Tendulkar (who was certain to be the first cricketer to reach fifty test centuries) to Rahul Gandhi (undoubtedly a future prime minister, if that's the road he chooses to travel down). His wife, who was sitting on my right, possessed that rare middle-aged beauty that the callow young can only look forward to, and rarely achieve.

I decided to flirt with her outrageously in the hope of getting a rise out of her self-possessed husband, but he simply flicked me away as if I were some irritating fly that had interrupted his afternoon snooze. I gave up the losing battle and began a serious conversation with his wife instead.

I discovered that Mrs Rameshwar Singh worked for one of India's leading fashion houses. She told me how much she always enjoyed visiting England whenever she could get away. It was not always easy to drag her husband from his work, she explained, adding, 'He's still quite a handful.'

'Do you have any children?' I asked.

'Sadly not,' she replied wistfully.

'And what does your husband do?' I asked, quickly changing the subject.

'Jamwal is on the board of the Raj Group. He's headed up their hotel operation for the past fifteen years.'

'I've stayed at six Raj hotels in the last nine days,' I told her, 'and I've rarely come across their equal.'

'Oh, do tell him that,' she whispered. 'He'll be so touched, especially as the two of you have spent most of the evening trying to prove how macho you are.' Both of us put nicely in our place, I felt.

When the evening finally came to an end, everyone stood except the man seated opposite me. Nisha moved swiftly round to the other side of the table to join her husband, and it was not until that moment that I realized Jamwal was in a wheelchair.

I watched sympathetically as she wheeled him slowly out of the room. No one who saw the way she touched his shoulder and gave him a smile the rest of us had not been graced with, could have had any doubt of their affection for each other.

He teased her unmercifully. 'You never stopped flirting with the damn author all evening, you hussy,' he said, loud enough to be sure that I could hear.

'So he did get a rise out of you after all, my darling,' she responded.

I laughed, and whispered to my host, 'Such an interesting couple. How did they ever get together?'

He smiled. 'She claims that he tied her to a lamp post and then left her.'

'And what's his version?' I asked.

'That they first met at a traffic light in Delhi . . . and she left him.'

And thereby hangs a tale.